Tease

Cloverleigh Farms
Series

Melanie Harlow

For Alice, Carrie, Heather, Helen, Laura, Lauren, Renee, and Tina, with appreciation and gratitude

You can't stay in your corner of the Forest waiting for others to come to you. You have to go to them sometimes.

A.A. Milne

One

Felicity

I T WAS A BAD DAY EVEN BEFORE I PICKED UP THE SCISSORS.

Not that I realized it. In fact, I was feeling pretty good that morning.

Sure, I'd just turned twenty-eight and was back home living with my parents, but that was only temporary. Tonight at my ten-year high school reunion, when people asked what I was doing with my life, I had a response all ready.

Me? Oh, I'm an entrepreneur, I'd say. *I started a vegetarian catering company and food blog called The Veggie Vixen. I made some of the appetizers tonight. Have you tried the zucchini fritters?*

I wasn't in the top echelon of lifestyle social media influencers or anything, and I still had a part-time job as a sous chef, but my follower count was growing steadily, and last night The Veggie Vixen had catered its first large-scale event: a wedding at Cloverleigh Farms.

My older sister Millie was the event planner at Cloverleigh, and even though the bride had been a bit difficult to work with during the planning—demanding a huge, high-end reception with all the frills on a bargain budget and asking why we couldn't "move a staircase" so she could make her entrance with the light hitting her a certain way—Millie and I had managed to put together a beautiful event for her, despite torrential summer rains that necessitated a last-minute switch to an indoor ceremony and cocktail hour. The bride and all her guests had raved about the food, flowers, and service all night.

So when I glanced at my phone and saw the notification from Dearly Beloved (the hottest wedding planning app out there) that I finally had my first review, I grabbed my glasses from my nightstand and eagerly tapped through to The Veggie Vixen's profile to see it.

YUCKY AND OVERPRICED!!!
Reviewed by He Put A Big A** Ring On It

I am not a vegetarian but I thought it would be cheaper to not serve meat at my wedding. I WAS WRONG. Everything was crazy expensive and tasted terrible. The cheese toasts were soggy and even the meatballs did not have meat. I did not want ugly gross boring vegetables at my wedding but that was exactly what I got. If I could, I would give no stars. Just ew. DO NOT RECOMMEND. I want a refund.

"Cheese toasts!" I shrieked. "My avocado, pomegranate, and chèvre crostini are *not* cheese toasts!"

I read it again and again, my entire body trembling with rage. Then I called Millie.

"Hello?" she said, her voice low and croaky, as if she'd been asleep.

"I did not serve anything soggy!" I shouted.

"What are you talking about? What time is it?"

"It's eight-thirty. The bride from last night left a shitty review on my Dearly Beloved page!"

"She did?" Millie sounded more alert.

"Yes! A totally horrible one-star review."

"Hang on. Let me grab my laptop."

I grabbed a fistful of my hair and yanked on it, wondering if it was possible to get a bad review taken down. You couldn't just tell lies in a review, right? Wasn't that like libel or something?

"Oh, Jesus," Millie said. "This is bonkers. She told me when she left how happy she was with everything." My sister started to laugh. "'Even the meatballs did not have meat?' They were vegetarian! What did she expect?"

"It's not funny, Mills." Throwing the covers aside, I got out of bed and went over to my dresser, where I began to rummage around in my makeup bag, looking for scissors. I needed scissors.

"You know what?" Millie said. "I have a notification that Cloverleigh Farms has a new Dearly Beloved review too." Then she groaned. "Looks like she was busy this morning. Why is she online posting bullshit reviews? Shouldn't she be packing for her honeymoon or something?"

"What does yours say?"

"It says, 'The peonies were wilted, the cheese toasts were soggy, the staff was rude, and the vodka was watered down. Everything was cheap cheap cheap even though I paid top dollar. I don't know how this place has so many great reviews, they ruined my wedding. My ceremony wasn't even in the place they'd promised me it would be. I want a refund.' That last sentence is in all caps, by the way."

My temper flared again, along with my nostrils. "Those. Were *not*. Cheese toasts!"

"Relax," Millie soothed. "It's obviously just an attempt at a money grab."

"But people on this app don't know that, Millie. They just see a one-star review and assume I serve bad food!"

"Who's really going to listen to a woman who refers to

herself as 'He Put a Big Ass Ring On It?' Right there, it's obvious her taste is questionable."

"Easy for you to say." I gave up on my makeup bag and stormed across the hall into the bathroom, where I began opening drawers and foraging through them. "Cloverleigh Farms has been around forever, and its reputation is established. It has a bajillion great reviews on Dearly Beloved already, but The Veggie Vixen is brand new—and now my only review says *yucky* and *just ew*!"

"If it bothers you that much, then respond to it. Apologize for her negative experience, say you always want your customers to be happy, and suggest she contact you directly. And if she really wants her money back, just give it to her."

"I'm going to be broke forever," I moaned, shoving cans of hair products around.

"No, you won't. You started a business. That means costs up front, but you're good, Felicity. You'll make money. What's all that noise?"

I slammed a drawer. "I'm in the bathroom looking for something."

"Not the scissors, I hope."

"You deal with stress your way, I deal with it mine."

"Felicity MacAllister, do *not* cut your hair. It's just one app."

"But it's the most important one for getting catering gigs and you know it. Engagement parties, showers, bridal luncheons—all those are booked through Dearly Beloved. Even people planning non-wedding events use that app."

I headed out of the bathroom and down the stairs. I was still in my pajamas—an oversized T-shirt I'd had forever that said, *Come to the nerd side. We have Pi*—but no one was home anyway. My dad was obsessive about his Saturday morning golf game, my stepmom, Frannie, ran a bakery downtown and was always out of the house before dawn, and my seventeen-year-old twin sisters Emmeline and Audrey were lifeguards at the public beach this summer. On Saturdays they had to report by eight a.m.

I had a fourth sister, Winifred, who was twenty-four—Millie, Winnie, and I were from our dad's first marriage—but Winnie lived in a downtown condo, right next door to her boyfriend, Dex, a firefighter and single dad.

Everybody was out there having a better life than me.

"You've got like two thousand followers on your Instagram," said Millie, ever the optimist. "That's a lot."

"Not really. And that's not the same as a review." Down in the kitchen, I opened the junk drawer. Spying a pair of scissors, I smiled gleefully. Then I picked them up, opening and closing them several times, my blood rushing faster. "Reviews are what bring in new business. I've been working my ass off to gain traction, and this just set me back at the starting line—no, it's worse than that! At least when I started out, I was on neutral ground. Now I'm on soggy ground. I'm sinking!"

"You're fine. Do you need me to come over?"

"I'm not fine. I'm humiliated and penniless, I'll never be able to move out of Dad and Frannie's house, and I can kiss the idea of getting a cookbook deal goodbye. I have *failed* at my dreams, Millicent. But at least I found the scissors."

"Don't do anything rash!"

I set my phone on the counter, grabbed a hank of hair in front of my face, and chopped some off. "Too late."

"No! Stop cutting your hair!" Millie shouted loud enough so I could hear her.

"Relax, I'm just giving myself a little trim." Enjoying the surge of adrenaline, I cut some more, right across the bridge of my nose. "Bangs are in."

"Not bangs! Anything but bangs!"

"I gotta go. I need a mirror." I hung up on her and took the scissors into the first-floor bathroom, where I haphazardly hacked off more of my long dark hair. I stuck to the front at first, but once my heart was really pumping, I decided to take some off the back too. I hadn't done this in *so long*—I'd forgotten how freeing it was.

Gathering it together in one hand, I positioned the scissors carefully. The blades came together again and again, severing the strands with a satisfying metallic *slice*.

Slice. Slice. Slice.

Several minutes later, the rush faded as I stared at my reflection. Sad clumps of hair littered the sink. "Oh, shit."

I tried to even out the bangs but only succeeded in making them shorter and more blunt. "Shit!"

The worst thing was that I should have known better. I'd been stress-cutting my hair since I was six, since the night I overheard the horrible thing, and it never ended well.

It felt empowering for a couple minutes, but it was never worth the trouble I got in once grownups saw what I'd done. Although, after my dad and Frannie got married, she'd sometimes sneak me over to the salon so a professional could attempt to mitigate the damage before my dad saw it, and she never got mad at me. She always understood.

But once I was a teenager, I refused her help—it was my stress, my hair, my problem. I wanted to handle it on my own, and it wasn't like I was a beauty queen in the first place. A funny haircut wasn't going to make much difference to my social status—the kids in the marching band and Chemistry Club weren't too judgmental about outward appearances— and my bloody noses were more embarrassing than my uneven bangs anyway.

But this put a *major* crimp in my plan to surprise everyone at the reunion tonight with my elegance and sophistication.

Maybe I could wear a hat. A jaunty beret, something that said 'I am still quirky, but I have more confidence now, and I don't care what you think of me.' Something that would force mean girls like Mimi Pepper-Peabody to remark, "Wow. You've come a long way since high school."

God, I wanted that to be true.

I mean, I was practically going on thirty. Weren't you supposed to have your shit together by this age? At twenty-eight, my dad had two kids and was serving his country as a Marine. Frannie was running a pastry shop and planning her wedding. Even Winnie, four years younger than me, had a solid handle on her life, including a job she loved and a sexy firefighter boyfriend. Millie was four years older, but she was established in her career and owned a house. Even the twins had jobs, boyfriends, and normal haircuts.

I felt like the last MacAllister standing. It brought back memories of being the last kid picked for teams in gym class. I could still feel the rest of the kids looking at me and the other non-athletes from their side of the gym. The cool side. The chosen side.

Would tonight be the same thing all over again?

Resignedly, I cleaned up all the hair in the bathroom and swept the kitchen floor. Then I made myself a cup of coffee and checked my phone—Millie had called twice and left several text messages in all caps.

STOP CUTTING.

THIS IS NOT WORTH IT.

YOU DON'T NEED BANGS, YOU NEED CAFFEINE.

MAYBE A SHOT OF WHISKEY.

I called her back. "Hey."

"Did you?"

"Yes."

"Your reunion is tonight, right?"

I sighed and took a sip. "Yes."

"Why don't I pick you up and we'll go downtown, grab some coffee, and beg a salon to fit you in for an emergency appointment?"

"It's not really an *emergency*," I countered, although the mirror might disagree.

"Is it better or worse than Dad and Frannie's wedding day?"

"Worse," I admitted. "But better than the night before the SATs."

"Send me a pic," she said in her bossy big sister voice.

I winced. "That's probably not a good idea."

"*Send me a pic.*"

"Fine, but be nice." I moved closer to the window, like better lighting might help. After snapping a selfie, I sent it to Millie.

My sister gasped. "Sweet Jesus."

"I said be nice!"

"Okay. Don't panic. What are you wearing tonight?" Millie had gone into executive event planner mode, and her tone was no-nonsense.

"I don't know." Fashion was not my area of expertise. "Got any advice?"

"Wear a fabulous short dress with a great pair of heels. Show off your legs. That will distract from your hair."

"I don't own fabulous dresses. I've spent almost every night for the last five years in a kitchen. Can I borrow something from you?"

She laughed. "Felicity, my dresses are not going to fit you."

"I could stuff my bra."

"You'd have to stuff a lot more than that," she said wryly.

I sighed, envious as always of Millie's full, feminine shape.

My body was mostly angles and edges, while hers was all soft, sexy curves. "I wish I had a date tonight. That would make it easier."

"I've got another wedding here, but maybe Winnie would go with you."

"Show up with my little sister?" I almost choked on my coffee. "That's worse than going alone."

"What about Hutton?"

My heart skittered a little at his name. "He said absolutely not the first time I asked. But I guess I could ask him again."

Hutton French had been my best friend in high school, a socially awkward math nerd like me who preferred books to people, played in the marching band, and could have lettered in fidgeting if it was a Varsity sport. (Actually, we both lettered in cross country—running is the one sporty thing I am decent at, probably because it does not involve balls, nets, or hand-eye coordination.) The one big difference between Hutton and me was that when I got nervous, I blurted odd things, and when he got anxious, he clammed up.

But he never made fun of my bad haircuts or bloody noses, and I never minded his aversion to social events or occasional panic attacks in crowded places. I learned to read the signs and knew how to look out for him. Together we co-captained the Mathletes Team and co-founded the Chemistry Club, and on Friday nights, he'd sometimes come over and sit at the kitchen counter while I baked, and then we'd watch sci-fi movies, polishing off whatever I'd made.

We even had our own secret code, which was really just a pigpen cipher used centuries ago during the Crusades by the Knights Templar. For a while, we passed encrypted notes to each other during classes just for fun, and we thought it was hilarious when kids grabbed them and threatened to read our "love notes" out loud. It felt like we were pulling one over on them when they couldn't decipher the text, although I'm not sure it did anything for our social status.

(And frankly, even if someone had cracked our code, what we mostly passed back and forth were quotes from *Star Trek*.)

My family was always convinced we were secretly in love and teased me endlessly, but our relationship was one hundred percent platonic. Honestly, I'd been shocked when he asked me to go to the senior prom—to this day, I have a hunch his mother bribed him with a fancy telescope or something—but we ended up having a good time, and he looked *so cute* in his suit and tie. We even danced once, and when the song was over, he said, "That wasn't as bad as I thought it would be." I think we shook hands at the end of the night.

There *was* that one night in the library when I thought he might kiss me—and I'd wanted him to—but true to form, I'd blurted something stupid and the moment passed us by.

After high school, Hutton had gone to M.I.T. to study math and physics, and later he made a billion-dollar fortune thanks to some algorithm he'd created. In fact, he was the youngest self-made American billionaire ever. He lived in California for years, but he was in town for the summer, staying in a gorgeous cabin about twenty minutes from town.

"I'd call him up right now," Millie said.

"He *hates* the phone."

"Why?"

"Because it involves talking to people. He likes numbers more than words."

Millie laughed. "Guess that's why he's a billionaire and we're us. Somebody asked me the other day what he does—*everyone* is talking about him—and I didn't even know what to say."

"My answer is always, 'He co-founded a cryptocurrency exchange called HFX.' But don't ask me to explain it." I sipped my coffee. "Whenever he tries to tell me what it is, I get lost."

"How can that be? You're a math whiz too, Miss I Skipped First Grade. We all know you were doing complex algebraic equations when the rest of us were learning B says *buh*."

I laughed, leaning back against the counter. "The kind of math Hutton does is way beyond algebra. You don't get to be a billionaire solving for x."

"Speaking of which, you'd think a billionaire would want to spend his summer vacation somewhere more ritzy than northern Michigan," Millie said.

"Well, his family is here, and Hutton's not really the ritzy type—although I assure you, the place he's staying in is *not* your typical cabin in the woods," I said with a laugh. "It's got like four bedrooms, three decks, a gourmet kitchen, one of those indoor/outdoor fireplaces, cathedral ceilings, huge windows. When you look out, all you see are trees."

"Nice." Her tone grew playful. "Sounds like you're there a lot."

"We hang out a few times a week," I said, trying to keep my tone neutral. Things between Hutton and me were still completely platonic, but there was something different about our chemistry this summer. Something simmering beneath the surface. Sometimes I thought about just going for it—kissing him to see what would happen.

But I always lost my nerve.

Hutton could have any woman in the world. I'd seen photos of him with actresses, supermodels, heiresses. Gorgeous, famous women I could never compete with. Why embarrass myself by trying?

"A few times a week, huh?" she teased. "That sounds like dating."

"No dating, we just hang." I rinsed out my coffee cup and put it in the dishwasher. "He doesn't love going out in public, which was the case even before he was a celebrity, but now it's even worse. People just stare with no shame. Women flirt outrageously. Guys ask for stock tips."

"Really?"

"Yes." I laughed as I went up the stairs. "He runs in the park super early to avoid having to deal with people, but there's this group of old ladies who gather in the park to do their Prancercise, who call themselves the Prancin' Grannies, and they adore him. They prance right up to tell him all about their single granddaughters."

Millie snorted. "Stop it."

"His own mom is even worse."

"Does she still have the shop downtown? The one that sells all the crystals and candles?"

"Yep. Mystic on Main. She's constantly trying to set him up on dates with her customers." I entered my room and flopped back onto my bed. The glow-in-the-dark stars I'd pasted on the ceiling were still there, as if my parents had known I'd be back. "Like she'll call him and say she has a computer problem at the shop, or she can't reach something on a high shelf, and when he shows up to help, there isn't really a problem, but there's a woman she wants to introduce him to. He gets so mad."

Millie laughed. "Does he ever talk about Zlatka?"

I ignored the little bolt of jealousy that always shot through me when I thought about Hutton and Zlatka, a stunning Lithuanian supermodel and the latest Bond girl. They'd dated for a few months this past spring, and the media had eaten it up. "No."

"I wonder if it's true what she said about him."

My belly cartwheeled. "I have no idea, and I'm not asking."

Millie laughed. "No, I guess there's no way you can be like, 'Hey, I heard you like to tie women up and boss them around in the bedroom.'"

"People just like to talk."

"Especially about that stuff," Millie said. "Although if you see any whips, chains, or blindfolds in his closet, let me know. It seems so opposite his quiet personality, but you never know what people are like behind closed doors."

I was curious about that closed door but needed to focus on my problem. "Anyway, what am I going to do about tonight?"

"Why go at all? Just don't show."

"Because I'm catering some appetizers, which I had to *beg* to do, because the reunion chairwoman wanted to go with *one* caterer, and she didn't want everything vegetarian. But I thought it would be good publicity."

"Maybe you can just drop them off."

"I don't want to be that person, Millie." My voice rose as I sat up. "I don't want to be intimidated by people. I want to prove to myself that I can hold my head up in front of Mimi Pepper-Peabody, even with terrible bangs."

"Okay, okay." Millie's tone was more gentle. "Who the heck is Mimi Pepper-Peabody?"

"She's the reunion chair, a girl I went to school with. Beautiful, popular, you know the type."

"A mean girl?"

I sighed. "That's tricky. It's not like she was outwardly mean to my face, but she had a way of cutting you down without looking like she was doing it. If I got a bloody nose in class, instead of privately asking me if I needed a tissue, she'd yell out, 'Ew! Felicity's nose is gushing buckets of blood, and it's so gross!' And everyone would either laugh or say how disgusting it was."

"Um, that's outwardly mean."

"Yeah, I guess it is." I played with the frayed hem of my T-shirt. "But she was so popular, she could get away with anything."

"Well, tonight's your chance to tell her to go fuck herself."

I laughed. "That's not my style."

"Fine. So go show her that being popular in high school doesn't mean shit once high school is over. And you never know, maybe she lost her looks. Maybe karma caught up with her and all her hair fell out from bleaching it too much. Maybe she has ten big warts on her nose."

"Nope. I see her around town and she looks the same as she did back then." I could see my reflection in the mirror over my dresser. "And so do I."

"Still. She can't make you feel bad about yourself if you don't let her."

"I won't let her," I decided, pushing my glasses up my nose.

No doubt that would be easier if I had America's youngest self-made billionaire on my arm. Maybe I hadn't come that far since high school, but Hutton had, and some of his shine might rub off on me.

I closed my eyes and imagined myself walking into the reunion with Hutton, me decked out in a minidress and heels, Hutton wearing the hell out of a suit and tie, jaws dropping all around the room.

Could that really be Felicity MacAllister and Hutton French, Mathletes and band geeks? They're so cool, so polished, so classy!

Smiling, I opened my eyes and dialed his number.

Two

Hutton

I USED TO THINK I WAS MAGIC.

As a kid, I honestly believed I could control the world just by doing certain things.

Touching my nose as I entered a room.

Stepping out of bed with my right foot first, never my left.

Refusing to ride on the left side of the back seat in my dad's car, only the right. This often meant I had to race out to the driveway early in order to beat my big sister Allie, who did not have magical powers no matter where she sat in the car, but did have an incredible knack for pushing my buttons.

If the trip involved the highway, I had to sit with my arms crossed without saying a word until ten cars passed. If I saw a tractor or motorcycle, I had to start over.

If the trip in the car did *not* involve the highway, I had to hold my feet off the floor the entire time, or at least until we passed two stop signs or one traffic light.

By doing these rituals but never speaking of them (or else the magic would cease to work), I was ensuring that all stayed right in my world, which was pretty fucking great back then.

In fifth grade, I was one of the most popular kids in school. I was good at math and baseball. I was on student council and in the band. I won the paper plate award for Most Likely to Go to Space and also an Astounding Attendance certificate, because I never missed a day of school. (Only I knew that was because being absent or even tardy would alter the balance of the universe and possibly weaken my powers, not because I was never sick.)

Then a bunch of really shitty things happened, including puberty, and my brain was completely rewired.

That's when I started to hate the phone.

Or more specifically, the feeling of dread I experienced when faced with being the sole focus of someone's attention on the other end of the line. You were granted no time to think before you had to answer questions—it was like a fastball coming straight for your head. You couldn't see their reactions to anything you said. You had no idea how they might be judging you. You had no opportunity to weigh the risk of any possible response. In contrast to a text or email, a phone conversation exposed you completely.

I avoided them at all costs.

So when my cell vibrated in my back pocket as I was about to leave the house, I almost ignored it. If it mattered, the caller would leave a voicemail. Then I'd listen to the message and decide if it *actually* mattered and merited a text from me or—even better—a response from my assistant back in San Francisco. There wasn't much that could make me answer or make a call in real time.

But when I saw who was calling, I took it. "You know I hate the phone."

"I do," said Felicity, "and I'm sorry. But I didn't think I could convey the urgency of this matter in a text."

I headed from the kitchen into the garage, pulling the door shut behind me. "Are you okay? Is your nose bleeding?"

"No, it's not that."

"Good. The memory of that last one still haunts me." I

slid behind the wheel of my SUV, recalling the way her nose had suddenly and violently started to bleed while we were out for dinner one night back when she lived in Chicago six years ago.

I'd been in town on business, and I'd been looking forward to catching up with her, since we really hadn't seen each other much since going away to college—I'd spent my summers on campus at M.I.T. and Felicity had spent hers working for her family at Cloverleigh Farms. I knew she'd abandoned her pre-med studies at Brown to follow her heart and attend culinary school, but I wondered if she'd changed in other ways too.

Did she still love sci-fi? Did she still hate thunderstorms? Was she still close to her family? Did she still cut her hair when she was stressed? Would things still feel easy between us, or was she so different that I wouldn't feel okay around her anymore? What if she felt like a stranger?

Thankfully, the moment I saw her enter the room and smile at me, I knew everything would be fine. She raced over to give me one of those hugs I'd never quite known how to return, and even the way she smelled was familiar—like summer at home. She still wore glasses. Her brown hair still looked like she might recently have trimmed it herself. I could still make her laugh.

And my heart still did that strange quickening thing when she got close to me, the thing that tied my tongue and heated my insides and put troubling questions in my head, like, *What would it be like to kiss her? What would she do if I took her hand? Should I tell her I want to be more than friends?* But my nerves had always been stronger than my attraction. I was positive she'd think I was crazy and look at me differently if I acted on those urges or spoke those words aloud.

See, I might not be magical anymore, but I have a horrible superpower that, when combined with my mathematical talent, allows me to enumerate any number of catastrophic outcomes for a given situation. And my brain loved listing all the possible ways things could veer off track if I made the wrong move with Felicity.

But I was hoping that night in Chicago would be different.

After all, I was older. I was more mature. I'd had some dating experience. I'd had sex with *three different women* in college, and one of them even said I was "surprisingly great" in bed for someone so quiet. (It wasn't all that surprising to me, since I'd done extensive online research on how to please a woman. I was excellent at research.) I'd also been seeing a therapist for my anxiety, and he'd noticed how often I mentioned Felicity . . . was there something there? He'd challenged me to find out.

But I hadn't gotten the chance. Felicity had some kind of blood vessel disorder that had always given her these fuck-awful bloody noses, and it was clear about thirty minutes into our dinner that she hadn't outgrown them. We'd spent the rest of the evening in the Emergency Room.

I took it as a sign that reaching across the table would have been a disaster. That the universe had saved me from catastrophe while also protecting my friendship with Felicity. That was something I did not want to mess with.

And when I got home, I ghosted the therapist. Fuck that guy.

"Yeah, that was a bad one, sorry," she said. "Hope they got the stains out of the tablecloth. But this doesn't involve blood, I promise. It doesn't even involve talking on the phone!"

I switched the call to Bluetooth and backed out of the garage. "What does it involve?"

"Doing me a favor."

"I'm listening."

"Okay, but before I tell you what it is, you have to promise to at least *consider* what I have to say."

"You're not really nailing this sales pitch, MacAllister."

I headed down the driveway, which wound its way through birch and evergreens and sloped down the hillside toward the highway.

"Sorry, let me try again." She cleared her throat. "Hey, Hutton! How are you?"

I smiled. "Okay, considering I'm on the phone."

"Did you run in the park this morning?"

"Yes."

"Were the Prancin' Grannies out and about?"

"In full force. They just got matching T-shirts, which they were very excited to show me."

Felicity laughed. "Oh yeah? What color?"

"I'd call it Pepto Bismol Pink. And they're bedazzled—which is a new word I learned today."

"I'm sure that addition to your vocabulary will come in handy in your line of work. So what are you up to?"

"I'm going over to my sister's house to watch the kids so she can get a haircut. Neil is working today." Allie's husband was a cop who worked twelve-hour shifts. I'd offered him a job working security for HFX, but neither he nor my sister had wanted to move—their oldest was in elementary school, my sister was a child therapist with a growing practice, and my parents lived right around the block.

"That sounds like fun." Felicity paused. "What about tonight? Do you have plans?"

"Why?" I asked, even though I had a hunch about what was coming.

"Because I'm going somewhere really fun, and I was thinking maybe you'd like to go with me!" she said with exaggerated excitement.

"You're not talking about the reunion, are you?"

"There will be food and drinks and music," she went on, like I hadn't spoken, "lots of people we haven't seen in ten years—"

"I'd gladly go another ten without seeing ninety-nine-point-nine percent of them."

"—and I'm making zucchini fritters!"

"Felicity, you already asked me if I'd go to this thing, and I said sorry, but no."

"Don't you like zucchini?"

"I like zucchini just fine. But I didn't like high school that much, I don't like social events at all, and the thought of having to make small talk with any of those people makes me want to eat rat poison."

She sighed. "Yeah. I know."

"Also, I have other plans tonight."

"What are you doing?"

"I promised my dad I'd come to his barbershop quartet poker night."

"That's *social*," she objected.

"It's *slightly* social, and I don't really want to do it," I said, easing onto the highway toward town. "But there will only be four old guys there, and we'll be occupied with the card game. There will be snacks and beer, but no small talk. Minimal eye contact. No one asking for selfies. No prancing grannies. Possibly I'll have to endure some old-timey four-part harmonies, and I'll definitely be subjected to a lot of dad jokes, but I'll live."

"I love that your dad is *actually* a barber in a barbershop quartet."

"The Clipper Cuts are available for wakes, weddings, and everything in between. They will meet all your entertainment needs."

Felicity laughed. "Well, while you're enjoying the snacks and harmonies, spare a thought for me trying to survive high school again, this time *alone*."

"Just skip it, Felicity." Avoidance was my specialty.

"I can't," she said.

"Why not?"

"Because I'm catering some appetizers and it will be a good business opportunity. Plus, I might have to do some damage control." She got all worked up telling me about a bad review she'd gotten this morning on some app. "And it's all lies! That bride *raved* about everything all night."

"Want me to buy the app and shut it down?"

She gasped. "Oh my God, can you? No, wait. Don't do that—it's a really helpful thing for a lot of people and businesses. Just not for me at the moment."

"Your business is going to be fine," I told her. "But I know how it feels to have people talking shit about you, and I'm sorry." There were endless rumors about me out there—I was a cold-hearted robot (not really), I was an arrogant prick (occasionally), I was an undercover Robinhood who stole from the rich and gave to the poor (half-true), I was a commitment-phobic player (I guess also half-true . . . I avoided commitment, but I wasn't a dick), I was shy and reserved in public but dominant and controlling in the bedroom.

Actually, that one I liked.

"Does that mean you'll come with me tonight?" she asked hopefully.

"No. But if there are any leftover zucchini fritters, bring them over tomorrow. You can tell me how it went."

She sighed. "Fine. But if I change my mind about the app, would you really buy it and shut it down for me?"

"In a heartbeat."

"Thank you. Have fun with your family."

We hung up, and I felt guilty that I'd refused her request for a favor. I believed in doing good things for good people, and Felicity was as good as anyone I'd ever known.

Still, a high school reunion? A room full of people staring at me? Judging my every word, or worse, my awkward silence?

Fuck that.

A few minutes later, I pulled up in front of my sister's house and parked on the street. Before getting out of the car, I glanced at my phone and noticed a text from my business partner, Wade Hasbrouck.

His home address was San Francisco, but since it wasn't even eight a.m. there, I knew he wasn't in California. Wade was a night owl, which used to cause some friction between us when we were roommates at M.I.T., since he was not a particularly quiet night owl, and I was an early riser. His family had a lot of money and owned several luxury homes around the globe, and he hopped from one place to another as easily as he hopped from bed to bed, which was why his marriage of two years was already on the rocks.

Yo, his text said. (I truly hated the media stereotype of the dudebro tech billionaires, but the image fit Wade to a T.) **Date with Sam final. July 28. Can't push it back. Gird your loins, bruh.**

Sam referred to Uncle Sam, and the date I was hoping to push back—again—was the date I had to appear in front of the House Financial Services Committee in D.C. They wanted testimony regarding regulation of the digital-asset industry in general and our crypto exchange in particular.

My gut clenched. Today was the 9th.

I had just under three weeks.

While I'd known for months this was coming, the idea of having to give a public, live, televised statement and field questions on the fly was almost enough to make me want to cash out of HFX and go underground.

But what kind of person is so fucked up he can't even handle the *thought* of defending the business he'd helped build, especially if it meant losing half his net worth? Not that money was everything. I'd never set out to get rich, and I knew better than to think money could solve all your problems. In fact, I liked giving it away just as much as I liked earning it—what was the point of being a billionaire if all you did was horde your riches? Collect yachts and cars? For fuck's sake, how many Porsches does one person's ego need? I wanted to do things that mattered.

But most of all, I wanted what money couldn't buy.

I wanted to be the kind of guy who could testify without breaking a sweat—at least not visibly. The kind of guy who could conquer his fear of being put on display and subjected to pressure. The kind of guy whose nervous system didn't react like he was walking into a den of angry lions every time he thought about all the eyes in the room on him.

The uncontrollable thoughts. The racing heart. The sweating, the nausea, the inability of my head to find words and my mouth to form them. The blurry vision. The dizziness. The refusal of my lungs to take a full breath. The sheer terror of knowing that I could publicly humiliate myself in a hundred different ways, expose myself as deficient. A failure. A fool. A fraud.

Actually, give me the fucking lions.

I'd take my chances with them.

I walked up the driveway to my sister's side door and paused before knocking, my fist in the air—were those my parents' voices I heard through the open kitchen window? My dad's loud belly laugh confirmed it a second later.

Allie pulled the door open, a gleam in her eye. "What'cha doin'?"

"Deciding whether I want to come in. Are Mom and Dad here?"

She nodded. "They stopped by after their Saturday morning power walk. Matching track suits and all."

"Any way I can avoid them?"

"Why do you need to avoid them?"

"They're just *a lot*. Mom's all over me about what she calls my emotional avoidance issues, trying to set me up on dates with her kooky clients right and left, and I'm already hanging out with Dad later tonight."

She grinned. "Poker night?"

"Yeah."

"Lucky you. But you can't leave. I need to be at the salon in twenty minutes, and Mom and Dad both have to work today. They just popped in to see the kids real quick." She sighed heavily. "They love popping in."

"I told you not to buy a house right around the block from them."

"I know, I know." She threw a hand up. "But it's a good location and the price was right. We're not all billionaires."

"Fuck off, I told you I'd help you with a house. You refused."

She smiled triumphantly. "I did, and it gave me great pleasure. So thanks for that. Anyway, you covered my student loans, and that was a lot." She patted my chest. "You get free therapy from me for life."

"Just what a guy wants, his big sister bossing him around and calling it good for him."

"Speaking of which, did you call the woman I told you about, Natalia Lopez? The one who does the acceptance and commitment therapy? She's always booked super far in advance but as a favor to me, she said she'd get you in."

"No. I don't call people."

"Hutton! You didn't like cognitive behavioral therapy, and this is another option. A different approach. Why not try it?"

"Because I don't need it."

"So testifying in front of Congress won't be a problem then? How many times are they going to let you get away with pushing it back?"

Rather than tell her about the text from Wade, I pretended to throttle her by the neck as we walked into the kitchen, which smelled like bacon and waffles.

My parents sat at the table in their matching track suits, his royal blue, hers bright purple. They were well into their sixties but didn't look it. My father still had a full head of thick dark hair, which was only slightly gray above his ears, and a bushy brown mustache that was his pride and joy. My mother's long blond hair, chatty exuberance, and brightly colored clothing made her look more like a Hollywood sitcom psychic than a grandmother.

If anyone asked what their secret was, they had different answers. My father swore it was his hobbies that kept him young—the man had more hobbies than anyone I'd ever known, from gardening to tai chi to his barbershop quartet—and my mother claimed it was their enduring love that kept them so energetic. I think it was a combination of both, since my father's hobbies often took him out of the house, which he'd once confided was quite conducive to a good marriage.

My niece, Keely, was on my mom's lap, tearing apart a waffle and shoving it into her mouth like only a two-year-old can. My nephew Jonas, who was four, was squeezing a steady stream of syrup over everything on his plate—waffles, bacon, sliced strawberries. The oldest, Zosia, was six, and she was concentrating hard on cutting her own waffle under my dad's watchful eye.

"Hutton!" he boomed, glancing at me. "Still coming tonight?"

"Do I have a choice?"

"Nope, I already told the guys you'll be there." He grinned. "They're excited to have a celebrity at the game, but a little worried about your deep pockets."

"I'm not a celebrity, Dad," I muttered, taking a coffee cup down from the cupboard.

"They should be worried about him counting cards, not placing high bets," said my sister, filling up my cup from the pot.

"Hutton has never cheated a day in his life!" My mom was outraged at this attack on my honor. "And he knows that nothing good ever comes from taking a penny you didn't earn. It brings bad luck."

My sister and I exchanged a look. Our mother was famously superstitious—which one of my therapists thought explained my belief in magic powers as a kid. He might have been right, but it wasn't really the breakthrough he thought it was and definitely didn't merit the price tag of those sessions. Thousands of dollars just to be told our parents can fuck us up? People called cryptocurrency a racket, but therapy was a hundred times worse.

I gave Allie a lot of shit about that.

"But what if you find a penny on the street, Grandma?" asked Zosia. "Isn't that good luck?"

"Depends if you find it tails or heads side up," she answered seriously. "The ancient Romans believed if you saw a coin heads up, it was lucky, but if it was tails up, you should turn it over and leave it for the next person."

My sister laughed. "I'll keep that in mind in case I come across any ancient Roman coins. In the meantime, I'm gonna predict that being a math genius gives Hutton the edge at the poker table tonight."

"The only edge being a math genius might give someone at the poker table is knowing they should quit early and go home with all their money," I said, taking a sip of coffee. "The reason casinos are so huge is because most people have no idea how probability works."

"Hutton." My mother was studying me intently, like she was trying to read my mind. This was a habit of hers. "Are you okay?"

"I'm fine."

"You don't look fine."

"I'm fine, Mom."

"Look at him, Stan. Does he look fine to you?"

My dad shrugged. "I suppose so."

"You don't think he looks sort of pale and sad around the eyes?"

"Sad around the eyes?" My father squinted at me. "Maybe a little."

"I'm getting a sense of loneliness and discontent within your aura."

Allie snickered as she washed her hands at the sink.

"Stop it," I said. "My aura is fine."

"You don't have to pretend with us, sweetheart." My mom's voice softened. "We're your family."

"I'm not pre—"

"Money can't buy happiness, you know," she went on. "True happiness comes from our connection to others and to our higher selves. It doesn't come from things like yachts or private jets or fancy cars."

"I don't own any of those things, Mom."

But she was on a roll. "It comes from allowing yourself to be loved and offering love in return. Isn't that right, Stan?"

"That's right, Barb." My dad took my mother's hand across the table.

"And you don't need to be rich or famous or brilliant to find love." Her eyes misted over. "You just have to accept yourself as you are, and open your heart."

"Actually, I think being rich, famous, and brilliant makes it harder," said Allie. "You'd get a lot of people wanting to be close to you, but maybe for the wrong reasons."

"I'm not saying it's easy to find," my mom clarified. "I'm just saying that we're all worthy. Don't you agree, Hutton?"

"Yes," I said, mostly just to get her to stop talking.

My mother didn't understand. No one did.

I'd tried to have relationships. I'd attempted to let people in. But dating was a fucking nightmare. Even maintaining friendships was hard because I rarely accepted invitations. And when I did, the amount of energy it took to appear confident enough to just hang out and make conversation was exhausting. But I was good at it, so nobody ever understood why I hated clubs and parties.

I was overreacting, Wade always said. I was being too antisocial. Too introverted. Too picky. Too dramatic. Everyone gets anxious sometimes. Couldn't I just take some drugs or something? Go to a shrink? Didn't I like getting laid?

My response was usually something along the lines of, *That's not how it works, asshole.*

I'd tried the meds, but they gave me headaches. Therapists just wanted to explain the fight or flight response to me again, as if I didn't understand it.

And of course I liked getting laid.

I was good at sex. It was a relief to let my body take over, let it hijack my brain and call the shots. Also, I was an excellent student of female pleasure, and as a high achiever, I was deeply gratified by a woman's orgasm—the louder the better.

But sex wasn't a miracle fix for everything that was wrong with me.

I might have been worthy of love, but I wasn't wired for it. Simple as that.

After my parents left for their walk, I took the kids to the park. There were no Prancin' Grannies in sight, but there were a few stroller moms who gave me the usual looks that made me feel like they were all talking shit about me.

I did my best to keep my head down and enjoy the time

with the kids—I pushed Keely on the swings, watched Jonas jump off the slide instead of slide down it, and scored Zosia's cherry drop off the bar a perfect ten. We stayed for over an hour before the kids' faces started to get pink and I realized I'd forgotten to put sunscreen on them like Allie had asked.

"Come on, guys," I said. "Your faces are getting red, and your mom is going to get mad at me about it."

Back at my sister's house, I heated up a couple cans of SpaghettiO's for lunch, which was the extent of my cooking skills. When they were done eating, I smeared sunscreen on their faces, and we went out to the backyard.

My sister pulled into the garage as I was filling a small plastic pool on the lawn with water from the hose. The kids stood with their feet in it and sucked on bright green popsicles that were melting fast in the July heat, dripping down their chins and hands onto their shirts, which already had orange spots from the SpaghettiO's.

Allie smiled at the kids as she approached. "Wow. Look at you guys."

"I said I'd watch them. I didn't say I'd keep them clean."

She shook her hair like she was in a shampoo commercial. "Do you like the new cut?"

I squinted at her. "Looks the same to me."

She stuck out her tongue. "Hey, someone in the chair next to me at the salon mentioned she was going to her ten-year reunion tonight. Is it yours?"

"Probably."

"You're not going?"

"No."

"Why not?"

I focused on the water pouring from the hose. "I already have plans."

"*Poker night*? Those are your big plans?"

"I didn't say they were big. I just said they were plans."

She tilted her head, the way I imagined she did in therapy sessions before she pushed on an emotional bruise. "Is Felicity going?"

"I think so." And in a dumbass move that I can only blame on sun poisoning, I said, "She asked me to go with her, but I said no."

My sister's glare was fierce, and she thumped me on the shoulder. "Hutton! How could you say no? She was your best friend in high school. She was your prom date."

"I remember."

She stuck a hand on one hip. "And do you remember what you went through before asking her?"

Of course I did.

"Because *I* do. You agonized over it for weeks. It got so bad, you came to *me* for advice. I had to talk you into it."

"Because it was scary. I didn't know what she was going to say."

"But she said yes, and you had a good time."

For a moment, I was back in that hotel ballroom, working up the nerve to ask her to dance to a slow song, forcing myself to do it, even though I was positive she'd only said yes to going with me because she hadn't wanted to hurt my feelings.

But her face lit up, she took my hand, and I held her in my arms as we swayed awkwardly on the floor. It was heaven and hell at the same time. I was torn between wanting that song to go on forever, and wanting it to stop so I could quit freaking out over how I smelled and whether I'd worn the right shirt with my suit or whether she really liked the red wrist corsage I'd given her or would have preferred white. When the song ended, I said something stupid, which I spent days agonizing over, although now I couldn't even recall what it was. At the end of the night, instead of kissing her like I wanted to, I shook her hand.

Then I agonized over that too.

But I did have a good time. There was no one else I'd ever wanted to hold that close. I often thought about doing it again, usually late at night with a hand in my pants.

"Look, it's nothing to do with Felicity," I told Allie. "I always have fun with her."

"Of course you do." She rolled her eyes. "We all know how you feel about Felicity, Hutton. It's been obvious for years. And despite your messy hair and your ugly mug and your terrible personality, she genuinely likes you too. I don't get why you two aren't a thing."

I glanced at her. She looked like our mom, the way she was standing there with her weight on one leg, hip jutting out, hand parked on top of it, blond hair gleaming in the sun as she gleefully pushed my buttons.

So I did what any self-respecting little brother would do—I turned the hose on her and sprayed her down.

Three

Felicity

AFTER PREPPING ALL MY APPETIZERS, I JUMPED IN THE SHOWER and washed my hair. As I blew it dry, I kept hoping maybe the shampoo and conditioner might perform some miraculous trick and it wouldn't look so haphazardly chopped, but no such luck.

I threw it in a ponytail and hunted through my closet for something to wear, but after an hour, I gave up, drove over to Winnie's condo, and banged on her front door.

"I need a fairy godmother," I told her when she pulled it open.

She grinned as Dex's daughters, nine-year-old Hallie and six-year-old Luna, appeared behind her. "How about three of them?"

"Even better."

"Dex is out running errands, so we're having girl time," she said, shutting the door behind me. "Come on upstairs!"

Fifteen minutes later, I came out of the bathroom in my fourth dress.

"How about this one?" I did a little twirl for my audience of three, who sat on the edge of Winnie's bed.

"Yes," said Hallie, her brown eyes thoughtful as she tapped her chin. "It's definitely the best so far."

"I like it." Golden-headed Luna clapped her hands. "Blue is my favorite color."

"It is a great shade for you." Winnie got up off the bed and moved behind me, pulling the zipper all the way up to the top. "There. Now it fits a little better."

"Thanks." I went over to the full-length mirror on the back of her closet door and studied my reflection. The dress was cornflower blue with small white flowers all over it. The skirt was short and flared, and the neckline was deep and round. It would have looked better if I'd had more chest to fill out the top, but even with three fairy godmothers, the chances of going from a B to a D cup by seven o'clock tonight were slim. "I do like the color. You don't think the top is too . . . baggy on me?"

"Hmm." Winnie studied my reflection too. "Do you have a push-up bra?"

"What's a push-up bra?" asked Luna.

"It's a bra that pushes up your boobies and squeezes them together," said Hallie. "So they sort of bulge out like water balloons. Mom wears them."

I laughed. "I might have something at home."

"Good. Okay, now the shoes." Winnie went over to her closet and came out with three pairs of heels. "I think the nude strappy ones will be the best, but the platform sandals could also be cute. How much standing do you have to do?"

"I don't know," I said, sitting on the bed to slip into the platform sandals since they looked the most approachable. "But I don't want to have trouble walking, and I'm definitely not used to heels."

"I like those," Winnie said with a shrug when I was buckled into the tan leather sandals with a woven platform. "But it's not a very dressy look. How fancy is this event?"

I shrugged. "The invitation said dressy casual."

"That's two different things," Hallie pointed out.

I looked over my shoulder at her. "Exactly. Why do fashionable people make things more difficult than they need to be?"

"I think this look works for *casual*," Winnie said hesitantly, "but if you want to go a little dressier, maybe try the heels."

"I want to look elegant and sophisticated," I said.

My sister nodded. "Then go for the heels."

I slipped my feet into the spiky things, strapped them on, and wobbled over to the mirror. "Well?"

"They look perfect," Winnie said. "But can you get around in them okay?"

I wobbled to the door and back. "I'll manage."

"Good." She glanced at my sloppy ponytail and uneven bangs. "Now what are we going to do about that hair?"

My posture deflated slightly. "I don't know. I shouldn't have cut it."

"I agree," said Winnie, "but that ship has sailed, so let's figure out what we can do. Take it down and we'll look at it."

I bit my lip. "It's not pretty."

"I've seen your self-serve haircuts before, sis."

"This might be one of the worst." But I yanked the scrunchie from my hair and let it fall in all its zig-zagging glory.

Behind me, one of the girls gasped. Maybe both of them.

Winnie's mouth formed an O. She covered it with her hands.

"Why did you do that to your hair?" Luna wondered.

"It's hard to explain," I said, trying to rearrange my pitiful bangs to be more even. "Sometimes I just have this urge to cut it and I can't stop myself. Like when I'm upset about something. And I think cutting my hair will make me feel better." I spun around and faced them, worried that I was putting ideas in their young, impressionable minds. "But it doesn't. It only makes me feel worse."

"I have an idea," said Luna.

"You do?"

She nodded happily. "Space buns."

"Space buns?"

"Yes!" Hallie said enthusiastically. "That's a great idea! Space buns wouldn't show how it's all crazy at the ends."

Winnie laughed. "You know what? She might be right. Unless you have time to go get a professional trim."

"I don't," I said. "I barely had time to come here. I have to get my fritters and crostini in the Cloverleigh ovens before the restaurant there opens at five, pack everything in the warming bags, load the car, haul it over to the banquet hall by six, then have everything set out by quarter to seven."

"Space buns for the win," said my sister. "Hals and Loony, can you grab me a comb, two elastics, and some pins?"

"Yes!" Both girls jumped off the bed and raced for the bathroom.

"Can you make space buns look elegant?" I asked as Winnie used the comb to part my hair down the center.

"I'll do my best." Her tone was not terribly reassuring.

Fifteen minutes later, I had two buns perched on my head like Mickey Mouse ears. There were a lot of pieces hanging out, but Hallie said that was okay. Space buns didn't have to be perfect. Winnie had even managed to trim my bangs so they looked slightly less maniacal.

"Thank you so much," I said.

"Want me to do your makeup too?" Winnie asked.

"Would you?"

"Of course! What else are fairy godmothers for?"

Hallie and Luna were like surgical nurses, bringing Winnie different bottles and compacts, brushes and palettes, standing at the ready for the next command. Highlighter. Bronzer. Mascara.

Finally, I was pronounced done.

"Well? What do you think?" I asked the girls.

Luna smiled angelically at me. "I think you'll be the most beautiful lady at the party."

"Me too," Hallie said.

"Thanks." I gave them all hugs. "I don't know what I'd have done without you."

"Me neither," Winnie said with a laugh. "You better get going."

I traded the painful heels for my sneakers and wrapped them up in my shorts and T-shirt, tucking everything under my arm as I followed them downstairs. They walked outside with me, and we ran into Dex coming up the front walk.

"Dad!" Luna hopped off the porch and ran up to him. "Look at Felicity!"

"Hey, Felicity," he said.

"Hi, Dex."

Luna yanked his shirt. "Doesn't she look pretty? She's going to a party."

Dex smiled dutifully at me. "Very pretty."

"But that's not the complete outfit," Hallie was quick to explain. "She's not going to wear those shoes, and she definitely needs a push-up bra for the dress, but we helped do her hair."

Dex's face turned crimson as Winnie reached around Hallie and put a hand over her mouth. "Bye, Felicity. Have fun."

"I'll try," I said, laughing as I headed for my car.

"Just be yourself!" my sister shouted.

That probably worked all the time for someone like Winnie, I thought on the drive home. Being herself. Everyone loved Winnie. She was sweet and pretty and charming. She could talk to anyone, always knew what to say, and her nerves never showed.

I wondered what that was like.

Back at home, I dug through my underwear drawer and fished out the most padded bra I owned. I'd bought it on a whim but had never had the nerve to wear it—it felt like false advertising.

But I put it on beneath the sundress, and poof—my B cup breasts did suddenly resemble water balloons. Not big ones or anything, but there was a definite bulge happening above the neckline. Excited, I put some lipstick on and studied my reflection. Not bad. Actually, I thought I looked pretty good. The awful haircut wasn't obvious, Winnie had done something with my makeup that made my brown eyes look wide and luminous, and I had at least two curves.

I wished Hutton could see me.

"It's going to be fine," I told the girl in the mirror. "You *have* come a long way, even if you don't feel it. And there's nothing wrong with being a work in progress."

Happy with the way the girl smiled back at me, I rushed out of my room and raced down the stairs. Maybe that girl in the mirror wasn't Mimi Pepper-Peabody or a Lithuanian supermodel, maybe she wasn't even very elegant in her glasses and space buns, but she could get through tonight with her head held high.

She forgot the bag with the heels in it, so she'd have to get through it in sneakers, but really, she was more comfortable in sneakers anyway. She would be herself, and everything would be fine.

Of course, that was before the vodka.

I'm not quite sure how it happened.

I was only going to have a few sips of a cocktail to steady my nerves, which had seemed solid enough on the drive over, but had grown more shaky as the clock ticked closer to seven.

Really, it was Mimi Pepper-Peabody's fault. She strolled over with a clipboard as I was setting out my appetizers on a table, looking like Reunion Organizer Barbie with her long, shiny, blond waves, her strapless little black dress, and her black patent leather heels with the bright red bottoms. "Hi there," she said with a megawatt smile that lacked an ounce of genuine warmth. "I'm Mimi Pepper-Peabody, soon to be Mimi Van Pelt." She held out her hand so I could admire the diamond engagement ring twinkling on her finger. "I'm getting married."

"Congratulations," I said.

"Thank you." The smile stayed plastered on her lips. "And you are?"

"I'm Felicity MacAllister," I said, glancing down at the name tag I wore. "We spoke on the phone? I'm the Veggie Vixen."

Mimi looked confused for a moment, then burst out laughing. "I'm *so* sorry, I thought you were one of the students I hired to help set up. You look so young with your hair in those things—what do you call them?"

"Space buns," I said, touching one of them self-consciously.

"Space buns, yes. My little cousin likes to wear her hair like that. Of course, she's eight." More condescending laughter as she patted my sleeve. "But don't worry, it's cute for you."

I glanced at her long, French-manicured nails and hid my hands behind my back. My cuticles were horrible. "Thanks."

"But you should tell your stylist not to cut your bangs so short. They look a little silly."

I bit my bottom lip.

Mimi snapped her fingers. "I remember you now—you used to get those awful bloody noses in the middle of class! Do you still get them?"

"Sometimes."

She shuddered. "How embarrassing. Hope that doesn't happen tonight."

"Would you like to try an appetizer?" I picked up a platter of zucchini fritters and restrained myself from throwing it at her.

"No, thanks. So you're in food service now?"

"Catering, yes. And a food blogger." I gritted my teeth and asked the polite question. "How about you?"

She tossed her hair. "I'm a lifestyle blogger and influencer. How many followers do you have?"

"I just hit two thousand."

Her smile was superior. "I have three thousand, four-hundred-eighteen. I'm growing *really* fast."

"Oh . . . that's cool."

"Let me know if you need any tips on building a following. Good to see you, Felicity—you haven't changed a bit." She strolled away, leaving the overpowering scent of her perfume behind.

I was still angry when people started arriving a few minutes later—at Mimi for being just as terrible and beautiful as she'd ever been, at myself for letting her make me feel small, at Winnie for talking me into space buns, and even at Hutton for refusing to come with me tonight. Needing something to take the edge off my mood, I marched over to the bar and asked for a vodka soda with lime.

"Make it a double," I told the bartender. "And easy on the soda."

"You're twenty-one, right?" He looked warily at my space buns before glancing at my chest.

"I'm twenty-eight," I snapped. "Do you want to see my ID?"

"All good." He grabbed a glass and plunked some ice in it. "Just checking."

I took the drink back to my table and sucked down the whole thing in a matter of minutes. So I was a little buzzed by the time Mimi came around again, this time followed by a couple of her old friends from the cheerleading squad. Carrie was brunette and Ella was strawberry blond, but both wore their hair styled exactly like Mimi's.

I smiled at them and said hello, pleased when they added some of my appetizers to their plates.

"Mmm, crostini," said Carrie. She was wearing a black dress very similar to Mimi's, but one-shouldered. "What's on this?"

"Goat cheese, dates, walnuts, fresh thyme, and a little honey," I said, thrilled she hadn't called them cheese toasts. "And those over there are watermelon, basil, and feta."

"Oooh," said Ella, who also wore a short, fitted dress in black. They looked like an army. Or a row of backup singers. "I'll try that watermelon one for sure. And what are those?"

"Zucchini fritters. Everything is vegetarian, and all the produce is local," I said with pride.

"This is so good," said Carrie, licking her fingers after polishing off a goat cheese crostini. "Mimi, you should try this."

"I don't eat bread or dairy." Mimi looked longingly at the appetizers on her friends' plates. She put a hand on her tummy. "The bloat, you know?"

"Live a little." Ella laughed. "One crostini isn't going to bloat you."

I thought for sure Mimi was going to protest, but she shocked me by reaching for a watermelon, basil, and feta crostini and shoving the entire thing in her mouth so fast, it was as if she was hoping no one would notice. Her eyes closed as she chewed and swallowed. "Wow. That is good." She eyeballed the rest of them on the tray. "How many calories are in them?"

"I'm not sure exactly," I said. "But the bread is sliced very thin, and compared to other cheeses, feta is very low in calories and—"

"Maybe just one more." Mimi plucked another one from the tray and gobbled it up.

Carrie laughed. "Told you they were delicious."

"They're pretty good," Mimi admitted. After stuffing a third and fourth crostini—goat cheese and date—and then several zucchini fritters into her mouth, Mimi picked up a business card. "The Veggie Vixen. But there's nothing very vixenish about you, is there?"

I rattled the ice cubes in my glass and tipped it up again, hoping for a few more drops of vodka.

"Do you cater weddings, Felicity? Mimi is engaged," Ella told me.

"I heard." I made myself smile at Mimi. "And yes, I do. And I'd love to talk about your wedding. I have plenty of dishes without gluten or dairy."

Mimi put the card back on the table. "Oh, Thornton would probably revolt if I planned anything vegetarian," she said with a condescending laugh. "He's such a man's man. You know how those millionaires are, with their hunting cabins and big game safaris. Such carnivores."

Her friends murmured their agreement, as if they were all engaged to carnivorous millionaires.

"But maybe some cute little things for one of my showers. I'm using Dearly Beloved to plan everything. Are you on that app?" Mimi set her wine glass down, and I watched in horror as she dug her phone from her purse. "I'll make sure I'm following you."

"Following me?" I squeaked.

"Yes. On Dearly Beloved." She snapped her fingers twice. "Keep up."

Suddenly there was nothing I wouldn't have said to keep Mimi from looking at that shitty one-star review on Dearly Beloved.

"I'm engaged too," I blurted.

Mimi looked up at me in surprise, fingers poised over the screen. "Are you?"

"Yes."

"To who?"

"To a hot billionaire."

Mimi's jaw dropped. *"You're* engaged to a hot billionaire?"

"Yes."

"Who?"

"Hutton French." The name popped from my lips before I could think.

"Hutton French?" The trio echoed with identical intonation. They exchanged surprised glances.

"The one from our graduating class who was dating Zlatka?" Carrie asked.

"They broke up," I said quickly.

"So where's your ring?" Mimi arched a brow and gestured toward my left hand.

I thought fast. "It's being sized. It's at the jeweler's."

"Hard to believe that guy from high school is now a famous billionaire," said Ella. "He was so . . ."

If she said *weird*, I was going to throw a fritter at her.

"Quiet," she finished. "And shy."

"But smart," I said. "He's brilliant."

"And gorgeous." Ella giggled, her cheeks turning pink.

"Like, I see his photos now, and I'm like, damn, why didn't you look this good back in high school?"

"He did," I told her, setting my empty glass on the tray of a passing server collecting them.

"I heard he was back in town," said Carrie. "My nana saw him at the park."

"So where is he now?" Mimi demanded, looking around. "Why isn't he here?"

I wrung my hands. "He's very busy with work."

"What exactly does he do?" Ella asked. "I've read the articles about him and all, but I'm embarrassed to say I have no idea what cryptocurrency is."

"It's complicated." I glanced toward the bar, dying to excuse myself and get another drink.

"It's too bad he couldn't be here tonight," Mimi said with a suspicious look in her eye. "You'd think he'd want to support your little business venture and all."

"He's *very* supportive," I said. Which would have been fine, except that I added, "He's coming later."

Mimi smiled like she still didn't believe me. "How nice. I can't wait to congratulate you both in person."

Shit! Now what was I going to do?

"If you'll excuse me, I'll just go call him and see if he's on his way. Nice chatting with you." Grabbing my purse, I turned and walked away from them. As soon as I was out of the room, the sneakers came in handy, because I bolted to the end of the hall and ducked into the coat closet. Since it was summer, it was dark and empty—I slammed the door behind me and leaned back against it, breathing hard.

I had to think. Should I call him? He might have his phone off. I could text him, but it would be hard to explain myself in a text. And I wasn't sure he'd view the situation with the same urgency I did. Could I pretend I was having a bloody nose and beg him for a ride to the ER? He'd show up, but he might be mad when he got here and there was no blood. Could I give myself a bloody nose? I briefly considered punching myself in the face.

Then I sank to the floor and sat cross-legged, my phone in my lap, the tips of my thumbs between my teeth.

Curse my big mouth!

Every time I got nervous, I spewed something weird or shocking. And just like stress-cutting my hair, it often got me into trouble. Or ruined what could have been a nice moment.

Like my first kiss.

If I closed my eyes, I could still smell the public library study room and picture the table where we'd been sitting. Our AP calc exam was the following morning, and Hutton and I were seated next to each other, working through the study guide.

We'd already been to prom together, and there were only a few days of school left. Once exams were over, all we had left was the graduation ceremony to get through. Lately I'd been a little panicked at the thought of losing him—the one true friend I had.

I kept looking over at him, and my stomach was doing this weird flippy thing. I liked the way his dark blond hair was messy and tousled in the front. He sometimes played with it while he worked. He was so intense when he studied, his blue eyes laser-focused on the page. He had a long, straight nose, nice ears, and when he swallowed, his Adam's apple bobbed. Sometimes he moved his jaw to one side or another when he was concentrating, and his lips would part. I'd never kissed a boy and wondered what kissing Hutton would feel like.

Absently, I rubbed my pencil eraser over my lower lip while I stared at Hutton's mouth.

He looked over at me. "What?"

I sat up straight and put both hands on the table, pencil down. "I didn't say anything."

"You were staring at me."

"No, I wasn't. I was staring into space. And thinking."

"About what?"

"Have you ever kissed anyone?" My stomach lurched.

Hutton's cheeks flushed and he dropped his eyes to his notebook. "No."

"Me neither." I picked up my pencil again and doodled in the margin.

"Have you ever wanted to?"

He went completely still. "Wanted to what?"

"Kiss someone."

He looked at me. His Adam's apple bobbed. "Have you?"

"Yes," I admitted.

Bob. "Me too."

Suddenly I was aware of how close we were sitting. And how no one else was in the study room with us.

He leaned forward a little. His eyes were on my mouth.

I thought he was going to do it. I was *positive* he was going to do it. I *wanted* him to do it. But then I panicked—how did you kiss a boy?

Like, where did your noses go? What did you do with your tongue? Were my glasses going to be in the way? Was my breath okay? How long were you supposed to keep your lips together? Should I move them or keep them still? Dammit, I was chewing gum! Should I swallow it? And what did this mean that I wanted Hutton to kiss me? Was I in love with him? If he kissed me, were we more than friends? What did he really think of me? My heart was pounding and I was sweating profusely and the seconds were ticking by, I could hear them on that old clock on the wall—tick, tick, tick—and he still didn't make a move, and I couldn't take it anymore, so I shot words into the silence like bullets.

"My mother didn't want me."

Hutton sat back and blinked. "Huh?"

"My mother didn't want me. My real mom."

"The one that left?"

I nodded, my heart still pumping with fear.

"How do you know?"

"I heard her say it one night when I was about six."

He looked uncomfortable, then rubbed the back of his neck. "Fuck."

"She left about three weeks later. And she never came back." *So it must have been true,* I left unspoken.

Hutton didn't say anything. His eyes dropped to his lap.

"God, what am I *doing*?" I put my pencil down and covered my face with my hands. "I'm sorry. Forget what I said. I'm sorry." My entire body burned with embarrassment. "I have no idea why I just dumped that on you."

"It's okay."

Picking up my pencil again, I stared at my page of problems and pretended the numbers weren't blurry.

After a moment, Hutton went back to his calc problems too—or at least I thought he did. But about five minutes later, he ripped a page out of his notebook, folded it in half, and slid it toward me.

I glanced at him. "What's this?"

"Open it."

I unfolded the page and laughed when I saw a message written out in pigpen cipher text. "You wrote me a note I have to decode?"

"You remember how?"

"I think so." It took me a minute to recall the grid symbolizing the pigpen's geometric substitution of the alphabet. But a few minutes later, I had it.

"I have been and always shall be your friend," I read out loud, my throat constricting as I reached the last word.

"It's from *Star Trek*."

"I know," I said, slightly insulted. But I was really touched.

"Thank you. That means a lot." I blinked away tears once more.

"You okay?"

"Yeah. I think—I think graduation is messing with me. And maybe the fact that we're going separate ways in the fall. You've sort of been the best friend I've ever had." I gave him a tentative smile. "What am I going to do without you?"

"No matter where I am, I'll always be there when you need me."

"I'll use the code like a bat signal," I said. "Then you'll know it's really me."

He laughed. "I'll do the same."

"And let's make a deal—we can't ignore the code, okay? If one of us uses it to reach out, we drop everything and come to the rescue."

"Deal."

And just like that, my problem was solved.

Four

Hutton

AT FIRST, I WAS TOTALLY CONFUSED.

The text from Felicity came in just as I was grabbing a beer from my parents' fridge. But what she'd sent was a photo of something—a sheet of white paper with a bunch of nonsense symbols on it. I was about to text her back and ask if she'd lost her mind when it hit me.

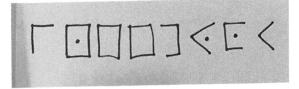

It wasn't nonsense. It was code—the pigpen cipher.

I smiled—I couldn't believe it had taken me more than five seconds to recognize it. "Hey Dad," I called. "Are we starting right this second?"

"Nope," he called back from the den off the kitchen. "Harvey's not here yet."

"Harvey's always late," said my mom, pulling a tray of cocktail wieners baked in crescent roll dough from the oven. "He moves so slowly, I'm convinced he was a sloth in his last life."

I set the beer bottle on the counter unopened and rummaged around in the junk drawer for a pencil.

"Speaking of past lives," she went on, "I did a reading for the most beautiful woman this afternoon at the store."

"Did she think she was Cleopatra?" Women *always* thought they were Cleopatra.

"Yes, but she wasn't. I've met the woman who was Cleopatra, and she lives in Tucson. But she was remarkably lovely, and I think she was latching onto Cleopatra because she's lonely and looking for love. I invited her to stop by tonight."

I stopped searching and looked at my mother. "You didn't."

"She's slightly older than you, but—"

"How old?"

"Forty, but she's a young forty." For some reason, my mother sort of fluffed up her chest when she said this. "What are you looking for in that drawer?"

"Something to write with—found it." I pulled out a stubby pencil with a dirty neon yellow eraser top. "I need a piece of paper too."

She handed me the spiral pad she used for writing her grocery lists. "Here."

I flipped past her list and quickly sketched the cipher's substitution grid from memory—and within minutes I was decoding Felicity's message.

I need you, she'd written.

Immediately, I remembered the night in the library when I'd almost kissed her—the note I'd passed and the promise we'd made.

"Shit," I said.

"What's wrong?" My mother glanced over at me as she placed the pigs in a blanket on a serving plate.

Exhaling, I gave the beer one last, longing look before sticking it back in the fridge. "I have to make a phone call."

I went out the back door into the yard, pulling the kitchen

door shut behind me, so my mother wouldn't be tempted to eavesdrop. The air outside was warm and humid, and smelled slightly metallic, like there might be a storm coming. I slapped at a mosquito before dialing Felicity's number.

"Hello?"

"I got the bat signal. What's up?"

"Okay, before I tell you, will you promise to honor the deal?"

"Why do I have a bad feeling about this?"

"Do you promise?"

"Yes."

She sighed with relief. "Thank God. Because I have to get out of this closet soon, and I can't face Mimi again without your help."

"What closet? Where are you?"

"I'm at the reunion," she said, "but I'm hiding in the coat closet because I did something bad. I mean, I said something I shouldn't have."

"About what?"

"About you. Well, about us."

"What did you say?"

She exhaled. "I said that we're engaged."

"You said *what?*"

"I said that we were engaged. Well, I said that I was engaged to a hot billionaire, and then when Mimi asked who, I said you. You're the only hot billionaire I know."

She thinks I'm hot was what registered first, and it fired up my insides a little. "Thanks. But why did you lie about being engaged in the first place?"

"I couldn't help it, Hutton," she said. "Mimi's been so mean and terrible all night, first when it was just the two of us, and then in front of her friends, and I just couldn't let her get away with it anymore. She kept bragging about her own engagement to some rich dude who hates vegetables, and making me feel bad about myself, and then she was going to look me up on Dearly Beloved, and I had to say something to stop her before she saw that awful review. So I said I was engaged to you," she finished, sounding out of breath. "Also, there may have been some vodka involved."

"I'm not surprised."

"I'm sorry, Hutton. I panicked."

"It's okay," I told her. "Do you need me to come pick you up?"

"No, I need you to come here and be my fake fiancé."

My gut clenched. "Is that really necessary? Can't you just say I'm out of town?"

"It's sort of too late for that. I already told her you were coming."

I groaned, rubbing my temples with my thumb and middle finger.

"I'm sorry, okay? I'll straighten it all out eventually, but can you please, *please* come here tonight and pretend like we're getting married?"

If it were anyone else, I'd have refused to do this insane thing. But Felicity was special to me, and after all, I had made a promise. I checked my watch. "It's quarter to eight. I won't be there for at least forty-five minutes. I have to go home and change."

"That's fine."

"What am I supposed to wear?"

"Something billionairy. A nice suit and tie. You don't happen to have a diamond ring lying around, do you?"

I laughed. "I'm not that kind of billionaire."

"Is there any chance you could find one?"

"Where the hell would I find a diamond ring at eight o'clock at night?"

"I don't know. Can't you borrow jewels for the night like Richard Gere did in *Pretty Woman*?"

"Richard Gere had more notice than I did. Jewelry stores are closed."

She sighed. "It's probably fine. I told Mimi the ring was at the jeweler's being sized."

"Jesus Christ, Felicity. How am I going to keep all the lies straight?" I was starting to sweat.

"Those are the only ones I told so far! We're engaged, the ring is at the jeweler's, and you're coming here later. I swear to God, I will make it up to you, Hutton—I just need this one night."

"One *hour*," I said.

"One hour will be perfect," she said. "I'll send you the venue address, and then you can text me when you get here. I'll even come out and meet you so you don't have to walk in alone."

"Thanks."

"Thank *you*, Hutton. I mean it. You're the best friend in the world."

I hung up and went back into the kitchen, where my mom was spooning French onion dip from the plastic carton into the dip end of a chip-and-dip bowl. "Everything okay?" she asked.

"Yeah, but I have to go."

"Where?"

I clenched my jaw. "My high school reunion."

"Really?" She sounded pleased.

"Yeah. Felicity is there, and she needs me to . . . show up," I finished. There was no way I could explain the real situation.

"A date with Felicity? I think that's wonderful!"

I chose not to take the bait. "Can you apologize to Dad for me?"

"Of course. Maybe I'll introduce Cleopatra to Harvey. He's been so lonely since Edna died last year."

"Good idea."

She set her spoon down, came over, and kissed my cheek. "You just go, darling. I can't wait to hear all about it. But are you going to change first?" She looked at my jeans and T-shirt with some dismay. "And maybe fix your hair a little too?" She started fussing with the front of my hair.

I pushed her hands away. "Stop it, Mom. I have to go."

"Only trying to help." She smiled. "Say hello to Felicity. I always had a feeling about the two of you. Past life soul mates if I ever saw them."

"We're just friends." Pulling my keys from my pocket, I headed for the back door again.

"Don't fight it, darling. Tomorrow we should do a tarot reading for you, feel out where this might be heading. And take an umbrella! The leaves are upside down, and that always means a storm."

I yanked the door shut behind me, drowning her out.

Just under an hour later, I texted Felicity from the banquet center parking lot. **I'm here.**

I'll meet you right outside the front door! she texted back.

Before getting out of the car, I checked myself out in the visor mirror. Was my hair neat enough? My tie straight? My scruff under control? If I'd had more time, I'd have shaved or at least trimmed it up. At least I'd ironed my shirt. I wasn't that good at it, since I usually had my shirts pressed at the dry cleaner, but my suit coat would cover it up. I grabbed it from the back seat, shrugged it on, and locked up my car before walking slowly toward the banquet hall entrance.

With every step, a sense of dread built beneath my skin. My chest grew tighter. My breath quickened. Inside were a bunch of people I didn't know at all, but who would be eager to judge me. They'd know who I was. They'd heard things about me. They probably thought I didn't deserve the money. Surely, they'd notice the way I was sweating. They'd ask questions and I'd stumble over my answers. Maybe I'd stumble over my own feet. I'd forget names. They'd think I—

"Hutton!" Felicity came running toward me and threw her arms around my neck, clinging to me like she was drowning. "Thank you so much for coming! You look amazing."

It surprised me when she didn't let go right away, and it felt good to be held that tightly. For a moment, I stayed completely still with my arms around her back, her chest pressed against mine. When I inhaled, I smelled her perfume—it wasn't the same one she used to wear, but I liked it. That scent and the feel of her in my arms took the edge off my nerves.

But when Felicity stepped back, she could see I wasn't entirely okay. "I'm sorry, Hutton." She reached out and took my hand, squeezing it. "Forget this. You don't have to come in."

It wasn't the first time I'd stood in a parking lot with a woman and hadn't wanted to attend a social event. But in those instances, I'd been told things like, *You're being ridiculous. Stop being selfish. You need to get over yourself.* It meant a lot to me that Felicity understood—so much that I would try to get over myself . . . for an hour. Near an exit. With a cocktail.

"Are you saying you don't want to be engaged to me anymore?" I teased.

"No. I'm saying that I realize how ridiculous this whole thing is. And it's not fair to you."

"It's really fucking ridiculous. But let's do it anyway."

"Really?" Her smile lit up her face.

"Yeah. As long as I don't have to talk much."

"I'll do all the talking," she said, tugging me by the hand toward the venue. "Promise."

"Then it's a deal." I let my eyes wander over her. She looked so pretty—her bangs looked like she might have gone at them with the scissors at some point today, but her eyes were huge and luminous, and her lips were full and pink. The dress she had on showed off curves I didn't realize she had, and the hem was shorter than she normally wore. I glanced down at her feet. "You made me wear a suit and you've got sneakers on?"

"That wasn't the plan, but yes."

"It's okay. You look beautiful." I opened the door for her.

She stopped abruptly in the doorway and looked at me. "I do?"

For a second, I was afraid I'd said something wrong. My collar felt tight. "Yes. But it's not that I don't think you look beautiful other times. I always think you're beautiful. I just meant that right now you—"

"Hey." She smiled again and put a finger over my lips for a moment. "It's okay. It was a nice compliment. You've just never said that to me before."

"Oh." I relaxed a little. "Well, I meant it."

Her cheeks grew slightly pink. "Thank you."

I followed her through the lobby into the room where the reunion was taking place, and immediately my shoulders and neck tensed up again. At least a hundred people were there, seated at round tables, filling plates at the buffet, waiting in line at the bar, standing in groups with drinks, chatting and laughing and having fun. It was so *easy* for some people, I thought, grateful when Felicity took my hand. Why was it so fucking hard for me?

The music was loud as Felicity led me between some tables and across the wooden dance floor. She nodded and smiled at people as we passed them, but I kept my eyes on her. Eventually we reached the line for the bar, and she turned to me. "Drink?"

"Yeah." I tugged at my collar with my free hand.

"Stop fussing. You look perfect. I love that navy suit on you. And your blue tie matches your eyes."

"Thanks."

"But you just made it crooked. Let me fix it." She faced me and straightened my tie with both hands, gently putting the knot back in place without making it too tight. "How's that feel?"

"Good." Our eyes met, and my heart thumped even harder.

"Next up," the bartender said, breaking the spell. "What can I get you?"

We ordered drinks—a Manhattan for me, a vodka and soda for her—and took them over to a small table set apart from the buffet. "This is mine," she said, gesturing to the platters of appetizers and a stack of business cards. "We can just stay over here, away from the crowd."

"Okay." Taking a sip of my cocktail, I indulged in an old habit—immediately locating the nearest exit and planning my escape route in case I had to leave fast.

While Felicity fussed with the display of food on the table, I recalled something a therapist once told me about using body language to exude dominance and control. Power posing, it was called. You sort of stood and moved like you had a fuck ton of confidence, and the idea was that not only could you fool others, but you could fool yourself.

It sounded like bullshit, and I fired her.

But just in case she was right, I decided to assume a more cocksure stance. That was a word I liked—cocksure. I widened my feet. Puffed up my chest. Scowled a bit, like anyone who came near me had better have a damn good reason to approach.

"Well, well. Look who showed up." A woman in a black dress with long blond hair and a stocky, dark-haired guy in a suit sauntered up to the table. The woman looked vaguely familiar, but even if she hadn't, she was giving off a scornful, superior air that broadcast exactly who she was.

"Mimi." Immediately, Felicity set her drink down and slipped her arm through mine. "You remember Hutton."

"Not like *this*." Mimi laughed as her eyes darted over my hair, my suit, my shoes. Then she held out a hand. "Nice to see you again."

I didn't want to touch her, but I took the hand she of-fered—it was cool and reptilian. "Hi."

"From band geek to billionaire," she said with a laugh. "Who'd have thought?"

"Me," said Felicity. "I always knew he'd be a huge suc-cess. He's brilliant."

"This is Thornton Van Pelt, *my* fiancé," said Mimi, giving her tone a slightly combative edge, as if getting engaged was a competitive sport.

"Good to meet you," said Thornton, looking bored.

"We're planning a June twentieth wedding, next year." Mimi took the lead with a declaration of a date. "What about you?"

"This year." Felicity pressed tighter to my side. "Next month."

"Next *month*?" Mimi's jaw dropped. "August?"

"Yes." Felicity looked at me adoringly. "We just can't wait."

I had no idea if I was supposed to reply or not, or what I would say if I did.

Thankfully, Mimi kept going. "I'm just surprised I hav-en't heard the news, what with Hutton being so famous and all," she said.

"We're very private," said Felicity. "We didn't announce it."

"When did it happen?" Mimi asked.

"Weeks ago," Felicity replied. "After he moved back."

"Really." Mimi looked back and forth between us. "That's sort of sudden."

"Well, we've practically been best friends since we were twelve," said Felicity.

"But you were dating Zlatka up until very recently, weren't you?" Mimi pinned her laser beam eyes on me.

"That's another reason why we didn't announce it," Felicity said, patting my arm. "We didn't want to hurt anyone's feel-ings. Right, sweetie?"

I was pretty sure Zlatka didn't have that many feelings, but I nodded and took another drink, like a cocksure badass would.

"Tell me about your ring," demanded Mimi.

"Oh, it's so beautiful," gushed Felicity. "A diamond solitaire. Really classic and stunning. Hutton has incredible taste."

"How big is the diamond? Mine is two carats." She thrust her hand out.

"Mine's three," said Felicity quickly. "And the diamond is conflict-free. Ethically sourced."

Mimi looked pissed. "Cut?"

"Round."

"Band?"

"Platinum."

"Color and clarity?"

That one threw her, and she fumbled. "Color and what?"

"Clarity." Mimi snapped her fingers twice. "Keep up."

"Uh, I forget," Felicity mumbled.

"You *forget* the color and clarity of your diamond?" Mimi's eyes narrowed, and beside me, I felt Felicity stiffen.

"F and VVS one," I said, recalling Wade's incessant rants about the ungodly expensive ring his then-girlfriend had wanted—probably to get back at him for all the cheating.

All three of them looked sharply at me.

"F and VVS one?" Mimi repeated. "Did you hear that, Thornton?"

Thornton checked his watch. "Yeah. Isn't that what you have?"

"No," she said, giving him the side eye. "It isn't."

"Hutton spoils me silly." Felicity tipped her head onto my shoulder. "But what does it matter, right? The ring isn't the most important thing. It's just a piece of metal and rock. The real worth is in the love you share."

"Tell that to her," said Thornton, tipping up his glass to finish off his cocktail. "I'll be right back. I need another drink."

Mimi didn't even look at him as he walked away. "What about your dress? Where's it from?"

"Paris," Felicity said. "It's French."

"I *know* where Paris is," she snapped. "How about the reception?"

"Cloverleigh Farms, of course. But it's very intimate—just immediate family."

At this point, Mimi had to concede victory. "Sounds like you've got it all worked out."

"We do." Felicity put her hand on my chest. And left it there. "We're very happy."

"Well, congratulations on keeping it a secret." Mimi crossed her arms. "That must have been hard."

"Well, it's actually still sort of a secret." Felicity laughed nervously. "We haven't really announced anything official yet, so if you wouldn't mind keeping it quiet?"

"Say no more." Mimi's eyes suddenly gleamed. "If you'll just excuse me, I'm going to find Thornton."

I turned to Felicity as soon as we were alone. "You know she's going to tell everyone she knows, right?"

She sighed, her shoulders drooping, her eyes dropping to the floor. "Yeah. I'm sorry."

"You don't have to apologize to me." I glanced out at the crowd. "But if she starts spilling the news right now, we might be swamped with people trying to get the scoop."

Her eyes met mine, a little panicked. "You're right. Let's get out of here."

I put my drink on the table. "You never have to ask me to leave a party twice. What about your appetizers?"

"I can leave them." She grabbed her purse from beneath the table. "I'll pick up the platters tomorrow, and my warming bags are already in the car. Let's just go."

This time, I took *her* hand and pulled her through the crowd, into the lobby, and out the front door. I moved quickly, and Felicity had to hustle to keep up with me. When we were out in the parking lot, we slowed to a walk and she started to laugh. "I think we're safe. God, that was fun. Did you see her face?"

I had to laugh too. "I had no idea what was going to come out of your mouth next."

"Me neither."

"Where are you parked?" I asked.

"Right here." She pointed at the nearest row. "You?"

"I'm over there." I gestured toward the far side of the lot. "But I'll walk you to your car."

"Thanks." She took a deep breath and looked at the darkening sky. "Smells like a storm is coming, doesn't it?"

"Yeah." We walked a few car-lengths. "You still hate them?"

"I don't really hate them, they just . . . put me on edge." She glanced at me. "You going back to poker night?"

"Hell no." I told her about my mother inviting Cleopatra over, and she laughed.

"Well, you can go home early and tell her I kept you out late."

Going home was exactly what I wanted, except . . . I didn't really want to leave her. "Do you want to come over?"

"Sure. Have you eaten?"

"No. Want to order in?"

"Or I could make us something. Do you have any food at your house?"

"I'm not sure." My housekeeper did my grocery shopping for me, but since I didn't cook, I never paid much attention to what was in my fridge or pantry.

"I'll hit the store on my way over," she said, pulling her keys from her purse. "My cooking is better than takeout." She unlocked her car, the lights flashing in the dark. "I'll see you in a few?"

"Sounds good." I opened the driver's side door for her, and she tossed her purse onto the passenger seat. Then she surprised me by putting her arms around my neck and pressing her body full-length against mine in a giant hug.

"Thanks a lot for coming here tonight," she said. "I know it was hard for you."

The words *hard for you* buzzed through my head as my cock came to life in my pants. Could she feel it? I was an expert in concealing my inner thoughts, but hiding an erection was a trickier task. "I didn't have a choice, remember? You used the code."

She leaned back so I could see her face, but she kept her arms looped around my neck, her hips resting on mine. "I promise I won't use it again unless it's a real emergency. Anyway, you were amazing." She kissed my cheek, which did nothing to stop the rush of blood to my crotch.

"It was all you. I only said three words."

"Really?"

"Yes, I said 'hi,' I said 'F,' and I said 'VVS one.' Some of that might not even count as words."

She laughed, finally letting me go. "I guess I did do all the talking—all the lying, I mean. Which is going to turn into a big mess tomorrow once Mimi opens her mouth. But don't worry." Her eyes met mine, her smile fading. "I promise to clean it up."

"I trust you," I told her. "And actually I enjoyed watching you take her down a notch every thirty seconds."

She smiled again, a little wickedly. "Not gonna lie, it felt pretty good. And if I never get engaged for real, at least I'll have the memory of tonight."

I didn't like thinking about Felicity with anyone else—I never had. "Hey," I said, a protective urge swelling in my chest. "Why don't I follow you to the store? We can shop together."

She looked surprised. "You hate shopping."

"I hate shopping *alone*. But I won't be alone—I'll have you. And I want to buy the groceries, since you're cooking for me."

"Okay," she said with a smile. "Follow me."

I walked over to my SUV, tossed my jacket in the back seat, and got in. A minute later, she drove by and waved at me, and as crazy as it sounds, my heart started to race as I followed her out of the lot. Like this was turning into a real date or something.

But it wasn't—we were just going grocery shopping and then back to my place to eat and hang out. It wasn't like anything would happen. It wasn't like there was anything different between us. All that stuff she'd said about me inside—that I looked great, that I was brilliant, that I spoiled her—was made up. And the things she did, like straighten my tie and hold my hand and touch my chest and lay her head on my shoulder . . . it was just for show.

She didn't know how I really felt about her. And I couldn't ever tell her. If I told her, it could go sideways in a hurry, and everything would be ruined.

I'd made my mind up about this years ago.

There was just one problem, I thought, my cock twitching in my pants again as I recalled the way she pressed her body against mine when she'd hugged me—twice.

I couldn't stop thinking about getting her naked.

Five

Felicity

"**G**OD, I LOVE YOUR KITCHEN." I PAUSED HALVING A PINT of cherry tomatoes to take a sip of white wine. "I feel like I'm in a dream right now."

"That's because you gave me the shitty job." Hutton had to look away from the pungent onion he was chopping.

"Sorry. Even I hate chopping onions." I laughed and gestured to our surroundings, wine glass in hand. "But if I got to do it in this kitchen every day, even that job wouldn't feel so bad."

Hutton glanced around, like he'd never really noticed the gorgeous wood floors, the elegant ebony-stained cabinetry, the gleaming marble counters, the stunning Thermidor range and stainless appliances. "Yeah. It's nice."

I swished one bare foot across the floor's smooth surface—I'd ditched my sneakers and socks because I loved the satin feel of them beneath my soles. "It's more than nice. It's probably good I *don't* have this kitchen. I'd never leave my house."

"You're welcome to use mine whenever you want. But not

if you make me chop onions." He pushed the cutting board toward me. "Here. I'm done."

"Thanks." I glanced at him, and my belly did the funny flip-flop thing again. He looked *so good*. He'd taken off his coat and tie, loosened his collar, and cuffed up his sleeves. He had this one lock of hair that refused to submit to any product or stay off his face. It was always springing forward onto his forehead in a way that made me want to brush it out of his eyes.

It was easy to imagine this was what our life might be like if we really were a couple. My skin warmed, and I quickly focused on my tomatoes.

"What's my next task?" he asked.

"Is the water boiling?"

He moved behind me to look at the pot on the stove. "Yes."

"Okay. I need a large sauté pan."

He opened a large lower drawer and stared into it. "I have a bunch of pans. I'm not sure which one you need."

Laughing, I turned around and peered into the drawer. "You *do* have a bunch—and they're very nice. Did they come with the house?"

"No. The house was furnished, but I hired someone to stock the kitchen with anything I might need."

My jaw fell open. "That's a thing?"

"Sure—for a price." He watched me pull out a shiny stainless sauté pan and place it on a burner.

"So you just say, 'I want a kitchen full of beautiful things, here's my credit card?' And you don't have to shop for anything yourself?"

"Exactly. That's the best part about making a lot of money—you can pay people to do the things you don't want to do, like shopping."

"You should have just asked me," I said. "I would have enjoyed it, and I would have done it for free."

"I wouldn't have let you do it for free."

"Then I would have taken your money and blown it on good food and wine for us. I need olive oil," I said, turning on the heat beneath the pan.

He went over to the pantry and brought me a tall glass bottle. "What else?"

"Dump the gnocchi in the water and keep an eye on them. Let me know when they float to the top."

He did what I asked, watching the little pillow-shaped blobs so diligently I had to smile.

"So what's the worst part?" I asked, adding the garlic, onions, chopped zucchini, and the kernels from two ears of corn to the pan.

"Huh?"

"You said being able to pay people to do things you don't want to do is the best part of making lots of money—so what's the worst?"

He thought for a moment. "People assume things about you. Like that you're greedy or a scammer or you cheated somehow. Especially with crypto, because it's not easy for the average person to understand."

"Like me. I don't get it at all," I confessed with a laugh, stirring my veggies.

"Oh shit—I didn't mean that to sound insulting," he said quickly.

"Relax." I touched his arm. "I know what you meant. And it's true—if you're not in the banking industry, crypto is not easy to understand. And when people can't understand something, especially when it relates to huge sums of money, it seems sketchy."

"There *are* sketchy people in crypto. And U.S. regulators love to find them and shut their operations down. But I'm not one of them. And HFX isn't perfect, but the industry is moving so fast, it's hard for regulators to keep up. If they wanted to work with us, they could—we could find the balance between growing the industry and preventing crimes and enforcing laws they want in place. But they're often more interested in playing gotcha."

"It probably sells more newspapers," I said, adding the tomatoes to the pan.

"And gets them re-elected." Hutton frowned at the boiling water. "I have to testify in front of the House Committee on Financial Services."

My eyes widened. "The House, meaning U.S. Congress?"

"That's the one. I haven't said anything about it because I was hoping to delay it. Or better yet, avoid it altogether."

Grabbing the bottle of wine from the island, I poured us both some more and handed Hutton his glass. "When will it happen?"

He took a long swallow before answering. "In about three weeks. July 28th."

"Holy shit. Alone?"

"No, there will be five other CEOs there."

"Well, that helps, right?"

"I guess. Unless everyone else sounds like they know what they're talking about and I sound like a fucking idiot."

"You won't." I reached over and rubbed his shoulder. "Can't your partner testify instead of you? Wade?"

"He'll be there, but Wade doesn't do what I do. He's East Coast old money, a member of the club, knows all the right people—but that's not necessarily helpful in this situation. Wade had the capital to invest at the start and he's good with people, which is why we're a good team, but he doesn't know the back end like I do. The things are floating, by the way." He pointed at the gnocchi.

"Good. Got a colander?"

Hutton hunted around until he found one, and I drained

the gnocchi before adding it to the pan with the vegetables. "So do you have a *choice* whether or not to testify?" I asked.

"Not really. I mean, I could cash out of HFX and abandon the algorithm I created along with the company I co-founded. But that would look fucking terrible. Like I was a criminal or had things to hide."

"So you have to do it?"

"I have to do it."

"Well, I think you'll be great," I said, putting a smaller stainless pan on the stove to brown some butter for the sauce. "I have full confidence in you."

He laughed. "Are you forgetting who I am?"

"Not at all! I know exactly who you are. You got this." I patted his chest, although he was going to think I was insane if I kept touching him. I wasn't normally so physically affectionate, but he'd been so good to me tonight, and he looked so cute, and his body was so warm and firm. I wondered what he looked like with his clothes off. He worked out every day— it had to show, right? He was lean, but he probably had nice muscles. Those masculine lines and ridges.

My face heated as I imagined his body above mine. The lights off. The door closed.

Stop it, I scolded myself, turning away and taking a quick sip of cool wine. *He rescued you tonight because you're friends. Because you used the code. Because you begged. You're not here because he wants you in bed.*

But when I glanced at him again, he was definitely looking at my bare legs.

When the brown butter basil gnocchi was done, we sat down at the table by the window to eat.

"So were you shocked when you got that text from me with the encrypted message?" I asked.

"Yes. I'm ashamed to say it took me a minute to recognize it."

I laughed. "I had to write out the cipher key first."

"Same." Hutton picked up his wine glass for a sip. "But I think about that night in the library sometimes."

I stopped chewing for a second, then swallowed. "You do?"

"Yeah." He took a bite of his gnocchi. "I remember . . . what you told me."

"About Carla—my mother?"

He nodded. "Do you ever talk to her?"

"Not really. She reaches out every once in a while, but . . ." My voice trailed off. "It was pretty obvious when she left that *Mom* was a role she was done playing. According to her, she never wanted it in the first place. At least, that's what she said that night."

"That must have been hard. I always wondered . . . never mind." Hutton took another bite.

"What? You can ask me."

He hesitated again, but eventually spoke. "I guess I just wondered how that happened. How you overheard it—what she said."

"I was eavesdropping on a fight my parents were having after I was supposed to be asleep."

"Oh." He nodded in understanding.

"There was a huge thunderstorm that night, and those always made me nervous. I used to go to my parents' room and ask if I could sleep in their bed. Sometimes they'd let me, other times my dad would tuck me back into my bed again and stay with me until I fell asleep. But that night, when I got out of bed and crept into the hall, I heard them fighting."

"I'm sorry," Hutton said quietly.

"They fought a lot back then." I reached for my wine, but

I knew nothing would ever fully take the sting out of what I'd heard that night. Not wine, not distance, not time.

I took another swallow as their argument replayed in my head, as clearly as if they'd had it last night—my dad telling my mom they couldn't afford her out-of-control spending, my mother lashing back about being neglected and ignored, my dad shushing her so they wouldn't wake up the kids, my mother calling him horrible names and accusing him of favoring his daughters over his wife . . .

You're drunk, Carla.

So what? What do you care? You don't! You've never cared about me. You don't love me. You only married me because I got pregnant! You did your duty after you knocked me up!

Knocked her up? That had thrown me. Had my daddy hit my mommy? Is that how you got a baby?

I did the right thing for our family, he insisted.

Fuck you, Mack! I never wanted your kids in the first place. I hardly want them now.

As I told Hutton about the argument, goosebumps blanketed my arms. "I heard her say, 'I never wanted your kids in the first place. I hardly want them now.' I remember curling my body into a ball underneath the covers, like I was trying to make myself disappear."

Hutton reached out and touched my wrist.

"He told her she didn't know what she was saying. That she didn't mean it. And she said he wasn't in charge of her thoughts and didn't get to decide how she felt about being a mother. She said she was sick and tired of her life. And when he said they could talk about it tomorrow and they should just go to bed, she said she'd already been to bed with someone that night, and it wasn't him."

"Fuck," said Hutton.

"It confused me. I didn't understand why my mother would have a bed somewhere else." I took a breath. "My dad said he was tired of the arguing and she should just say what she wanted, and her answer was, 'I want out.'"

"And she didn't want to take you guys with her?"

I almost laughed. "No. But she wouldn't have been able to anyway. The first thing my dad said was, 'The girls stay with me.'"

He smiled. "Good for your dad."

"He's the best. And that did make me feel good—at least my dad still loved me. But it messed with my head, you know? Hearing my mother say those things. Up to that point, I thought all moms wanted kids. Suddenly that wasn't true. My mother didn't want me." I sighed. "I went back into the bedroom and over to the desk where Millie had been working on a project for school, and I picked up the scissors. That was the first time I cut my hair."

"Ah."

"The next morning, everyone asked me why I'd done it, and I made something up. I never told anyone what I'd overheard."

"Never?"

I shook my head. "No. I was scared of getting in trouble. All I could think of was that a good girl would not have listened. I was young, but I knew eavesdropping was wrong. I didn't want my dad to be mad, I didn't want my sisters to be hurt, and I was too ashamed to tell my friends. When they asked me why my mom moved out, I lied and said she had to go take care of her sick grandmother in Georgia."

"That's a lot of baggage for a kid to carry around."

"It was. But I survived."

He nodded. "I'm curious. What made you tell me at the library?"

"Honestly?" I reached for my wine again and finished it. Plunking the empty glass down, I said, "I have to confess—it was kind of an accident."

Hutton got up, went to the wine fridge, and pulled out a new bottle. "What do you mean?"

"Well, you know how I sometimes say random things when I get nervous?"

"Like being engaged to a billionaire?" He worked the cork from the bottle with a noisy pop. "That our wedding is next month?"

I laughed. "Exactly. The library was one of those times."

"What were you nervous about at the library?"

Heat rushed my face and I put my hands over my cheeks. "It's too embarrassing. I can't tell you."

"Come on." He poured us both more wine.

"You're going to laugh at me."

"I won't. I promise."

I took a deep breath. "Okay. I was nervous because I thought you might kiss me."

"And you didn't want me to." He sat down again.

"What?" I stared at him in disbelief. "No! I totally wanted you to. But I'd never kissed a boy before, and I had no idea how to do it. I was like, 'What if it's awkward? What if my glasses get in the way? What do I do with my gum?' Then I panicked."

He started to chuckle. "Sorry, I know I said I wouldn't laugh, but the two of us were having the exact same moment of panic. I wanted to kiss you and couldn't bring myself to make a move. My head was racing with all these ways it could go wrong, and I wasn't sure you even wanted me to kiss you in the first place. I thought maybe I was misreading the signs."

"You weren't," I said, shaking my head. "God, can you imagine what we must have looked like? Sitting there on the edges of our seats, our faces inches apart . . ."

"I was sweating buckets," said Hutton. "It was probably dripping off my forehead."

"I didn't notice. But it felt like an eternity went by and nothing happened, so I figured you must not see me like that.

I had to say something to break the tension, and for whatever reason, the thing about my mom came out."

"I remember having no clue what to say. So I wrote the encoded note."

I smiled. "That was the perfect response. It made me feel better."

"Good."

We sat there for a moment, not touching our food or wine, just looking at each other. It was like time had rolled backward, and we were in the library all over again. If I were someone else, I thought, Millie or Winnie or anyone else, I'd get up and sit on his lap. I'd straddle his thighs and put my hands in his hair and tell him it's time we gave ourselves a second chance at that first kiss. Just thinking about it made my heart beat faster.

But then he said, "It's probably good that we didn't mess around back then. Don't you think?"

I blinked, then recovered fast. "Oh, yeah. Definitely. It would have made things weird with us."

"Right," he said, but there was something unconvincing in his voice. "I mean, it's hard to say for sure, but you're probably right. It might not have been worth the risk."

I reached for my wine and he picked up his fork.

He'd said *might*.

Might wasn't a certainty. Might left room for doubt. Might created space for hope.

Beneath the table, I crossed my fingers.

After dinner, I loaded the dishwasher while Hutton put the leftovers away and then cleaned the stainless pans by hand. I laughed as I watched him at the sink, sleeves rolled up, scrubbing away with a sponge. "I bet you're the only billionaire washing pots and pans tonight," I teased.

"Probably," he said.

"I think it's good." I patted his shoulder. "Shows character. Like you haven't forgotten where you came from. Hand them to me and I'll dry."

Side by side, we got everything washed, dried, and put away. When only our wine glasses were left, Hutton glanced at the half-empty bottle. "Do you want to stay a little longer? Finish the wine?"

I hesitated. "If we finish that bottle, I won't be able to drive home."

"So stay over," he said. "I have plenty of guest rooms."

"A sleepover?" I feigned being scandalized, touching my fingertips to my chest. "Before we're married? What would the townsfolk say?"

He laughed, grabbing the bottle and emptying it into our glasses. "They're probably already talking about us. Come on, let's go out on the deck. I don't think the rain has started yet."

Outside, the air was thick with the sharp, ominous scent of ozone. I sank into the cushions at one end of an outdoor couch, and Hutton sat down next to me, on the center cushion.

Close.

There were no other houses nearby, no lights in the woods, no noise except for the crickets and warm, summer wind rustling through the branches. I tucked my feet underneath me and smoothed my dress over my thighs. "It's so dark out here. So isolated."

"That's what sold me on the place."

I laughed, poking his shoulder. "You're such a grumpy old man."

"I'm twenty-eight. I'm a grumpy *young* man."

"Fine. You're a grumpy *young* man." I sipped my wine. "But you know what? You have to deal with a lot of people wanting to be up in your personal business all the time, so I shouldn't criticize. You deserve privacy when you want it."

"Can you please tell my mother that?"

I laughed. "I wonder what happened with Cleopatra tonight."

"No idea. She said she was going to introduce her to Harvey. He's my dad's widowed friend."

"Aw, that's nice. She just wants people to be happy."

"You can be happy without a serious relationship," Hutton said, a tad defensively.

"True." I took another sip of wine and thought I heard thunder rumbling in the distance. "Unless you're lonely, or you really want a family."

"I'm never lonely," he said.

"What about a family?" I asked. "Do you ever think about getting married? Having kids?"

Hutton set an ankle on the opposite knee. "Not really. I don't know if I'd make a good dad."

Surprised, I shifted to face him, my knees bumping up against his thigh. I rested my elbow along the back of the couch and propped my head in my hand. "What makes you say that? You're great with your nieces and nephew."

"Yeah, but being an uncle is different. It's less pressure. You can just have fun with them. You're not really responsible for their upbringing." He paused. "I don't know if I'd have the temperament to be a good dad. I get really irritated and impatient sometimes. I can be irrational and stubborn. My brother-in-law, Neil, is so easygoing and relaxed."

"All different kinds of people can be great dads. My dad was stubborn too. He *definitely* got irritated. And he had such a foul mouth, the swear jaw would be overflowing by the end of the week." I laughed at the memory of his stuffing dollar bills into it after a lengthy rant that included several F bombs. "He wasn't perfect. But he was an awesome dad."

Hutton set his wine glass on the table, then folded his arms. "What about you? Do you want kids?"

"I do, but I need to figure some stuff out first."

"What kind of stuff?"

I lifted my shoulders. "How to be in a healthy relationship."

He laughed shortly. "I've got no advice on that front. I'd be an even shittier husband than father."

"What makes you think that?"

"Experience."

"Oh yeah?" I nudged his leg. "Is there a wife you're hiding somewhere? As your fake fiancée, I should know this."

He gave me a sideways grin. "No, I've never been married. But I've tried to have relationships, and I suck at them. I have literally been *told* that I suck at them."

"That's not nice."

He shrugged. "It's honest."

"I guess I'd value kindness over honesty in that situation."

"Didn't matter. And I didn't even really care."

I looked at what was left of my wine and swirled it around. "Are we talking about Zlatka?"

"She's the one who told me I sucked most recently, but she's not the only one who felt that way—and I never blamed them. No one wants to date a recluse who hates going places."

"That's all it was? You never liked going out?"

"That was a lot of it. But there were other problems too. I'm not good at talking about things. I'm better at—never mind." He leaned forward and picked up his wine again. Finished it in one long swallow.

"What?" I nudged him again. "Tell me."

"I'm better at the physical stuff than the emotional stuff."

My core muscles contracted, and I dropped my eyes to my lap. "You mean sex stuff?"

"Yeah."

"Well, that's important too," I said, wondering exactly

what he was good at and whether it was wrong of me to want to find out. "Good physical chemistry with someone."

He set his empty glass back on the table. "Actually, I don't even think Zlatka and I were that compatible when it came to sex."

"Why not?"

"Certain things I liked, she didn't."

I took a breath for courage. "Such as?"

He paused. "Let's just say that Zlatka does not like being told what to do or not do, and I enjoy that kind of control."

I poured the rest of my wine down my throat.

"But there were other problems. She constantly accused me of avoiding any situation or conversation I didn't want to be in, and she was right. I do avoid those. Eventually, our relationship fell into that category."

"You don't miss her?"

"Fuck no. She was exhausting. And I've never missed anyone." He met my eyes. "I mean, except for you. There have been many times in my life when I've missed you."

I smiled. "Really?"

"Yes."

"I've missed you too." Our lips were not that far apart, and I was not chewing gum this time. If I leaned toward him a little, would he—

Lightning flashed above the trees behind him, the sound cracking like a rifle shot a second later. "Oh!"

He put a hand on my leg as the rumble of thunder followed. "You okay?"

"Yes. Sorry." A little sheepish, I lifted my shoulders. "Storms still make me jumpy."

"Let's go in." Hutton stood up, grabbing our empty wine glasses from the table. "I'll show you the guest rooms, and you can take your pick."

"Are you sure it's okay for me to stay?" I followed him into the house.

"Yes. I could call and ask my mom, but I'm pretty sure she'd be in favor of it," he joked, sliding the glass door closed with his elbow.

"Mine too. Actually, I *am* going to text her and let her know I'm staying here, just so she doesn't worry."

"Good idea."

The first bedroom Hutton showed me was on the main floor, its door right across the hall from the master suite. It had a queen-sized bed made up with pretty white eyelet bedding and its own bathroom. "This is perfect," I said, sinking down on the bed.

Hutton lingered in the doorway. "The other two bedrooms are on the lower level, if you'd like more privacy."

"Listen, I've been living with my parents and two teenage sisters for six months. This is heaven."

He laughed. "Okay. Can I get you anything?"

"Got a spare toothbrush? Maybe an old T-shirt I could sleep in?"

"Be right back."

While he was gone, I texted my mom that I was staying at Hutton's and would be home in the morning. I noticed that I had notifications from Dearly Beloved and Instagram, but I ignored them and turned my phone off—I'd deal with the outside world tomorrow.

I'd just set my phone on the nightstand when Hutton appeared holding a folded white shirt, a toothbrush still in the package, and a travel tube of toothpaste on top. "Will this work?"

"Yes. Thank you." I stood up and took everything from him, and our hands touched in the process. A jolt of heat shot up my arms.

He stuck his hands in his pockets. "Need anything else?"

"Nope. I'm good." Thunder boomed loudly from outside, and I jumped.

"You okay?"

"No." I laughed, embarrassed. Without thinking, I made a quick joke. "Can I sleep in your bed tonight?"

Hutton's face went white.

"I'm kidding," I said, my face growing hot. "Because of what I told you earlier. Don't worry, I won't—"

"You can if you want to."

"—actually crawl into your . . . huh?"

"You can sleep in my bed. If you want to. I mean, if you're scared."

What if I'm not scared and I just want to be close to you?

But I couldn't bring myself to say the words.

Instead, I just smiled. "Thanks. But I'll be fine."

"Okay. Goodnight." He left the room quickly, pulling the door shut behind him.

I stood there for a moment staring at it. What just happened? Did I just reject an invitation? Did he *want* me to crawl into his bed tonight? Or was he just being nice?

Why were we so bad at this?

I kept obsessing over it as I took out my space buns, washed my face, brushed my teeth, and traded my dress and push-up bra for his T-shirt. The clean white cotton felt cool and soft against my skin. Staring at myself in the bathroom mirror, I wondered what to do. There had been moments tonight when we'd edged close to crossing the line. I knew I hadn't imagined it.

But he'd also said things that led me to believe he didn't want to risk our friendship just to mess around—and I didn't either. What we had was rare.

What I wanted was reckless.

Turning off all the lights, I slipped between the sheets and stared into the dark. Rain drummed on the roof, punctuated by the occasional flash of lightning and growl of thunder.

Would one night of engaging in some questionable behavior ruin years of friendship? Maybe it wouldn't. Maybe we could just get a little naked and see what happened. Let our lips meet. Let our hands wander. Let go of our inhibitions in the dark.

Thunder boomed, so powerful it shook the house.

"This is crazy," I whispered to myself, but I threw the covers back, swung my feet to the floor, hurried over to the door and threw it open.

Then I gasped.

Hutton stood there in the dark—shirtless—his hand raised as if he'd been about to knock.

Six

Hutton

"OH!" Felicity's hands flew to her cheeks. "I was just . . . um . . ."

My mind hopefully stepped in where her tongue left off.

Wondering if you want to get naked?

Curious about what your body would feel like on mine?

Thinking about fucking you in ten different ways?

Great, me too.

But what she said as her eyes wandered over my chest was, "Thirsty."

"Right," I said. "That's why I'm here."

"It is?"

"Yes, I thought you might be thirsty and I forgot to tell you there are bottles of water in the fridge. Why don't I just get you one?" I turned away from her, my heart pounding, and walked quickly across the great room into the kitchen. Pulling the fridge door open, I stood there for a moment and let the cool air hit my bare chest. I stared at the contents, completely forgetting what I was looking for.

She knows, asshole. She totally knows why you were knocking on her bedroom door without a shirt on. I'd been standing there trying to be cocksure for five full minutes, vacillating over whether I should knock or not, imagining all the possible ways it could go.

The thing was, I was sure of my cock, but my cock wasn't all that sure of me.

It was a huge risk, making this kind of move when you'd known someone as long as Felicity and I had known each other. It wasn't like Zlatka approaching me at a party and saying, "I want you. Let's get out of here." That was unmistakable.

Was Felicity flirting tonight or just being familiar? Had I imagined the physical attraction? What would she say if I told her I wanted to make her feel safe during the storm, possibly by distracting her with an orgasm or two? I knew I could deliver, but was she—

"Hutton?"

Startled, I turned around to see her standing there in my T-shirt and bare feet, her hair in disarray. In my fantasies, she'd whispered my name in the dark like that a thousand times. Of course, if this were my fantasy, she'd be on her knees right now. Or I'd have her back against the fridge. Or up on the counter with my tongue between her thighs.

"Sorry, didn't mean to scare you." She smiled gingerly. "Did you find the water?"

"Water. Yes." Turning around again, I closed my eyes and took a breath, then grabbed a plastic bottle and shut the fridge. "Here you go."

"Thanks." She took the water from me but made no move to leave the kitchen. Even in the dark, I could see her gaze wandering over my chest and shoulders and stomach. My drawstring pants hung low on my hips, and her eyes strayed south. "I guess I'll . . . go back to bed."

"Wait."

She looked up. "Yes?"

Ten different questions popped into my head, and unfortunately the one I went with was, "Did you cut your hair today?"

She touched the jagged ends. "Oh. Yeah. This morning, after I saw the bad review on that app. It looks terrible, I know. It's all uneven."

"Not at all. There's beauty in asymmetry too."

She smiled, but with nothing left to say, and neither of us brave enough to cross the line, standing there started to feel a little torturous. Finally, she broke the silence. "Night."

"Night." Cursing my lack of nerve, I watched her walk away from me. A moment later, her bedroom door clicked shut.

I went back to bed and lay awake for a long time, listening to the raindrops pummel the roof, like little fists on my brain. I'd fucking blown it at least five different times tonight. I'd spent years thinking about her and wondering what if, and then tonight when I'd actually had the chance to do something about it—multiple chances—I'd backed off.

But maybe that's how it was supposed to be. Maybe my subconscious was doing me a favor and getting Felicity in bed would wreck things beyond repair. I'd ruined enough relationships in my life, hadn't I? This one was worth protecting.

Tomorrow morning, I'd go for a long run and give myself a heavy lift session to work off some of the testosterone and frustration. Then I'd get myself off in the shower while I thought about what it might have been like if I'd had the nerve to knock on that bedroom door tonight. The way she'd taste. The sounds she'd make. Her legs around me. Her back arched. Her perfect breasts beneath my lips.

Before I could stop myself, my hand crept inside the waistband of my sweatpants. Fisting my cock, I stroked myself while I imagined her body under mine. I'd lick every inch of her skin, tease her with my fingers, fuck her with my tongue.

My breathing grew heavy and fast, and I was grateful for

the noise of the storm. I worked my hand harder, quicker, tighter, fantasizing about sliding into her for the first time—she'd be wet and warm, eager for me, begging for my cock. Her hands in my hair, down my back, on my ass, pulling me in deeper. She'd cry out in pain or pleasure or maybe both, because I'd never hurt her but I wouldn't be able to hold back—I'd wanted her for too long and she was finally mine and I wanted to make her come, I wanted to feel it and hear it and watch her take it all from me, harder and faster and *fuck, fuck, fuck*—I barely suppressed a groan as all the tension was released in thick, pulsing beats that left a mess on my stomach.

Ashamed of what I'd done—she was right in the room across the hall!—I snuck into my bathroom, cleaned up, and got back into bed, where I tossed and turned the rest of the night.

"Hutton."

It was Felicity's whisper. For a second, I thought I was dreaming.

"Hutton." Now her hand was on my shoulder. Had she changed her mind and come to my bed after all? "Hutton, wake up. Someone is here."

My eyes flew open. My room was bright—it wasn't the middle of the night, it was morning, and Felicity wasn't here to seduce me. In fact, her forehead was creased with concern above the top of her glasses. I struggled to make sense of what she was saying. "Huh?"

"Someone is here, knocking on the door. I think it might be your mom."

"My mom?" That was not sexy at all. I propped myself up on an elbow and blinked. "Here?"

"Yes. And maybe some other people." She stood up and

glanced out toward the hall. "I heard pounding and shouting, but I didn't want to answer the door."

I noticed Felicity still wore my T-shirt and also that her nipples were hard, poking at the cotton. Under the covers, my dick sprang to life.

Bang! Bang! Bang!

"Hutton! Are you in there?" That was definitely my mother's voice.

Moaning, I fell back and put my pillow over my face. "Go away, Mom."

"I don't think she's going away. She's been knocking for several minutes."

"Fuuuuuuck." I tossed my pillow aside and sat up, messing my hair with one hand. "Why is she here so early? What time is it?"

"It's after ten."

"Is it? I never sleep this late."

"Me neither. But I had trouble falling asleep last night."

"Me too." I looked at her chest again, and she folded her arms.

Nice. Now she thought I was a pervert.

"Was it the storm that kept you awake?" I asked.

"It was a lot of things."

"Hutton, darling, open up! I looked in the garage and saw your car, so I know you're here!"

I groaned as I got out of bed, thankful that at least my mother's yelling had deflated my erection—mostly. Heading for the bathroom, I said, "Give me a minute."

"I'll get dressed," Felicity said.

"No rush. I'm just going to brush my teeth and then try to get rid of her."

But two minutes later, when I opened the door, I found it wasn't just my mother—it was also my sister, my brother-in-law, my nieces, my nephew, and all four members of the

Clipper Cuts: Stan, Harvey, Buck, and Leonard, decked out in their red and white striped coats and straw boater hats. Harvey held a big white bakery box. Before I could stop them, they all shuffled into the house and stood there looking at me expectantly.

"What's going on?" I asked, running a hand over my bed-head hair. "Why are you all here?"

"We were at the house rehearsing for the FitzGibbons' fiftieth anniversary luncheon when we heard the news," my father said. "We gathered the troops and rushed right over."

"Is it true?" my mother asked breathlessly, hands clasped in prayer.

"Is what true?" I asked, looking at the crowd's rapt faces in confusion.

"There she is!" My mother's face lit up, and her eyes misted over. "It's true! It's true!"

I glanced over my shoulder to see that Felicity had come from the direction of the bedrooms, wearing the blue dress from last night, her hair a mess, her legs and feet bare. It was obvious what this looked like.

Hurrying over, my mom took her by both hands then wrapped her in a giant hug. "Sweetest Felicity, this is better than a dream!"

"It is?" Felicity looked at me with wide, panicked eyes over my mom's shoulder.

Taking her hand, my mother dragged Felicity over to me and looked at the two of us side by side. Then she wiped her eyes. "I don't know if I can contain my emotions. The two of you—after all this time—engaged to be married!"

My jaw dropped. Felicity made some sort of squeaking sound.

My sister came over and mock-punched my gut before giving me a hug. "You jerk! Since when can you keep a secret from me?"

My brother-in-law, Neil, threw his arms around me and thumped me on the back. "You should have said something, man."

"But it makes perfect sense now!" my mom exclaimed with a laugh. "No wonder he always protested so much when I tried to help him find love. He'd already found it!"

"But why was it a secret?" asked Zosia, eyeing the box of donuts. "I don't get it."

"Because when you're someone like Hutton, the media is always prying into your business, and taking a relationship public puts a lot of pressure on it," said my sister. "Right, Hutton?"

"Uh, yes."

"And the sad eyes and discontent aura I sensed yesterday must have been his yearning to share the news with us, but feeling protective of his blossoming love! But in retrospect, it was right there." My mother took my hand and placed Felicity's palm in mine. Her eyes filled with tears. "Gentlemen. A song please?"

But before we could protest, the Clipper Cuts gathered into formation before us, and Harvey blew a note on the pitch pipe.

"Congratulations to you," they sang in four-part harmony to the tune of Happy Birthday, "Congratulations to you. Congratulations on your engagement, congratulations toooooo youuuuuuu," they crooned, drawing out the last two notes while shock coursed through my veins.

Everyone cheered as Felicity and I exchanged a frantic look.

"Pic!" my sister shouted, holding up her phone. "Everyone in!"

The Clipper Cuts eagerly crowded in behind us while my family squeezed in on the sides. Neil held Jonas in his arms, and my mother scooped up Keely and set her on one hip.

Allie snapped one, then scrunched down in front of us and took another selfie-style so she could be in it too. "How about smiling this time?" she suggested with a laugh. "Hutton and Felicity, you two look like you've seen a ghost."

I couldn't even attempt a smile. I have no idea what shape Felicity was able to make with her face. For fuck's sake, I didn't even have a shirt on.

"Now one of the happy couple," my mother said.

I held up one hand. "Mom, really, this isn't the—"

"Oh, now don't be shy," she chided, clasping her hands beneath her chin. "Put your arm around her, Hutton! You're in love! And the poor girl is trembling with excitement."

I looked at Felicity—she did look shaken and scared—and immediately put my arm around her shoulder.

"Um, Mrs. French, everyone, there's something I need to explain," Felicity began.

"Please. Call me Mom." My mom's eyes grew tearful again. "And there's nothing to explain. It's the oldest story in the book—boy meets girl, they're just friends for years, then they realize that there's always been something more there . . ." She wiped away tears. "It's like the universe has answered all my prayers. Now I can stop worrying about you, Hutton."

"You can?"

"Yes." She laughed delightedly. "No more trying to set you up, because clearly you've realized that your soul mate has been right here all along."

Felicity shook her head. "I'm so sorry about this, but—"

"Don't be sorry." My mother smiled. "We understand wanting to keep the news to yourselves. It's only natural to want to hold a secret like that close to your heart. But now that it's out," she went on excitedly, "I can't wait to celebrate! And is it true the wedding is next month?"

"Uh . . ." Another panicked look passed between Felicity and me. "Where did you hear that?"

"Oh, the news is everywhere," said my sister. "Online, local morning news, social media. You've been secretly engaged for weeks, and you're having a very intimate wedding at Cloverleigh Farms in August. At least five friends texted me the headlines and asked if it was true." She laughed. "I had my doubts, but Mom was positive the universe would not play such a cruel trick on her."

"And I was right! Just look at them—it's *obvious* what's been going on," my mother said with a wink, gesturing at my shirtless chest and Felicity's bare legs.

"Hope we didn't interrupt," said Neil with a laugh.

"Say cheese!" My sister snapped another pic. "How about a kiss?"

"A what?" A tremor went through Felicity, and I tightened my arm on her shoulders.

"A kiss!" My mother clearly loved the idea. "For the camera. For prosperity. For love!"

"Exactly," my sister said, aiming her phone at us. "Kiss her, Hutton."

I looked into Felicity's eyes and saw a multitude of emotions—fear mostly, but also a familiar warmth, and possibly even a little hope. Without thinking, I lowered my lips to hers.

My mother sighed, my sister *awwww'd*, Zosia *ewwww'd*, and the Clipper Cuts launched into "Let Me Call You Sweetheart."

But I barely heard any of it, because for the first time, I was actually kissing the girl I'd been wanting to kiss since I was fifteen. Her lips remained closed, but they were just as soft and sweet as I'd imagined them, and even though the kiss was as chaste as it had to be with such a big audience, I didn't want it to end.

"Okay, I got the picture," my sister said.

But we didn't stop.

"Get a room!" shouted Neil.

"That's gross. Can we have the donuts now?" asked Zosia.

I lifted my head and opened my eyes—Felicity's expression was one of total astonishment. "I'm—I'm confused," she whispered.

"Come with me." I grabbed her forearm and yanked her toward the back hallway, my mind clicking.

"I was kidding!" Neil yelled with a laugh.

"Oh, let them go," my mother said. "They probably need a moment to themselves—we barged right into their love nest unannounced."

Inside my room, I closed the door and spun around. Felicity's face was drained of color except for two splotches of red on her cheeks. "Oh my God," she said. "I'm so sorry."

"Don't be."

But Felicity had started to pace along the foot of my bed. "I shouldn't have opened my big mouth to Mimi. I knew this would happen. I just didn't think about the consequences of your family hearing the news and being so happy about it! And it's not just them."

"What do you mean?"

"When I turned on my phone this morning, I saw that Winnie had sent me a bunch of headlines about us—we're front page news!"

"We are?"

"Yes! My follower count skyrocketed overnight. I've got tons of DMs. My notifications on Dearly Beloved are blowing up. And my mother—Frannie, I mean—left me a voicemail, which I haven't listened to, but I can imagine what it's about." She stopped moving and put her hands up to her face. "Now I have to tell everyone the truth—that I made it up. This is so embarrassing."

"Okay, hang on." My mind was spinning. "Maybe we don't have to tell everyone that."

"Huh?"

I ran a hand through my hair. "Maybe we can just—go with it."

"Go with it?"

"Yes—for a little while at least."

Her head drew back. "Why?"

"You heard my mother. She's finally going to leave me alone. Maybe everyone else will too."

Felicity stared at me like I was nuts. "Are you serious?"

"Yes. I'm tired of being harassed by everyone around me about my lack of a personal life. I've got a lot of work to do to get ready to testify, and if people think we're engaged, they'll give me the space to do it," I said. What I *didn't* say was, *Also, being your fake fiancé will mean I get to spend a lot of time with you, acting like you belong to me, perhaps in ways that don't always involve clothing.*

"For how long?"

"Just while I'm here," I said. "I only rented the house for three months. I have to be out by August fifteenth."

She did the math. "So one month?"

"Right." I felt strangely liberated by the idea of inhabiting this *other* version of me for thirty days—the guy I would be for her if I could. "What do you think?"

She smiled. "I think there's going to be a lot of disappointed Prancin' Grannies out there."

"So you'll do it?"

"Of course I will."

"It'll mean lying to your family . . . are you sure you're up for that?"

She chewed her bottom lip for a moment. "But we're not *hurting* anyone. My family will actually be overjoyed. The only problem will be when we have to end it. But I guess we could just call it off when you go back to San Francisco."

"Sounds reasonable."

"Except that I said we were getting married next month! Shit!" She thumped her head with the heels of her hands.

"Look, let's not worry about that right now."

"But we have to get the story straight, Hutton. We need a script." Felicity shook her head, her eyes wide. "Otherwise I'm liable to go rogue."

"We can come up with a story." I glanced at the closed door. "For now, let's just try to get rid of them."

Felicity laughed. "Maybe if we just stay in your bedroom, they'll take a hint."

My stomach muscles tightened at the thought. "I wish."

I threw a shirt on before we went back out to the kitchen, where my hopes of brooming everyone out the front door were quickly crushed. Coffee had been brewed, Neil was cracking eggs into a frying pan on the stove, my sister was peeling oranges, and everyone was enjoying the donuts.

"Come sit, you two," said my mother, setting out two full mugs for us on the marble island. "We want to hear all about how you popped the question."

"That's private, Mom." I slid onto the edge of a stool next to Felicity.

"Come on, just tell us," Allie cajoled. "And let's see the ring."

Felicity played with the fingers on her left hand. "The ring is actually still at the jeweler's. It's being sized."

"Grandma says this means you've gotten over your emotional devoidance issues," said Zosia, licking pink frosting off the top of her hand. "Is that true?"

"Emotional *avoidance* issues, and don't say that." My sister gave her daughter a stern look.

"Just tell me—did he get down on one knee when he proposed?" My mother's eyes grew dreamy. "Was it romantic?"

Felicity glanced at me, and I nodded, figuring I'd take my cues from her. "Yes," she said, her voice growing more confident. "He got down on one knee and it was very romantic."

"Where were you?" Allie wondered.

"Here." Felicity glanced over her shoulder. "Out in the woods."

"You proposed in the woods?" My mother seemed excited about that. "That makes sense for an earth sign like Taurus. And what sign are you, Felicity?"

"I'm a Cancer. My birthday just passed—in fact, that's when he asked me to marry him." Felicity was enjoying the story now. "On my birthday."

"Oh, that's perfect." My mother nodded happily. "An earthy bull is a wonderful match for a sensitive crab."

Allie snickered, and I rolled my eyes. "Mom, calling someone a sensitive crab is not a compliment," I told her.

"I'm saying you're going to be good together," my mother said defensively. "Both Taurus and Cancer are very family-oriented. But a Cancer might struggle with someone who isn't in touch with his feelings, Hutton, so you'll have to take care not to let her down. She'll snatch her feelings right back into her little crab shell."

"Let's talk about the wedding," Allie said. "It's going to be at Cloverleigh Farms?"

"I think so," said Felicity. "I just need to confirm some details with my sister Millie. She's the wedding planner there."

"What's the date?"

"Um, that's one of the details to be confirmed." She looked at me. "We're hoping for August."

My father looked at me. "So are you moving here for good, son? Or will you two move to San Francisco?"

I cleared my throat. "Plans are up in the air right now."

"Can I come to the wedding?" asked Zosia hopefully. "Please?"

"Of course you can," said my mother.

"Out of curiosity, what's the rush?" Allie glanced at Felicity's mid-section. "Is there anything else you want to tell us?"

"*No,*" Felicity and I answered at the same time.

"Alexandra, the reason for the rush is obvious," my mom said with a sigh and dramatic gesture at us. "They're in love! And they're perfect together, don't you agree?"

My sister laughed and picked up her coffee. "I agree. A bull and a crab are a match made in heaven."

We made it through breakfast by changing the subject any time someone tried to ask about the wedding or our future plans. Felicity was awesome at steering the conversation away from us. She asked my mom how things were going at her store and promised to come in for a reading soon. She asked my dad how his garden was this summer and said she'd love to come by and pick some tomatoes. She asked Neil what it was like working for her uncle Noah, who was the county Sheriff.

"He's a great guy," Neil said. "That's your uncle?"

"He's married to my stepmom's sister," Felicity explained. "But I grew up in that family, so they're all aunts and uncles to me."

"The Sawyers are wonderful people," said my mom. "In fact, I can't wait to speak with Frannie about the wedding and everything."

"Not yet, Mom," I said, noting the look of alarm on

Felicity's face. "This news sort of got out unexpectedly, so give us a chance to talk to the MacAllisters first."

"So where can I see your next singing performance?" Felicity asked the Clipper Cuts, smoothly switching topics.

It was incredible—like watching her tap dance for a solid hour when she'd never had one lesson.

Finally, I told everyone they had to go because I had work to do. My mother was the last one out. I shut the door behind her and leaned back against it. My left eyelid was twitching. "Jesus."

Felicity covered her cheeks with both hands. "That was . . . a lot. Are you okay?"

"Yeah. You?"

She nodded. "You think they bought everything? I feel like your parents were convinced, but sometimes your sister would look at us like she wasn't sure."

"Allie is pretty shrewd, but mostly I think she was just amazed I'd kept a secret from her. I usually tell her everything."

"I love that you're close to your sister. I think that's cool." Dropping her arms, she sighed. "Okay, come on. Let's get the kitchen cleaned up and figure out how we're going to handle my family."

The thought of having to do this all again in front of the MacAllisters was almost enough to make me pull the plug on this insane scheme, but then I remembered how good it felt when I kissed her. How badly I wanted to do it again.

I followed her to the sink.

"I'll wash, you dry?" she suggested.

"Sure. But—hang on." I rubbed the back of my neck. "That kiss."

She glanced up at me. "What about it?"

"I didn't see a way out of it."

"No. Of course not." She looked down at the island and traced a long vein in the marble with a fingertip. It was a minute before she spoke. "Isn't it amazing that this was formed millions of years ago because of heat and intense pressure?"

But I couldn't answer, because I was too busy wondering what it would feel like if she traced a vein on my skin that way—slowly, deliberately, with awe. I had a particular vein in mind.

Eventually she looked up at me. "I didn't mind when you kissed me, Hutton."

"You didn't?"

She shook her head. "At least now we know what it's like, right?"

"Right."

She went back to tracing the vein. "In fact, we'll probably have to do that kind of thing again."

My heart stumbled over its next beat. "Kiss?"

"Yeah. I mean, people are going to expect it if we're engaged." She peeked at me. "Won't they?"

I nodded, feeling like the universe had rewarded me for being bold.

"So I was thinking, maybe we should practice."

Blood rushed straight to my cock. "Right now?"

"Maybe not right this second, but you know . . . soon." Her shoulders rose. "Don't you think it would be a good idea?"

"Yeah. Soon. Practice. Good." Like a fucking caveman.

"Great." She smiled and picked up a plate to rinse it.

"You should move in," I blurted.

The plate slipped from her hands and clattered back into the sink. "Huh?"

"You should move in with me." I raked a hand through my hair. "It would make things more real, more believable. Don't you think?"

"Um. Yes. Definitely, it would make it more real." Her cheeks had grown pink. "It's just—I don't—I didn't know if you . . ."

"Didn't know if I what?"

"If you, you know, *wanted* to make it more real."

My heart was beating way too fast. "I do."

Her lips hung open for a minute, then she closed them. Offered me a smile. "Okay. I'll go home this afternoon and get my stuff. It will be nice to get out of my parents' house, even if it's just for a few weeks."

"Great."

We continued doing the dishes in silence, but inside, I was freaking out.

She was moving in—today. She wanted to practice kissing. What else might be allowable inside the parameters of this act?

My skin prickled with heat as my eyes wandered from her head to her heels.

This could get complicated.

Seven

Felicity

"I**T'S TRUE?"** WINNIE'S VOICE ROSE TO A FEVER PITCH.

"Yes." I sat on the edge of the bed I'd slept in and tested out the words. "It's true. Hutton and I are engaged. I'm moving in with him."

"I can't believe it! Why didn't you say something yesterday? I'm freaking out!"

"Sorry. I wanted to, but Hutton and I had agreed to keep it quiet for a while. You know how he is." I bit my lip, feeling guilty for lying to my sister. But Hutton had come to my rescue last night, and he'd asked me for this favor—I could come through for him.

"I remember him being quiet and shy, yes, but I didn't realize you two were a *thing*. You always swore there was nothing there! The words 'just friends' have come out of your mouth a million times! You were like a broken record."

"It was true," I said defensively. "Right up until recently. When he came back to town this summer, we realized we had feelings for each other we'd never admitted to."

"God, we are *so* different. I'd have tattooed his name on my body by now."

I laughed. "Probably."

"You know everyone saw it except you two." Now her tone was smug.

"Yes, well, now we do." Leaning sideways, I attempted to peek across the hall into Hutton's bedroom, where he was changing into workout clothes, but he'd shut the door.

"This is so amazing. But you know me—I'm going to need every single, solitary detail, and I'm going to need them now."

"I don't have time right now, but I'll tell you at dinner tonight. Hutton and I are hosting everyone here, and I'm going to cook."

At first when I'd asked Hutton if we could invite my family for dinner, he'd gone pale—it wasn't that he didn't like my family, but we'd just gotten rid of *his* family, and this would be a lot of peopling in one day. But I'd talked him into it, promising we'd get our story one hundred percent straight before they arrived and that he would not be left alone to make small talk with anyone. Also, I told him it would be much better to get the news out to everyone all at once rather than have to go through it multiple times.

"Are Mom and Dad coming?" Winnie asked.

"Yes. I just talked to Mom."

"Did she cry?"

"Yep," I confirmed, pangs of guilt hitting me again. "Burst into tears the minute she answered the phone, but she's happy. She's at work and the bakery is super busy, but she made me promise to tell her everything the moment she gets here."

"I can't wait until dinnertime," Winnie wailed. "Can't you tell me sooner?"

"I really can't," I said. It was the truth—Hutton and I still had to get the story straight. "But I promise it will be worth the wait. I'll text you Hutton's address and you can come around four."

Winnie sighed heavily. "Fine. But call Mills right now, okay? She's losing her mind."

I bit my lip. Millie was the one person I was worried about—she had an innate bullshit detector, and she knew me better than anyone on the planet. "I will."

"God. You're getting married, Lissy. *Married.*" She was choked up. "I can't believe it."

"Me neither."

"I'm so happy for you. How awesome to fall in love with a friend. And how sweet that you two have been friends since, what, high school?"

"Middle school," I said. "He moved in the middle of seventh grade." I could still see him standing in the doorway of Mr. Krenshaw's honors math class, the guidance counselor's hand on his shoulder as she introduced him. He stared at the floor the entire time, his floppy hair covering the top of his face.

The only empty seat in the room was next to me, and when Mr. Krenshaw pointed him in my direction, he looked right at me, and the first thing I thought was that he had the clearest blue eyes I'd ever seen. There was something so gentle in them, and I instantly knew he wasn't a jerk like other middle school boys. I had the sense he might not fit in easily, so when I saw him alone at lunch, I invited him to sit with me. He didn't say much, but he sat next to me at the table that day . . . and just about every day afterward.

"But we weren't super close right away," I said. "That took time."

Winnie laughed. "Yes, you guys have been very good at taking your time—until now. Suddenly everything is lightning fast. Are you really getting married next month?"

"Um, hopefully. I still need to talk to Millie. See if it's doable."

"Well, if it's not doable at Cloverleigh, let's talk about

Abelard," she said. Winnie was the wedding coordinator there. "I totally understand wanting to have it at Cloverleigh Farms, but if you can't get a date at such late notice, I might be able to help you out, especially if you can wait until September."

"Hutton will be gone by then," I said without thinking.

"Gone? What do you mean? Does that mean you're moving too? What about your catering business?"

My legs started to bounce nervously. "Not sure of anything yet, but Hutton only has this house for about another month. Where we'll live is one of the decisions we'll have to make."

"I saw that your follower count exploded."

"So did my DMs. Clearly getting engaged to a public figure helps your influencer status. I'm suddenly inundated with requests to collaborate."

"That's so exciting!"

"I have a bunch of new messages in my Dearly Beloved inbox too," I told her, suddenly feeling overwhelmed. "I haven't even looked at them yet. Anyway, I have to go, but I'll see you here at four. Feel free to bring Dex and the girls if you want."

"Will all of Hutton's family be there too?"

"No. We saw them for brunch this morning. It's just the MacAllisters tonight."

"Pretty soon, your name won't be MacAllister anymore. You'll be Felicity French! If you change your name, I mean." Then she sighed. "I'd like to be Winnie Matthews someday. You're so lucky."

"Thanks. I'll see you later."

We hung up and I sat there for a moment, unable to help the smile that crept onto my lips.

Felicity French sounded fucking awesome.

While Hutton worked out, I ran over to the reunion venue to pick up the platters I'd left there last night, and then home to pack. I was glad—for selfish reasons—that the house was empty. I wasn't ready to answer detailed questions yet.

Dragging my suitcase out from under the bed, I emptied some dresser drawers into it, added a few things from my closet and a couple pairs of shoes, then shoved my makeup bag, hair products, and some random other toiletries into an overnight bag. It wasn't everything, but it would get me through one month. After slinging my laptop case over my shoulder, I lugged everything downstairs.

But as I was struggling to get out the front door, I encountered Millie on the porch.

She stuck her hands on her hips. "Running away?"

It felt like I'd been caught with my hand in the cookie jar. "I was going to call you."

"And say what?"

"Um, that I'm engaged to Hutton?" It came out as a question and Millie burst out laughing. "What's so funny?" I demanded.

"You're not really engaged to Hutton," she said, shaking her head. "There is no *way* you've been secretly dating him for a month. I talk to you every day. I see you all the time. I just asked you about him yesterday. Now tell me the truth."

I shifted my weight nervously from foot to foot. "The truth is . . . complicated."

"Good thing I'm smart."

"And it's a long story."

"Good thing I've got time."

Unable to look her in the eye, I glanced around. It had stopped raining, and the sun was bright. Puddles were evaporating. Sidewalks were drying out. Birds tweeted. An airplane droned overhead.

Millie began tapping her foot.

"The thing is . . ." I hedged, and for possibly the first time in my life, I couldn't find any random thing to blurt. Maybe because I knew my big sister wouldn't accept the usual deflection. Exhaling, I gave up. "The thing is, I opened my big mouth at the reunion last night when Mimi Pepper-Peabody-soon-to-be-Van Pelt cornered me and made me feel bad about myself, and I said I was engaged to Hutton."

Millie's jaw dropped. "Oh, shit."

"Then I hid in a coat closet and begged him to come to the reunion and pretend it was true."

"And he did?"

I nodded. "He showed up in a suit and tie just like I asked and stood there while I said a bunch of ridiculous things to Mimi and her fiancé about our wedding, including the fact that it's taking place at Cloverleigh Farms at the end of August."

"I know. I read about it on dirty-little-scoop-dot-com."

"You read that tabloid crap?"

She shrugged. "I can't help it. I'm addicted to celebrity gossip."

I fidgeted, shifting my weight from one foot to the other. "I don't know how it all got out so quickly. It was just supposed to be a fun game for the night, a way to get back at Mimi for being such a twat-waffle. I told her not to say anything."

"Well, it's out there now. Somehow it—" Millie stopped. "Wait, did you say Van Pelt? Is that Mimi's fiancé's last name?"

"Yeah. He has a funny name." I thought for a second. "Thornton! Thornton Van Pelt."

"That's how it got out," Millie said. "The Van Pelts own a media conglomerate—websites, cable networks, newspapers, social media, online tabloids. I bet they own Dirty Little Scoop. Basically, you told the worst possible people your secret."

"Shit." My shoulders slumped, and my overnight bag slipped to the ground. "I had no idea."

Millie bent down and picked up my bag. "So that explains why you're a viral news sensation today. But the question is, why aren't you denying it? Why not just say it was a joke? Because Frannie and Dad and Winnie all think this is a real thing."

"Did you tell them it wasn't?" I asked, my voice catching with fear.

"No. I didn't want to say anything until I talked to you." She glared at me and hooked my bag over my shoulder again. "But you were ignoring all my attempts to reach out, so I had to hunt you down like a fugitive. Now *what* is up? Why didn't you tell Frannie and Dad the truth?"

"Because Hutton asked me not to."

Millie's brow furrowed. "Why?"

"I can explain, but I want to get off the porch before I run into them. Can we go for coffee somewhere?"

"We can," said Millie, "but you might run into a lot of people pointing and whispering. This is a small town without much else to talk about, and you guys just set it on fire."

"You're right. Okay, let's go to your house."

I followed Millie to her house, and we sat at her kitchen table with glasses of iced tea. Millie's house wasn't as big or fancy as Hutton's, but I'd always loved its cozy vibe, complete with white picket fence, covered front porch, and arched interior doorways. She had beautiful taste too—the hardwood floors and molding were stained a deep, rich brown, the walls were light and neutral, and her furniture was vibrant and colorful.

Her two cats, Muffin and Molasses, came into the kitchen, and Muffin jumped into my lap. I stroked her as I told Millie about the reunion, the evening at Hutton's house, and the hushed conversation he and I'd had behind his closed bedroom door while his ecstatic family—including the Clipper Cuts—made a celebratory breakfast.

"So wait . . ." She held up a hand. "You spent the night in separate rooms? Nothing happened?"

"Nothing happened, but . . ." I squirmed in my chair. "I sort of wanted it to."

Her eyebrows shot up. "Keep going."

"I don't know, something just seems different between us."

"All summer? Or starting last night?"

"Maybe it's been all summer. It's hard to say—I feel close to him, which is kind of crazy since we went a long time without seeing each other. But when he moved back and we started hanging out again, it was like no time had passed at all—and also like there was some new layer there."

"Sexual tension?" she prompted, a gleam in her eye.

My eyes dropped to Muffin's soft gray fur. "Yeah. But it's scary to think about crossing that line."

"That's understandable. You've been friends for so long, it's harder than crossing the line with a stranger." She took a sip of her tea.

I pushed my glasses up my nose. "And what if I'm wrong? What if he isn't into me that way? What if he really *was* knocking on my bedroom door to ask if I was thirsty?"

"Wait." Millie set her glass back on the table with a thump. "He knocked on your bedroom door after you guys had gone to bed last night?"

"Yeah." My face warmed. "Without a shirt on."

"He's into you that way," she said confidently.

"Also, he kissed me this morning," I confessed, a smile tugging at my lips.

"Oh?" Her eyebrows arched.

"It was just for show—his sister was taking pictures—but it was nice. Right after that was when he dragged me into the bedroom to say we should keep up the ruse so his mom and everyone else in town will stop bugging him about being single. He needs peace and quiet to work." I told her about the Congressional hearing. "He's really nervous about it."

"I don't blame him. That would be scary for anyone, but especially for someone with anxiety." Millie tapped her chin. "So the plan is to keep up the charade until he leaves for D.C.?"

"I think so. We haven't really discussed the ending yet."

"But you're not actually going to plan a wedding, are you?"

I glanced out her kitchen window. "I'm not sure. But I *am* moving in with him."

"You're *moving in with him*?" Her eyes bulged.

"Yes. He suggested it this morning, to make it look more real . . . right after I suggested we practice kissing."

She gasped. "This *is* nuts, Felicity."

"But it could be kind of fun, you know?"

"Lying to everyone?"

"Not that part, but—the moving in and the practice kissing and the make-believe at being in love and even the fake planning a wedding. I mean, what if I never do any of that for real?" I asked, growing flustered. "I'm not like you and Winnie. I've never had guys knocking down my door. I've had like three boyfriends ever, and none of them lasted more than a few months."

"That's because you break up with anyone that says 'I love you.'"

"We're not talking about the past," I said quickly.

"*You* brought it up."

"What if it never happens for me, Millie? What if it never feels right? Why shouldn't I get a chance to experience what it's like?" I'd gotten so worked up that Muffin was spooked—she jumped off my lap and ran away.

"Okay, okay. I'm sorry," Millie said gently. "As long as you're sure this isn't going to end badly, I'll go along with it."

"You have to." I begged her with my eyes. "You can't tell anyone it's not real. Please. Just let us have this for a month."

She crossed her heart, locked her lips, and tossed the invisible key over her shoulder. "I won't say a word. Especially because I think it *is* real—part of it, anyway."

"It's not real." I sat up taller in my chair and leveled her with a gaze. "It's pretend and it's temporary and we're just having a good time. Now are you coming for dinner? I'm cooking at Hutton's house—I mean, our house."

"I wouldn't miss it. I just hope I remember my lines."

"All you have to do is say you're going to help me plan a small wedding at the end of August. That's it."

"Doesn't give those bangs much time to grow out," she teased.

I glared at her and touched my forehead. "Not funny."

"It's actually not as bad as the photo you sent," she said. "I'm pretty sure you've done worse."

"Thanks." I paused. "I think."

When I pulled up at Hutton's—now *home*—I wasn't sure if I should knock or just try the door. I was still standing on the front step debating when he pulled it open. He'd cleaned up after his workout, and his hair was a little damp. "Was it locked?"

"I don't know," I said. "But I didn't just want to come in. I was going to knock."

"Felicity, you live here now. You don't have to knock. I'll get you a key." He reached for my suitcase and glanced at my car. "Can I help you with bags?"

"This is it," I said, stepping inside. "I didn't pack up everything, since this is, you know, short-term."

He shut the door behind me. "Did you run into anyone at home?"

"Yes. Millie." I sighed. "And I have to confess something."

"What?"

"She knows the truth."

His eyebrows rose. "She does?"

"Yes. I'm sorry. She just knows me really well, and she can smell bullshit a mile away. I couldn't keep up the act. But don't worry, she's going along with it." I smiled. "And unlike my younger sister Winnie, Millie can totally keep a secret."

"Does she think we're crazy?" He started wheeling the suitcase into the back hall.

"Definitely. But she—" I bumped into him, because he'd stopped moving.

To the right was his room. To the left was the room where I'd slept last night.

Behind him, I held my breath, hoping he'd choose right.

He went left. "Is this room okay?"

"Of course." I followed him into the room. "It's just . . ."

"What?" He faced me with a concerned expression.

"It's just, what if someone asks to see the house tonight? My family has never been here before. If they see all my stuff in a separate room, they might wonder."

He nodded. "You're right." He dragged the suitcase past me and across the hall into his bedroom. "Is this better?"

I lingered in the doorway, taking in the king-sized bed on the left, the twin nightstands with matching lamps, the chair in the corner, the sliding glass door leading to a private deck overlooking the woods. I'd been in here this morning, but hadn't looked at much beyond a sexy, sleeping Hutton tangled up in the sheets. "It's a beautiful room."

He went over to the dresser. "If you just give me a minute,

I'll clear out some drawers for you so you can unpack in here. There should be plenty of room in the closet too—it's huge. Sorry, I should have thought about this before."

"Don't worry about it."

He emptied the three dresser drawers on the left onto the bed. "Is that enough space?"

"Definitely."

He scooped up the clothes on the bed in his arms. "I'll just store these in another bedroom for now."

"Okay." I glanced at a door to my right. "Is that the bathroom?"

"Yes. There are clean towels in there too, if you want to take a shower."

"Thanks."

He stood there for a moment, staring at the blue dress I wore, like maybe he was picturing it coming off before my shower.

Which gave me an idea.

"Would you mind?" I turned around and presented my back. "It's hard for me to get this unzipped on my own."

"Oh. Sure." He dumped the clothing on the bed again and came up behind me.

I felt his hands at the back of my neck, making my pulse quicken. Slowly, he slid the zipper down, pausing at my bra line. A few seconds passed.

I held my breath, fighting the impulse to fill the silence with words that would ease the tension. *That's good enough. I can take it from here. Thanks for the help.*

Instead, I waited to see what he would do.

Then I heard the sound of the zipper again as he lowered it to my waist, his knuckles grazing my spine all the way down. My legs tingled.

Hutton paused, his fingers lingering on my tailbone. "Is that good?"

"Perfect. Thank you."

"No problem." Stepping back, he gathered up the pile of clothing on the bed and left the room, leaving me with a smile on my face and a galloping heart.

After closing the door behind him, I looked at my suitcase and the empty dresser drawers. Did this mean he *actually* wanted to share his bedroom with me?

Or was it all part of the act?

"I just can't believe it." Frannie's eyes misted up again, even though she'd already cried twice—once when she and my dad had arrived, once during the appetizers on the deck, and now she was tearing up over her tacos. Seated across from me at the kitchen table, she dabbed at her eyes with her napkin.

"Jeez, Mom. Again?" Emmeline, seated at the island with Audrey, Hallie, and Luna, shook her head. "It's not sad."

"I know, but . . ." Frannie took a breath and smiled at me, her eyes glassy. "It's overwhelming, how happy I feel about it."

"And how sudden it was," added my dad, who was next to her.

I smiled at them, trying not to feel bad. "It was sudden. I get it."

"But it's not like we didn't all suspect," gloated Winnie. She was seated next to our dad, with Dex at the end of the table nearest her. "You should have seen them back in high school," she said to him. "It was obvious this was how it was going to turn out."

"It's cool that you were friends for so long," Dex said.

"So how did you go from just friends to engaged so quickly?" Winnie asked. "Like when did it happen?"

On my left, Hutton grabbed his beer. To my right, at the

other end of the table, Millie picked up her wine and took a big swallow. I wasn't sure which of them was more nervous.

"Well," I said, launching into the explanation Hutton and I had agreed on as we prepared dinner, "you guys know we've been close since we were twelve. And even when we'd go for a while without seeing each other, we were always in touch. In March, when Hutton came home for a visit, we really reconnected. Then when he moved back in May, we started spending more time together."

"So it really wasn't sudden at all," Winnie said with a laugh.

"You realized what you'd been looking for was right there," Frannie said, blinking back tears again.

"Just like in a song," Audrey gushed. "Or a movie."

"Or a storybook," said Hallie. "Except not a fairy tale, because Felicity wasn't, like, a servant or a mermaid."

"Or in a sleep like death," said Luna. "Or stuck in a tower."

"Good thing, because she just chopped all her hair off. There wouldn't have been anything for a prince to climb." The two girls giggled at Hallie's joke, and the twins joined in.

"At least you got to be a prince," Dex said to Hutton. "When they put me in a story, I'm an ogre."

"Are you going to have a big wedding?" asked Audrey.

"No," I said firmly. "We'd like something very intimate at Cloverleigh Farms. Millie and I are working together on a date." I gave my older sister a look, silently begging her to corroborate.

"Yes," she said. "We'll work it out."

"But Cloverleigh must be totally booked for the season," Frannie said with concern.

"On weekends, the barn is booked up, yes," Millie said. "But since their event is small, we might be able to accommodate them somewhere else on the property."

"We could close down the bar and restaurant on a Sunday evening," Frannie said. "We've done that for private events before."

"Sure," said my dad.

"We know this is last minute, and we apologize," I said to them both.

"No need." My dad's eyes met mine. He wasn't an outwardly emotional guy—he was a Marine, after all—but the long, tight, bear hug he'd given me when he arrived told me how he felt. "We'll make it work. Nothing is more important."

I swallowed hard.

"Tell us about the proposal," Winnie pleaded.

"It was very romantic." I took a sip of my wine for courage. "We were on a walk in the woods here, and he suddenly just dropped to one knee."

"Had you been planning it?" Frannie asked Hutton.

"It was sort of spontaneous." That was his big line, and he delivered it well. I gave him a secret smile of triumph.

"Did he have a ring?" Winnie wanted to know.

"No, but we looked at photos online, and chose one together," I said. "It's being sized and we'll pick it up soon."

"So you've never even had it on your finger?" Winnie was excited about this. "It will be like getting engaged all over again when you put it on!"

I laughed. "I guess it will."

"Which jewelry store?" Frannie asked. "Is it one in town?"

Panic seized my throat—we hadn't actually decided which store.

"Tiffany." Hutton surprised me by answering. "It's at Tiffany in New York. We're going to fly there this week and pick it up."

"You are?" Winnie asked.

"We are?" I stared at Hutton.

"Yes." He met my eyes and gave me a sexy little smile. "Surprise."

"Oh." Frannie fanned her face. "Here I go again."

After dinner, it wasn't quite dark yet so we decided to go sit down by the fire pit. Hutton mentioned there was a corn hole set in the game room on the walkout level, and my dad and Dex were both eager to demonstrate their superior skills in front of their daughters.

They grabbed beers and went down to carry the boards outside, and I opened another bottle of wine. After pouring some for Frannie and Winnie, who followed the guys and kids downstairs, I offered some to Millie. "I'm just going to get the dishes loaded, and then I'll come down."

"I'll help you. I want to talk to you anyway." She glanced over her shoulder to make sure no one was in earshot. "Oh my God! I'm dying!"

I filled both our glasses with wine and set the empty bottle on the marble. "Do you think we pulled it off?"

"Definitely. Everyone was so excited because you guys have been friends for so long. I don't think they questioned it a bit—they *want* to believe it."

"Good." I took a sip of wine. "Although I do feel kind of bad about how happy Dad and Frannie are."

"They are happy. But you know what?" She leaned back against the counter, draping her hands over the edges next to her hips. "Hutton is happy too."

"What do you mean?"

"I mean he does not look at you like the feelings are fake."

I turned away from her and started rinsing plates. "They aren't *all* fake. We're good friends."

"You know what I mean."

"How does he look at me?" I couldn't resist asking.

"Like he can't believe you're real."

I looked over at her. "Stop it."

"I'm serious. The guy has a thing for you. Why else would he agree to this crazy scheme? Ask you to move in? Fly you to *Tiffany* in *New York* next week to pick up a ring?"

"I have no idea what that was about," I said honestly. "It was not part of the story we made up earlier."

"That's my point." She came over and started helping me load the dishes. "Not all of this is made up."

"Okay, maybe not *all* of it—there is an attraction there," I admitted.

She grabbed her wine and took a sip, her eyes sparkling with mischief over the rim of the glass. "Speaking of which, what are the sleeping arrangements Chez French?"

My cheeks burned. "I'm not sure. At first, he put all my stuff in the guest room, but then we thought that would look suspicious, so we moved it into his bedroom. But I don't know what's going to happen tonight. Like, when it's time for bed, which room should I go in?"

"Do you want to sleep with him?"

"Yes, but you're not supposed to want to bang your best friend *or* your fake fiancé, are you?"

Millie laughed. "I don't think there are any guidelines for this situation. You're going to have to make them up as you go along." She clinked her glass to mine. "Have fun."

Eight

Hutton

FELICITY SHUT THE DOOR BEHIND HER FAMILY AND TURNED TO face me. "So was it terrible?"

"No. It wasn't terrible. Actually, your family talks so much that I didn't really feel pressured to be *on* once we got through dinner."

She laughed. "We do talk a lot. And adding Dex's girls to the mix was another layer of chaos."

"It was fine. I'm fucking exhausted, but it was fine."

"Why don't you go to bed?" she suggested. "I can finish cleaning up."

"I'm not *physically* exhausted," I clarified, sticking my hands in my jeans pockets. "It's just a lot of work for me to be around a group of people, even people I like. Takes a lot of energy beneath the surface to appear cool and collected on the outside when your insides feel like a bunch of live wires."

She nodded. "I bet. Thank you for doing that for me."

"You're welcome. And you don't have to clean up. The housekeeper will be here in the morning, and she can take care of it."

"I'm just going to finish loading the dishwasher and take

care of the pans," she said, heading for the kitchen. "I've worked in too many restaurants to leave a mess."

"Can I help?"

"No. But you can keep me company and you can say it's okay to shoot some photos for my blog in here tomorrow. The light and surfaces are going to look amazing!"

I laughed. "Of course it's okay. This is your kitchen now too."

Her smile warmed my insides. "Thank you."

I sat down at the island. "So tell me more about your business plans. What's the ultimate goal?"

As she loaded the rest of the dishes into the dishwasher and washed the pans by hand, she spoke about her passion for creating colorful, delicious, nourishing recipes with seasonal ingredients—local as much as possible. "I love the combination of art and science that cooking takes, and I love the stories behind the places where ingredients come from—especially fruits and vegetables," she said, laughing. "I know it's not super sexy, but I think growing up running around Cloverleigh Farms really showed me the love and pride and passion families have for growing good things. And there are all kinds of small farms like that, passing down family traditions and recipes and methods. I'm fascinated by the human side of it. That's what I missed in the test kitchen. The stories."

I loved hearing her talk about her ideas and her passion as she moved around the kitchen, but it would have been easier to stay focused if she wasn't wearing a pair of black shorts that showed off a lot of leg. On top she wore a white tank top and a light blue button-down, which was now tied around her waist. Her breasts looked so round and luscious in the tight little top, I was practically drooling on the marble counter. Since the moment she'd suggested we practice kissing, I'd been anticipating what might happen tonight. Was she really going to share my bed, or had putting her clothes in my dresser just been part of setting the stage?

I concentrated on what she was saying, afraid I'd zoned out for too long.

"I guess my ultimate goal would be to write cookbooks," she said. "But I need to build a platform first in order for publishing houses to consider me. Unless you're already a celebrity, it's not easy to get a cookbook deal. You need something to make you stand out, a unique perspective, a fresh aesthetic."

"I know some people in publishing. I could put you in touch with them."

She smiled at me. "Thanks, but I want to do it on my own. I had this all planned out when I moved back. Frannie sat down with me, and we sort of mapped out the steps I should take. First, get my blog up and running. Next, start my catering business. Then, once I had traction and a bigger following—and some income—I could write the proposal for the book."

"That makes sense."

"I'm still finding my voice, you know?" She pushed her glasses up her nose before sticking her hands in the back pockets of her shorts. "I'm still building confidence in myself and figuring out what I want to say and why people should listen."

"I have faith in you," I told her. "You're smart and creative and intuitive. You'll find the angle."

"Thanks." Her voice grew softer. "I remember when I wanted to drop out of Brown and go to culinary school. Everyone told me I was crazy except you."

"I wanted you to do what makes you happy."

"I know. I appreciated that. Most people just brought up the money—didn't I realize I'd never make a doctor's salary working in a restaurant?" She mimicked the voices of those who'd doubted her judgment.

"Money isn't everything."

"I agree." She dropped her eyes to the counter. "Um, that thing you said. About New York?"

"Sorry about that." I frowned. "As soon as it was out of my mouth, I realized I probably should have asked you first."

"Hutton." She laughed, shaking her head. "Stop apologizing to me. You never have to worry that I'll take things like that the wrong way."

"Does that mean you want to go?"

A smile lit up her face as she rose up on her toes. "Of course I do!" Then she dropped back onto her heels, her expression worried. "But not to buy a ring, right? Just for fun."

"Don't you think we should get you a ring? Everyone keeps asking."

"Okay, but not a Tiffany ring. Something fake and cheap." She placed her palms on the marble island and gave me a serious look. "I mean it, Hutton. No expensive ring."

"Why not?"

"Because it's unnecessary. Let's just buy a decoy, okay? An imitation diamond for our imitation engagement. That's all we need." She shook her head. "Don't waste your money."

I didn't see it as a waste of money if it would make her happy, but I knew I wasn't going to win that argument—not tonight anyway. "Okay."

She looked relieved. "Thank you."

"Does the trip work with your schedule?"

"Well, I'm on the schedule at Etoile Tuesday through Thursday, but not in the kitchen. I have to man the booth at the Cherry Festival. And I'd say I could get someone to cover for me, but there's something kind of crazy going down Tuesday night that I can't miss."

"What is it?"

A mischievous smile appeared on her face. "It's a proposal. Etoile's head chef, Gianni, is going to propose to his girlfriend, Ellie Fournier. She's the daughter of the Abelard owners. But you can't tell anyone."

I laughed. "Who would I tell?"

"Anyway, I can't miss it. I think I'm the only other person that knows what's going to happen and when, and I promised Gianni I'd be there to make sure Ellie is where she's supposed to be at the right time." She thought for a second. "But I might be able to get someone to cover for me Wednesday and Thursday."

"Okay. You let me know."

"I'll ask Gianni tomorrow, but it will be kind of short notice to plan a trip, won't it?"

"It's not a problem. I'll get us there and back whenever we want."

"Do you own a private jet or something?"

"No private jet. But it's easy enough to hire one."

She laughed. "Spoken like a true billionaire."

Our eyes met, and the silence grew a little tense. She looked so damn good, and I wanted her so badly. "Ready for bed?"

"Yes."

I stood up. "Go ahead. I'm just going to make sure all the lights are off downstairs and the doors are locked before turning the alarm on."

"Need help?"

"No. I'm good." My heart was hammering as I went down the steps, because I had no idea which room she would choose. I figured by going downstairs, I was giving her a chance to decide what she wanted without pressure from me.

I knew what I wanted.

When I came back upstairs, all the lights were off. I locked the front door and headed for the back hall. Then my heart sank—the door to the guest room where she'd slept last night was closed, and the light was on.

Fuck.

Disappointed, I got ready for bed, noticing that she'd taken her cosmetics bags out of my bathroom as well. So maybe I'd been wrong about her feelings. Maybe putting her clothes in my room *had* only been for show. Maybe she really just needed help getting that dress unzipped. Maybe the whole kiss practice idea was more about believability than desire.

With my door closed and the lights off, I tossed the covers back and got into bed. I lay there for a few minutes, wondering if asking her to move in had been a huge mistake—was I going to survive a month with her under my roof? Under my nose? Under my skin?

I thought about her in bed just across the hall. The way she smelled. The curve of her shoulders. The pink in her cheeks when she was nervous. Those huge brown eyes, and the way they might look up at me if she was on her knees. The plush rosy lips parting, the tip of my cock easing into her sweet round mouth.

My hand slipped into my pants. Grimacing, I tightened my fist around my erection and wondered if this was my punishment for inviting her to live here, or maybe for this whole batshit scheme—doomed to jerk off every night while I thought about fucking her or going down on her or shoving my dick in her mouth. I stifled a groan, knowing it would serve me right.

That's when I heard the soft knocking at the door.

I yanked my hand from my pants and lifted myself up on one elbow, my heart a jackhammer in my chest. I stared at the door in the shadowy dark, wondering if I'd imagined it, if shame had me hearing things.

But a moment later, the door opened soundlessly and Felicity slipped inside like a ghost before closing it again. I blinked, vaguely making out the white T-shirt she wore— was it mine?—the dark hair swinging around her shoulders.

"Hi," she whispered.

"Hey."

"I was wondering if you wanted to practice now."

My cock, already standing at full attention, twitched with excitement. "Yeah. I do."

"Should I get in your bed?"

"Definitely."

She walked tentatively to the empty side and stood there for a moment, like she wasn't sure I meant *this bed right here*.

But I wanted her too much and I'd been waiting far too long to let my nerves keep this from happening. Now that I was sure she wanted this too, I reached out and grabbed her by the forearm. "Come here."

She laughed as I pulled her into bed with me and easily slipped her body beneath mine, stretching out on top of her, pinning her wrists above her shoulders. The laughter faded as she felt my erection thick and hard between us. "Oh," she whispered.

"Is this okay?"

She spread her legs and slid her heels up my calves. "It's more than okay. It's what I've been waiting for."

My body ignited as I crushed my mouth to hers like I'd dreamed of doing so many times. I wasn't sure if practice kissing was something you were supposed to ease into, perhaps with a few romantic lines first, but I couldn't hold back. I kissed her deeply and hungrily, teasing her lips open and stroking her tongue with mine. Between us, my cock grew harder and my hips moved instinctively, slowly rubbing my solid length along the sweet spot between her legs.

I moved my mouth down her neck as she tilted her head to one side and made soft, sweet little sounds of assent. I inhaled the scent of her skin, caressed it with my tongue, rubbed my lips against the hollow of her throat. Letting go of her wrists, I braced myself on one arm and slipped a hand beneath the cotton shirt, pausing with my palm on her waist to wonder exactly how much activity was allowable at this first practice session.

"Maybe we should discuss a few things," I said, sliding my hand up her ribcage.

"Like what?"

"Like what other things we should practice. For example." Shifting my weight to my side, I eased my hand over her breast, brushing one hard nipple with my thumb. "I could practice touching you like this."

She gasped, then sighed softly as I nuzzled her lips while teasing the stiff peak until she arched and moaned beneath my hand. I switched my attention to the second one, desperately hoping she'd let my tongue do what my fingers were doing.

She slipped a hand down between us, sliding her palm over my erection through my thin summer pajama pants. "And I could practice touching you like this."

A groan emerged from deep in my throat. I kissed her again, more savagely this time, pinching her nipple with my fingertips, twisting and tugging gently. My dick ached beneath her hand, and I yearned to feel her fist wrapped around it.

I grabbed the bottom of her shirt. "I could practice undressing you."

"I definitely think you should," she panted.

I whipped the shirt over her head and tossed it. I hadn't pulled the drapes all the way, and just enough moonlight seeped into the room to render her skin luminous against my dark gray sheets. I could see the gentle curves of her breasts and hips and thighs—secret, unfamiliar parts of her I'd only imagined.

Immediately I bent my head to her chest and slipped a hand between her legs, sucking one perfect little bud into my mouth as I rubbed my fingers over her panties. She cradled my head in her hands, her breath coming fast. I took her nipple between my teeth and flicked it with the tip of my tongue, thrilled when she gasped and cried out.

She reached for the drawstring on my pants. "My turn." Once she'd untied them, she shoved her hand inside and curled her fingers around my cock.

I shivered with pleasure at her touch, every nerve ending alive and humming, and dangerously hot. She worked her hand up and down my shaft, and my hips flexed impulsively, thrusting into her fist. Kissing her again, I willed myself to hang on to control and not explode all over her hand. To distract myself, I eased my fingers inside the edge of her cotton panties, gratified when she brought up one knee—an invitation.

I groaned at the warm, wet feel of her as I slipped a finger inside her snug velvet softness. This was not a good distraction from my orgasm—all I could think about was my dick pushing its way into this heaven, driving inside her again and again.

How far could this go?

"Hutton," she whispered against my lips. "You should practice taking off my underwear."

Popping onto my knees, I hitched my fingers beneath the cotton panties and dragged them down her legs. Then I lowered my head between her knees.

She gasped, hitching herself onto her elbows. "What are you doing?"

"Is this okay?" I kissed the inside of one delicious inner thigh, and then the other.

"I guess." She laughed nervously.

"You can tell me to stop, and I will."

But the tension in her limbs eased as I inched closer, pressing gentle kisses on her soft, sensitive skin. When I finally stroked her with my tongue, she moaned.

"Don't stop," she whimpered as I circled and swirled her clit with my tongue. "Never stop."

"You taste even better than I imagined."

"You've imagined this?" Her voice rose with surprise.

"Oh yeah." I swept my tongue up her center again, pausing at the top to execute a series of spirals and tricks that would make a gold medal gymnast proud. "I've played this movie in my mind a thousand times."

"You—" She struggled for words. "You never said anything."

I flattened my tongue and performed a few slow, deliberate strokes over her swollen clit. Her body quivered beneath me. "Not the thing you tell someone during calculus review." I licked her again. "Or in a text." I sucked her into my mouth, loving the cry of pleasure she gave me. "Or at the hospital emergency room."

She groaned. "God, don't remind me about that."

I laughed because I was so fucking happy. "It all worked out. I'm exactly where I want to be."

"Me too," she whispered, her fingers threading into my hair. "I'm exactly where I want to be too."

I worked my lips and tongue a little faster. Slid one finger inside her—then two fingers, using a little come hither motion as I sucked her clit into my mouth and flicked it with quick, fluttering beats.

"Your tongue—oh God—you're amazing. I can't—I can't—"

A moment later, she dropped her head back and gripped my head with both hands. Her cries grew wanton and desperate. Her fingers tightened in my hair. Her insides tightened around my fingers and within seconds, I felt her climax thundering through her body with rhythmic contractions and sweet little pulses against my tongue. I didn't stop until she pushed me away.

"It's too much," she panted. "You have to stop."

Grinning, I kissed my way up her body—hip, stomach, ribcage, collarbone, jaw. "I can stop."

"I don't mean stop forever, just maybe for a second, so I can breathe." She looped her arms around my neck. "But practice isn't over yet."

"No?"

She shook her head. "I think there are several more things we should work on."

"I'm open to suggestions."

"I thought you enjoyed being in control."

I laughed. "That's true."

"I'm not scared," she whispered. "I trust you. Tell me what you like."

There were all kinds of things I wanted to tell her, but for tonight, it was enough that she was here, that she wanted me, that she trusted me.

"Don't move." I bit her shoulder lightly before getting to my knees and reaching over to my nightstand to grab a condom from the top drawer.

"Wait." She sat up. "I think *I* should practice this part."

Surprised, I handed it to her. My pajama pants were still loosely clinging to my hips, so she took it between her teeth and worked them down to my knees. My cock sprang free, and I held my breath as she tore open the packet, tossed the wrapper aside, and slowly rolled the condom on with two hands. I was so hard it hurt.

Then she looked up at me with those dark eyes I loved to fantasize about. "How did I do?"

"A perfect ten." Impatient, I pushed her back and stretched out over her again. "But this next part is critical. Timing is everything."

"Could not agree more," she said, wrapping her legs around me.

I eased inside her, inch by inch, my heart a wild thing in

my chest, my breath trapped in my lungs. Felicity inhaled slowly, her eyes closing. When I was buried deep, I lowered my lips to her ear. "You feel so fucking good."

"Hutton," she whispered, her hands sliding down my back to my ass, drawing me in deep. "This can't be real."

I began to move, rocking into her with deep, slow strokes, paying attention to the way she arched her back and tilted her hips and used her hands to pull me closer. I wanted to know exactly what made her moan, what made her dig her nails into my back, what made her body tense up with mounting pleasure until she couldn't contain it anymore—she had to burst wide open. And I wanted to time it all perfectly, so that we could experience that explosion of ecstasy together.

But it was a tall order.

I was so fucking hard for her, and it felt like I'd been that way for hours—no, days. Months. Years. My ego needed her to think I was the best she'd ever had, but my body was like *Fuck you, ego, this is our gig.*

Luckily for me, Felicity's body seemed just as impatient as mine. Not only that, but we moved as if we'd been made for each other, like this wasn't the first time, like we were returning to a place we already knew. There was nothing clumsy or awkward, no fumbling, no apologies, no doubts. Being with her almost felt like a memory of something that hadn't happened yet—maybe a memory of a dream.

She was familiar to me, and yet she was a revelation.

Eventually, my ego had to step aside and let my body have its way. Closer. Harder. Faster. Higher. The tension built and the heat rose until sweat slicked our skin and the muscles in my body seized. Until her cries rang out and her hands clutched my ass and her hips met mine in thrust after thrust after thrust. Until the pleasure tore us apart at the seams and we came undone all at once, trembling and throbbing, pushing and pulling, desperate to hang on—to each other, to the moment, to the unbearable bliss of release.

When I opened my eyes, she was looking up at me, stunned and shaken. "That was . . . wow."

"Yeah. We probably got in a little more practice than we needed."

"No, I think it was good. Practice makes perfect, right?"

"That was pretty fucking close to perfect."

Her lips curved into an adorable grin that made my chest ache—but it was a good ache. A protective ache. I didn't want her to leave my bed. Would she stay the night with me?

"I wasn't sure if I should come in here." Her fingers played in my chest hair.

"Seriously?" I shifted onto my side so I wouldn't smother her, but I took her with me, so we were face to face.

"Yeah. I could not make up my mind about whether you wanted me like this or not."

"Convinced now?"

She giggled. "Mmhm."

"Good." I kissed her forehead.

"I even came in here while you were downstairs turning off the lights to steal a shirt. That was going to be my excuse if you caught me in your bedroom, and then I was going to attempt to seduce you. But you took so long coming back up that I lost my nerve."

I laughed, propping my head in my hand. "Sorry. I was trying to give you enough time to make the choice on your own about which bedroom to sleep in. I was hoping you'd choose mine, but I didn't want to pressure you. But please tell me you'll attempt to seduce me again."

She smiled. "Maybe. You'll have to wait and see."

"This is definitely a side of you I've never seen."

"There's a reason for that. We've always been such good

126

friends. I mean, we still are." Her tone grew a little frantic. "Right?"

"Of course we are." I tucked her hair behind her ear. "In fact, I'm really glad to hear you say that."

"Why?"

"I can't promise anything more."

"Because you suck at relationships?"

"Hey." I tugged at her hair, and she burst out laughing.

"Sorry—couldn't resist," she said. "But don't worry, I can't promise anything more either. To be perfectly honest, I suck at relationships too."

"I don't believe that."

"Believe it. I mean, I've never dated a Zlatka, so no one has ever told me that to my face, but my sister Millie said something today that hit pretty close to home."

"What did she say?"

Felicity played with my chest hair again. "She said the reason I've never had a successful long-term relationship is because I break up with anyone who says 'I love you.'"

"Is that true?"

"One hundred percent."

I'd expected her to deny it, so her honesty made me laugh. "And why is that?"

She didn't answer right away. "I don't really know. I've just always been that way. I suppose I figure things are going to blow up at some point anyway, so I might as well light the match."

It didn't take a psychiatrist to know it probably had something to do with her real mom abandoning her when she was so young, especially having overheard the fight with her dad, but if she wasn't ready to talk about it, I wasn't going to make her. Nothing worse than someone trying to be your therapist when you just needed a sympathetic ear—something my sister did not seem to understand.

"Well, I think Zlatka is into women too," I told her, "so if you'd like to date her, I'm sure she'd be glad to tell you exactly why you suck at relationships. Although, she's not likely to tell you she loves you—at least, she never said that to me—so maybe things would work out with you guys."

Laughing, she slapped my shoulder. "No, thanks. I don't need Zlatka in my life pointing out all my flaws."

"You have no flaws."

"Ha! I've got plenty. But I'm actually sort of glad for one of them tonight."

"Oh yeah?"

"Yes, if I had better impulse control, I might not have told Mimi we were engaged, and then I would not have just experienced the best two orgasms of my life."

My chest puffed up with pride.

She snuggled closer to me. "Tell me something about yourself that I don't know."

"Like what?"

"Something from before we met."

I thought for a second. "When I was a kid, I wanted to be a professional baseball player."

"You did? I didn't even know you played baseball."

"I quit right before we moved up here."

"Why?"

"I had a really bad game. Struck out three times in a row and cost my team the league championship." It was a memory I hated, so I tried never to go back there.

"Oh." Felicity rubbed my shoulder. "I'm sorry. That had to feel terrible."

"It did. I never played again. But it's not like I was going to play professionally anyway. I was talented, but I wasn't *that* good."

"Well, I'm glad you told me. The childhood baseball dream seems like something a fiancée would know."

"What did *you* want to be when you were a kid?"

"A hundred different things. A scientist. An astronaut. A pastry chef. A school librarian. I thought it would be cool to spend my days around kids and books."

"You'd be great at that, Miss MacAllister." Immediately I indulged in a hot fantasy about her. "Would you be a naughty librarian?"

She giggled. "Only for you. Hey, this is what we should do every night."

I reached down to her ass and squeezed it, pulling her against me. "I could not agree more."

"I don't mean *that*," she said, laughing. "I mean—yes, that too—but what I meant was that every night we should tell each other one secret. So that we know each other better than anybody else."

"You already know me better than anybody else."

"I do?" she asked, her voice rising.

"Are you surprised?"

"Kind of. I mean, I know we're close now, and we were close then, but there were a lot of years in between."

Turned on all over again by her skin on mine, I shifted her beneath me and settled my hips between her legs. "Doesn't matter. I've never been close with anyone the way I am with you."

She put her arms around my neck. "Are you saying that right now because you want to have more sex?"

"Yes." I kissed her lips. "But I also mean it. What looks like a six to you might appear as a nine to me. It's just a different perspective. Both things can be true."

"You're such a math nerd," she teased.

"I also like the numbers six and nine."

She laughed as I kissed my way down her neck. "I suppose both things can be true."

Nine

Felicity

WHEN I OPENED MY EYES, I WAS NAKED AND ALONE IN Hutton's bed. Instinctively, I reached for my glasses on the nightstand, but they weren't there, and I remembered I hadn't worn them when I set out on my errand of seduction last night.

Smiling, I fell back against the pillow and pulled the sheets up to my chin. We'd had so much fun—the kind of fun I'd always imagined having in bed with someone, but had never experienced. Sex was always so fraught with nerves and expectations—what if I was a disappointment? What if he was clueless? What did this mean for the relationship? How could I sneak out fairly quickly afterward because I liked to sleep in my own bed, or worse, how could I get him to leave so that I could have my bed to myself?

But there had been none of that with Hutton.

He'd made me feel sexy and beautiful, and he was the hottest, most skilled, most attentive guy I'd ever been with. I didn't have to worry about what this meant for the relationship, because there wasn't one, we were just pretending. And I didn't have to invent excuses for why I had to leave or come up with reasons why it was a bad idea for him to stay the night . . . I'd *wanted* to sleep next to him.

The bathroom door opened and Hutton appeared, dressed in running clothes. "Hey."

"Hi." I sat up and smiled, covers gathered in front of my chest. "Heading out?"

"Yeah. Want to come with me?"

I thought about it, but decided I didn't really feel like jumping out of bed and exerting myself right this moment. Mostly I just wanted to roll around in his sheets and relish last night's delight. "Nah, you go ahead. I might take a jog later or something."

"Okay." He leaned over and squeezed my foot under the blankets. "The housekeeper will be here in about an hour. I texted her that I had a guest staying with me, so she wouldn't be caught off guard by the naked girl in my bed."

I laughed. "Thanks, but I'm getting up in a minute here. I need to go into work."

"Isn't the restaurant closed Mondays?"

"Yes, but I have to check in with Gianni—I want to go over details for tomorrow night's proposal and ask him about getting Wednesday or Thursday off. After that, I was thinking of making a few dishes and taking some photos in your kitchen. Will you be around for dinner?"

"You're cooking? Fuck yes."

"Great." I smiled. "Say hi to the Prancin' Grannies for me. Will they be heartbroken about your engagement?"

"Probably. But maybe they'll stop bugging me about their granddaughters now."

"Good luck."

He waved, and I watched him head out, recalling his firm, muscular body on mine last night. I'd been right about his physique—there had been ridges and lines aplenty. But it wasn't just the way he looked. The guy could *move*. Not just his hips, but his arms, his hands, his mouth.

That tongue.

My core muscles clenched, and I closed my eyes. Warmth billowed beneath my skin, sending a tingle from my spine to the ends of my fingers and toes.

I couldn't wait for our next practice session.

I got dressed, packed up my laptop, and headed over to Abelard Vineyards. When I arrived, I headed for the lobby, waved at the front desk staff, and knocked on Winnie's office door.

At her desk, she looked up and smiled. "Good morning, future Mrs. French."

I grinned. "Morning. You busy?"

"Not too bad. Come on in." She gestured to the chairs opposite her desk. "What's up? You're not working today, are you?"

"Not officially." Etoile was always closed on Mondays. "But I need to check with Gianni on a couple things for this week." I couldn't tell her about the proposal—Winnie was *horrible* at keeping secrets, and Ellie was her best friend. Gianni had made me promise to keep the plan from my sister.

"Like taking some days off to go to New York on a shopping spree with your billionaire boyfriend?"

"It's not a shopping spree," I said, rolling my eyes. "We're just picking up the ring."

"Where will you stay?" She picked up her coffee cup with her pinky extended. "The Ritz? The Carlyle? The Pierre?"

"I'm not sure," I said. Then I couldn't resist adding. "But we're chartering a private jet to fly there."

Her jaw dropped. "Stop it! Aren't you high-falutin'?"

"Listen, Hutton works hard. He's earned the right to falute a little."

"I agree one hundred percent, and I look forward to faluting vicariously through you. But hey, if you stay at The Pierre, steal one of the bathroom robes for me. They're glorious."

Laughing, I shook my head. "I will not be stealing any bathrobes. Anyway, I wanted to make sure you can still help out in the Etoile booth tomorrow night."

"Yes. I'll be there. Six, right?"

"Perfect. The second thing is, I wondered if you might help me sift through some of these messages I'm getting from companies wanting to collaborate with me." I set my phone on her desk and shrank back, like it was emitting an offensive odor. "My follower count and inbox have gone bananas, I have no idea if any of these people are legit, and it feels kind of icky that all I did was get engaged to Hutton and now I'm insanely popular."

"I'd be glad to help you." She sat back in her chair and studied me thoughtfully. "But you don't have to say yes to any of them if you don't want to."

"Half the companies reaching out to me have nothing to do with food. It's like clothes or cosmetics or hair products. Can you imagine? *Me*, recommending hair products? I'm even fielding requests regarding my wedding day. Someone wants to send me a case of self-tanner!"

She laughed. "So say no."

"But is that stupid? What if it helps my business? I won't get a book deal without a platform."

"I get that. But ideally, you want to build an audience of people who would be interested in what you do, what you say, and who'd eventually buy your book. Recommending a self-tanner might earn you a little extra cash, but it probably won't build your audience. A better use of your time would probably be concentrating on putting out more content. And it's not like you need the extra cash for rent anymore."

I squirmed in my chair. "Right. I *am* going to put out more content."

"Good. So if it doesn't feel right to say yes to those offers, don't. But of course I can help you sort through it all."

"Thanks. I'm going to head over to see Gianni and then I'll be back." I left Winnie's office and headed for Etoile's kitchen, where I found Gianni going over inventory.

"Morning," I said.

"Morning." He nodded toward the coffee machine. "Coffee's hot if you want some."

"Thanks." I poured myself a cup. "All set for tomorrow night?"

"I think so." He grinned devilishly, his eyes lighting up. "She's going to be so fucking mad at me."

I laughed. "She'll still say yes." Ellie and Gianni had also known each other since childhood, but unlike Hutton and me, they'd been enemies and not friends. Still, they had fantastic chemistry, although it had taken being stranded for two days in a January blizzard at a roadside motel—which had resulted in an unexpected pink plus sign a month later—for them to realize they were good together.

"Just don't forget the final prop," he said. "Once she's wearing the ring, I need to throw a whipped cream pie in her face."

Shaking my head, I laughed again. "I really cannot wait to see this proposal go down."

"Speaking of proposals." He cocked his head. "What's this I hear about you being secretly engaged? Ellie was losing her mind yesterday."

"Oh. Yeah." My cheeks grew hot, and I gave him a weak smile. "Surprise."

"I can't believe you never said anything. When's the wedding?"

"Um, we're thinking next month."

Gianni's blue eyes popped. "Wow. That's fast." He glanced at my waistline. "Is there a reason?"

"Not that kind of reason," I assured him. "We just . . . don't want to wait, I guess."

"Don't let anybody make you feel bad about that," he said with the cocky assurance he always had. "People always think they know how everyone else should live their lives and make their choices, because that's the way *they* did it. But it's bullshit. There's no one right way to do things—it's all right in the end, as long as it gets you where you want to go. The journey looks different for everybody, and it *should*."

"Thanks," I said, wondering where exactly it was that I wanted my journey with Hutton to go. "I appreciate that."

"And Ellie mentioned you guys have been good friends for a lot of years, so maybe it wasn't that sudden anyway."

"It was slow *and* sudden." I smiled. "Both things can be true."

When I was done in the kitchen, I returned to Winnie's office and we did a little research into some of the companies requesting to work with me. Most of the offers I had no problem rejecting, but there were a few cooking-related, female-owned businesses that I thought sounded interesting, so we made a list and responded to them. Winnie suggested I respond to the awful Dearly Beloved review too.

"You think so? That's what Millie said."

"I would," she said with a shrug. "Show potential clients that you honestly care. Because the biggest priority is getting more reviews, and to get those, you need more business. I think you could do it in a way that shows your professionalism and character."

I decided to take my sisters' advice, replying to He Put A Big A** Ring On It with an apology, saying I was sorry she was disappointed, but that I stood behind my work and would therefore be glad to offer a refund.

"Perfect," said Winnie.

"I should go," I said, noticing the time. "I need to hit the market on my way home. I want to try a few new recipes and take some photos while the light is good in the kitchen."

"Let me know when those companies get back to you," Winnie said, stretching her arms overhead. "I think you made the right choices."

I tucked my laptop into my bag. "Thanks for the help."

"So I was wondering," she said with a put-on casual air, "do you have plans for the last Saturday evening in July? The 30th?"

I glanced at her and noticed she was staring intently at a plant on her desk, like she couldn't meet my eyes.

"Not that I'm aware of. Why?"

"No reason. No reason," she said in the same false, high-pitched tone. Then she sat there with her lips mashed together so tightly, it was as if she was afraid if she opened them, something might fly out.

I knew what it meant. "Winnie. Do you know something?"

She made sounds that might have been words but kept her mouth completely closed, like really bad ventriloquy.

"For heaven's sake, Win. You know something. Out with it."

"But I promised I wouldn't telllllll," she said, as if it pained her.

"You know you can't keep a secret."

She slapped one hand over her mouth. Then the other on top of the first.

"Winifred."

She slid off her chair and hid beneath her desk.

I rolled my eyes. "Fine. I'm leaving."

Her voice came from beneath her desk. "If I tell you, you have to promise me that you won't say anything."

"Okay."

She stood up and smoothed her skirt. "So while you were in the kitchen, I got a phone call from Hutton's mom."

I gestured for her to get on with it. "And?"

"She wants to plan a surprise outdoor engagement party for you guys here on the patio."

I gasped. "Shoot! On the 30th?"

"Yes. The crazy thing was, that date was booked right up until this morning! Literally, the event that was scheduled got canceled like ten minutes before she called. It was some kind of weird kismet."

"I bet Mrs. French loved that."

Winnie nodded. "She did! I haven't confirmed with her yet—but I feel weird going along with it because I know Hutton doesn't love parties. Although you'd think his mom would know that."

"She knows." I sighed.

"So will he be okay with it?"

"Are you kidding? He hates parties when he *isn't* the center of attention. This one will be torture for him."

"So should I make something up? Tell her that other event wasn't canceled after all?" She looked scared. "I could get in trouble for that."

"No, don't. She could easily go somewhere else, and then we'll have no control or inside information." I slung my laptop bag over my shoulder. "Go ahead and tell her yes. We'll get through it."

"You're sure?"

"I'm sure. But I'm not going to let it be a surprise," I warned her. "I have to tell him."

"Will he go right to his mom?" Winnie's brow furrowed. "She made me swear I'd keep it a secret."

"She obviously doesn't know you very well," I said with a grin. "But I'll make sure Hutton understands the situation."

"Thanks." Relieved, she smiled and sat back in her chair. "It's going to be a beautiful party, I promise."

"Keep it small," I pleaded. "Intimate."

"I told her the max the patio can accommodate is thirty. And Etoile is also open that night, so the kitchen can't handle too much more food."

"Thirty is perfect. Keep me posted."

On my way to the market, I called Hutton's cell.

"You know I hate the phone," he said when he picked up.

"I do. But I can't text and drive."

"Never do that. Did you talk to Gianni?"

"Yes, and he said it's not a problem. I can take Wednesday and Thursday night off. Ellie will cover for me."

"Good. I'll book the trip."

"Yay!" My heart danced with excitement. "I'm heading to the market, and I was wondering if there was anything in particular you'd like for dinner," I said, figuring I'd butter him up with his favorite dish before telling him about the party.

"Does it have to be vegetarian?"

"Nope. I can do anything."

"Steak."

I sighed. "Of course steak."

"Hey, you said anything."

"I did, and I will cook you a steak," I said with a laugh. "It's not that I don't think they're delicious—I know they are.

I just don't feel great after I eat meat, so I stick to other things. How's your day going?"

"Fine, although I have a call scheduled later this afternoon with Wade that I'm not looking forward to, and not just because I hate the phone."

"Is it about testifying?"

"Yes. He says he has more details about what questions I'll have to answer. He's in touch with committee members."

"Well, more details are good, right? The better prepared you can be, the more confident you'll feel. How was your run?" I asked, changing topics. "Did you see the Prancin' Grannies?"

"Yes. They tried to accost me the minute I got out of my car. I had my earbuds in, so I pretended I didn't hear them and just started running. They couldn't keep up with me."

I laughed. "Poor grannies. They just want your attention for a few minutes."

"They're vicious. You don't know them. In fact, now that they think we're engaged, they're probably going to come after you. Better watch your back for those pink bedazzled shirts."

I laughed as I pulled into a parking space in the grocery store lot. "I'll be on my guard."

Ten

Felicity

I SPENT ALL AFTERNOON IN HUTTON'S FABULOUS KITCHEN, creating some new recipes and photographing the results. At the market, I'd chosen the most brightly-colored, locally-grown foods I could find—apricots, raspberries, cherries, crisp greens, snap peas, broccoli, sweet cherries, radishes, honey. Next, I hit my favorite cheese shop and bakery, ducked into a reputable butcher shop for Hutton's steak, and finally I hit the wine store, picking up a couple bottles each of red and white.

This is why you have no money, I told myself. It was true—my love for good food and wine and my dedication to using seasonal produce and small-batch products always trumped my desire to grow my savings. I couldn't help it! But today, I was looking at it as an investment in my business, and in myself.

Hutton eventually wandered up from downstairs and opened his laptop at the kitchen table, where he sat and worked while I floated around in the kitchen, happier than I'd been in months. Even when I thought about that stupid Dearly Beloved review, it didn't bother me nearly as much as it had before. Everyone faced setbacks, right? When you put yourself out there, whether it was with a plate of food at a restaurant or a recipe on the blog or a new business or a cookbook, you had to anticipate criticism, both deserved and undeserved. The important thing was to keep believing.

And every time I looked at Hutton, my belly swooshed and my mouth curled into a smile and my heart fluttered wildly. He was so handsome and serious sitting there in his light blue button-down, frowning at his screen and sometimes tugging on his hair, just like he used to when we were teenagers studying calculus. I could hardly wait to go to bed tonight, change that expression to something different, hear that deep voice in my ear again, feel his skin on mine. Who would have thought our sexual chemistry would be so good after so many years of being just friends?

Around six, Hutton closed his computer and grabbed a beer from the fridge. "Want one?"

"No, thanks. But maybe you could open that bottle of Valpolicella for me?"

He opened the wine and poured me a glass. "Anything else I can do to help?"

"Nope. Just keep me company." I set the plate of vegetarian charcuterie I'd assembled earlier on the island. "Have a beer and a snack and hear me out."

He straddled a stool at the island and tipped up his beer. "Hear you out? That sounds ominous."

"Not really." I took a sip of my wine. "I just want to tell you about a little party."

One of his brows arched. "What party?"

"The surprise party your mom is throwing for us on the patio at Abelard Vineyards the last Saturday in July."

As soon as the word *surprise* came out of my mouth, he was shaking his head. "No fucking way."

"The patio is really lovely," I went on smoothly, sliding the onions from the cutting board into the pan.

"No."

"And the best part is, capacity on the patio is limited to thirty, so it has to be small." The onions began to sizzle.

"It's not the patio I'm objecting to. It's the surprise. Also the party."

"But Hutton, we're not even supposed to know about it—at least if Winnie plans it at Abelard, we'll have all the details in advance. We'll know the terrain, the menu, the timeline—all the relevant details. Even if Winnie pretended Abelard had no available dates, your mom would not give up," I said emphatically, facing him again. "She'll go somewhere else and we'll have no clue when it's coming."

Hutton grumbled something I couldn't make out and took another swallow from his beer.

"Our families are happy for us, Hutton." I softened my voice. "People want to celebrate. We know it's not really happening, but they don't."

"I know, but . . . a party? That was *not* part of my plan." He shook his head. "This engagement was supposed to get people off my back, not invite them to pile on."

"I know. I'm sorry."

He shoved a piece of baguette in his mouth and chewed grumpily. "When is it?"

"July 30th."

"Two days after my testimony."

"I realized that after Winnie told me the date," I said, applying a dry rub to his steak. "I know the timing stinks, but that was the one day Abelard could fit us in. They had a cancellation."

He brooded silently for a moment, watching my fingers on the meat. "You're right. My mother is not going to drop it."

"We're not even supposed to know about it."

He tipped up his beer again and looked at me. "Do *you* want this party?"

I flipped the steak and put the rub onto the other side. "It might be kind of fun. But I feel bad that your parents are going to spend money on it."

"Listen, my mother has been trying to throw me a party since I was twelve and I've said no every time. No birthday parties, no graduation parties, nothing. She will not care about the cost."

"So is that a yes?"

"Do I have a choice?"

I laughed. "Not really. Unless you want to call the engagement off before you go to D.C. End things sooner rather than later."

"No," he said quickly. "I can deal with the party. Let's stick to the original plan."

After dinner, Hutton had some work to finish, and I wanted to edit the photos I'd taken and create some content to post this week. We sat at the kitchen table with our laptops in comfortable silence.

"It's like the old days." I nudged his leg with my foot. "Sitting here working next to you like this."

"It's better," he argued, tipping his chair back on two legs.

I laughed and tucked a strand of hair that had come loose from my ponytail behind my ear. "How so?"

"Well, I used to sit next to you and wonder what it would be like to kiss you. I'd come up with all these crazy ways I could make it happen, then talk myself out of every single one of them." He shook his head. "I'd think up tons of things I wanted to say to you—I'd even practice my lines—but never actually be able to say them."

I smiled. "Do you remember what you said to me after we danced at the prom?"

His eyes closed. "Don't tell me."

"You said, 'That wasn't as bad as I thought it would be.'"

He groaned. "That is *not* what I rehearsed. I totally chickened out. Sort of like I did at your bedroom door Saturday night instead of telling you the real reason I was about to knock."

I feigned shock, my mouth forming an O. "You mean you weren't really coming to my room with no shirt on to see if I was thirsty? I'm aghast! You had me totally fooled!"

"That's it." He lunged for me, picking me up out of the chair and tossing me over his shoulder, heading for the bedroom.

"What is this?" I cried, hitting his butt with my hands. "Kidnapping?"

"We're not kids anymore." He entered his bedroom, where just one nightstand lamp was on, and tossed me onto the foot of the bed.

"Hutton, wait!" Lying on my back, I crossed my arms over my chest. "I have to take a shower. I never took one today and I've been running around and cooking and getting sweaty. I won't smell nice."

Bracing himself above me, he lowered his chest over mine pushup-style and buried his face in my neck. "You smell fucking great. And I'm only going to make you get sweatier."

I laughed as his scruff tickled my throat. "Compromise— how about you give me ten quick minutes in the shower and then you join me?"

"Five minutes." He stood up and adjusted the crotch of his pants. "Go."

I shrieked and bolted for the bathroom, whipping my shirt off on the way and slamming the door behind me. Hutton's bathroom was airy and luxurious, with a double vanity and a freestanding white tub beneath the window. Next to it was a glassed-in shower with multiple heads and a multi-color pebbled tile floor. But my eyes lingered on that tub.

I glanced back at the door—could I get Hutton into a bubble bath?

After turning on the faucet, I dug through my bag for my lavender and vanilla shower gel and dumped some in. It didn't create a *ton* of bubbles, but there were enough to make it look fun and smell good. Then I undressed, tossed my hair up, and slipped into the water.

I closed my eyes for a second, marveling that I was naked in Hutton French's tub, that in a moment, he was going to come in here and join me. Seventeen-year-old me would be *astonished*.

It set my mind spinning.

Less than five minutes later, Hutton barged in, buck naked with one hell of an erection. But he stopped short at the sight of me in the tub.

"What's this?"

"It's a bath." I smiled sweetly and splashed a hand in the water. "Come and play."

He inhaled, and his cock jumped. "What's that smell?"

"Lavender and vanilla. It's supposed to relax you."

"It's not working," he said, approaching the tub, his gaze roving hungrily over my skin. "In fact, I'm the opposite of relaxed right now."

"Then get in with me." I lowered my chin and looked up at him through my lashes. "I promise to make it all better."

He shook his head, his eyes still on my breasts. "Felicity, there's no way we're both going to fit in that bathtub."

"I'm not saying it won't be a tight squeeze, but I'm sure two people as skilled in geometry as we are can come up with a solution to this problem." I sat up and turned off the water. "For example, you can lie on your back and I'll lie on top of you—a parallelogram. Or you can sit, and I'll straddle your lap—more of a trapezoid. Or," I said, getting to my knees, "you can stand, and I'll kneel in front of you."

His cock twitched again. "And what do you call that?"

I licked my lips. "A blowjob."

Without further argument, he stepped into the tub.

I moved closer, running my hands up the front of his thighs. Then I pitched my idea. "Want to play a little?"

"Play?" His tone was intrigued but cautious. "Play what?"

I looked up at him and smiled wickedly. "My parents aren't home."

"Huh?"

"So you have to be quiet." I wrapped my fingers around his cock and brushed my lips with the tip, keeping my eyes locked on his.

"Oh, fuck." His Adam's apple bobbed. "You want to play teenage *us*?"

A laugh bubbled from the back of my throat as I angled my head in different directions, brushing the sensitive crown across my cheek, under my jaw, along my throat. "Yes."

"You do realize that teenage me already came all over your face."

I laughed again, splashing his legs. "Come on. Play with me. I have confidence in your grown-up self-control."

"That makes one of us."

I brought the tip back to my lips, opening them slightly, letting him feel my breath. "I've thought about this while we study. Have you?"

"Yeah." I could sense him concentrating hard. "And afterward."

"Afterward?"

"Late at night. When I'm alone in my bed."

"Tell me." I grazed the underside of his cock with my

tongue, and it thickened in my grasp. "What do you think about?"

"This. You, on your knees in front of me. My cock in your mouth." His voice was low and commanding, and it turned me on.

"Like this?" I took just the tip in my mouth, teasing him.

"Yes."

I sucked gently, then swirled my tongue around the crown, making his abdominal muscles flex. Opening my mouth wider, I took him in deeper, moaning softly. His hands curled into fists at his sides. I liked his hands. They were masculine and strong, and I remembered how his talented fingers had brought me such pleasure last night.

It gave me another idea.

"Show me," I said, sitting back on my heels. "What you do late at night. When you think about this."

"Are you serious?"

"Yes." I crossed my arms over my chest, like I was suddenly shy. "Or else."

He glared at me, but he took his cock in his hand, wrapping it in his fist and giving it several long, slow pulls. "Is this what you want?"

But I couldn't answer. I was mesmerized—by the muscles that worked as he stroked himself—arm and shoulder and abs. By the way he stood, like he wasn't ashamed—head up, chest proud, breath coming faster. And by the way his eyes remained on me, their shade of blue hotter and more piercing than a moment ago.

I started to breathe faster too. In fact, I think my breathing was more frantic than his. I could not get over that he was actually doing this in front of me—or how much I liked the sight of his hand on his cock, palm sliding over the darkened crown, fist working up and down the thick, veined shaft. I realized I hadn't seen his naked body in the light last night, and it was perfect. A work of art.

"Touch yourself," he demanded in a voice I'd never heard him use, a voice that couldn't be refused. Besides, he'd done it for me. And this was all pretend, right? We trusted each other. Why not just let go?

I lifted my butt off my heels and ran my hands over my breasts, down my stomach, up my thighs, never taking my eyes off him.

"Yes." His hand moved faster. Harder. "Yes."

Emboldened by his reaction, I let one hand glide between my legs, slowly caressing my clit with soft, circular motions, as if I was alone in the dark and not under his eyes in the light.

"Fuck," he growled through his teeth. "Fuck, that's hot."

"I'm thinking about you," I panted, sliding my free hand over one breast. "I love thinking about you when I do this."

His jaw clenched and he exhaled sharply, as if I'd said something to make him angry. "Is that true?"

"Yes," I said, because it was. He'd always been such a good fantasy, almost like a movie star—someone out of reach. "I'd pretend your hands were on me this way."

"My tongue." His eyes blazed with desire. "Did you think about that?"

"I am now." I rubbed myself a little harder, the muscles in my legs starting to hum. My eyes lingered on his erection.

"Fuck." He closed his eyes and stopped moving his hand, keeping it wrapped tightly around his dick. "This is going to be over too soon."

"Let me." I took him by the wrist and pulled his hand from his cock so I could take over. Curling my fingers around him, I lowered my mouth onto his thick, hard length, taking him to the back of my throat. I held my breath, keeping still for a moment, praying I wouldn't choke.

"Jesus," he breathed, his hands slipping into my hair.

I felt him pulse once—a warning—and tasted something salty sweet. I began to suck hungrily, using my hand to grip what wouldn't fit in my mouth.

He cursed again and tightened his grasp on my head, holding me still. "Are you sure?"

I glanced up through my lashes, moving my hands to his ass, digging my fingers into his skin and pulling him deeper. It was all the permission he needed, and he began to flex his hips, driving his cock into my mouth, his breaths loud, his groans escalating, his movements growing more and more frantic until his body tensed up and he stopped moving completely, except for the thick, pulsing throb of his orgasm, which erupted at the back of my throat.

He pulled out and I sat back on my heels again, wiping my mouth with my arm and catching my breath.

But I didn't have much time to recover before Hutton grabbed me beneath the arms and set me up on the edge of the tub. Dropping to his knees in front of me, he pushed my legs apart. "My turn," he said.

It took some serious balance not to go right over backward during the toe-curling, thigh-trembling, tub-thumping finish he gave me.

Teenage Hutton and Felicity would not have recognized themselves.

I was proud of us—for having the guts to cross the line, for being brave in front of one another, and for trusting that none of this would ruin what we had.

The game was fun, but it was just a game.

Eleven

Hutton

"TELL ME A SECRET," FELICITY SAID, snuggling up to me in bed.

"A secret?" Lying on my back, I put one hand behind my head and wrapped the other around her shoulders. I could still smell the lavender and vanilla on her skin—pretty sure I was never going to find those scents relaxing, especially now that my brain would associate them with what had just transpired in my bathroom. But at the very least, they'd bring back a nice memory.

"Yes. Or a story from when you were little. I like those."

I thought about it for a moment. "When I was young, I thought I had magic powers."

"Oooh! What kind of magic powers?"

Her reaction made me smile—I loved that she was more interested in the nature of my otherworldly abilities than in laughing at the idea. "I thought I could control the outcome of things—favorably for me, of course—or prevent bad things from happening, with certain actions."

"What would you do?"

"Typical stuff that someone with OCD does. Small

rituals like always putting my right sock on first, always sitting on the right side of the car, touching my nose as I entered a room, counting things."

"I didn't know you had OCD." She was playing with my chest hair again. I loved when she did that.

"I don't think I do, at least not anymore. If I'd been evaluated back then, they might have diagnosed me that way, but I never told anyone about my powers."

"Why not?"

"Because then they wouldn't work."

"Ah." Her fingers moved in slow, relaxing circles. "When did you stop believing in them?"

I didn't even have to think about it. "When my grandfather died."

Her hand stopped moving. "How old were you?"

"Eleven."

She propped her head on her hand and looked at me. "Is this the grandpa that gave you the signed Ray Bradbury paperbacks?"

I smiled—she remembered. "Yes."

"Tell me more about him. What was he like?"

My head filled with memories of the brilliant, fun-loving grandfather I'd known. "He loved puzzles, and we used to work on them together all the time. He loved baseball and never missed one of my games. He wore Pinaud Clubman aftershave, and sometimes I catch a whiff of it in a crowd and it's like he's right there."

"Maybe he is."

"Now you sound like my mother."

She laughed. "Do you still have the books he gave you?"

"Yes. They're not in pristine condition or anything—he read them over and over again, and I did too—but I'd never sell them anyway."

"Of course not. That kind of thing is priceless." She put her head down again. "I'm sorry you lost him so young."

"His death hit me hard. It wasn't sudden—we knew he was sick—but I was so sure of my ability to prevent anything terrible from happening that I was totally unprepared when it happened."

"Did you blame yourself?" she asked softly.

"Not exactly, but I started to doubt myself in every way. Soon after that was when I struck out three times during my baseball team's championship game. I remember thinking then that it was clear—I wasn't magical. I wasn't even that special or talented. And everyone fucking knew it."

She kissed my chest, then pressed her cheek against it, wrapping her arm around my waist.

"I remember coming home and lying on my bed, just staring at the ceiling and thinking, *I'm not who I thought I was.* The world didn't work like I thought it did. And maybe everyone else had known this all along, and I was just an idiot."

She hugged me tighter.

"We moved right after that. My parents wanted a change of scene, and I think they even thought it would be good for me. They could see something was off. I'd gone from a cocky, smart-mouthed fifth grader who only came home to eat and sleep into a kid who hated leaving the house." I exhaled. "But I think the move made it harder. I had to start over—without my magic powers."

"But then you met me," she said brightly. "And that was a good thing, right?"

"That was a good thing."

"Until I made you pretend to be my fiancé. Attend social gatherings. Host dinner parties."

"Yes, but . . ." Rolling over, I covered her body with

mine, eager to lose myself in her again. "It also has its perks."

The next morning, I woke up early and headed to the park for my run. I was hoping it was early enough to avoid the Prancin' Grannies—and I even parked in a different spot—but no such luck.

"There he is!" shouted one of them as I got out of my car. Before I could get my earbuds in or make an escape, they came prancing over, wearing bedazzled pink and indignant expressions.

"Hello, ladies." Reluctantly, I faced them down, reminding myself they were not lions, just old ladies. Ignoring the itch under my skin, I forced myself to ask the polite question. "How are you?"

"Fine, fine. We were hoping to catch you," said one with a head full of curls the copper color of a penny. "We want to hear all about your big news!"

"We know her." A granny wearing lipstick in the same shade of pink as their shirts nodded excitedly. "We're friends with her grandmother."

"Oh. You mean Felicity." My mind worked overtime to think of something more to say, and nothing came.

"Yes. Her grandmother is Daphne Sawyer," put in a granny with a neon yellow sweatband around her head. "She and her husband John own Cloverleigh Farms, but their kids run it now."

"I heard the wedding is going to be at Cloverleigh Farms." Another granny, this one with seriously thick penciled-in eyebrows, pushed her way to the front. "Is that true?"

"Uh, we hope so."

There was a chorus of sighs and murmurs about what a

beautiful place Cloverleigh Farms was, a few comments about other weddings they'd attended there, and a general air of smiling, nodding approval. They were also eager to establish their connections to the Sawyer family.

"I just love the Sawyers. So kind and welcoming."

"And so generous. When Hank had gall bladder surgery last year, they sent a pie."

"We always play in John Sawyer's charity golf outing. Such good people."

"Daphne still invites me to the annual staff Christmas party. We go every year, even though I haven't worked there in years." Copper penny curls paused. "I'll probably be invited to the wedding."

In the brief silence that followed, I could practically hear the ruffled feathers.

"Will it be a big wedding?" asked the one with the neon sweatband. "Lots of guests?"

"No," I said firmly.

"Why not?" The smiling, nodding approval was replaced with narrowed eyes, hands on hips, and accusatory stares.

"We want to keep it small," I said, rubbing the back of my neck.

"Small!" Copper penny curls was offended. "When you're a local celebrity? That's no fun!"

"You should do something spectacular," said penciled eyebrows. "Like fireworks."

"Oooh! My grandson flies those planes that tow banners," neon sweatband told me. "You should do that."

"My Alfred drives those horse-drawn carriages that take tourists around," said a short granny in the back. "Something like that would be nice and splashy."

"Yes," added the one with bright pink lipstick. "Isn't a small wedding just a bit selfish of you?"

"Selfish?" I repeated, dumbstruck.

"Everyone in town is so happy for you! We feel proud that such a brilliant, successful young man chose a hometown girl to settle down with!"

"It shows real character!"

"It shows that no matter how much money you make or how famous you get, what matters is family."

"Yes! Friends and neighbors are an extension of family."

"And in a small town, everyone is family."

They all chimed in with agreement, like a gang of street urchins in an old movie. "Yeah! That's right! You tell him, Gladys! Atta girl!"

"So if you're not going to let us share in the joy of your big day, we just don't know how to take it." Neon sweatband shook her head and put her hands on her chest. "Our hearts might break."

"You think about that, sonny." Pink lipstick nodded once. "Come on, girls."

They pranced away in a huff.

After my run, I went home to clean up and grab something to eat. I was hoping Felicity would be there so I could tell her about my encounter with the Prancin' Grannies, but her car wasn't in the driveway when I pulled in. It was funny how empty and silent the house seemed without her.

I showered and dressed, then discovered a Post-It note on the fridge. *Eat anything you want in here! I've already photographed it!* Beneath the words was a note in our secret code. Smiling, I puzzled it out—*XOXO Felicity.* I pulled the note off the fridge and stuck it in my pocket.

After I ate, I sat down at my desk in the downstairs guest room I used as an office to get some work done. I was sketching a rough outline for my testimony when my phone rang.

Assuming it was Felicity, I smiled and answered it without thinking.

"Hello?"

"Dude," Wade said. "You answered. Is that a thing now?"

Fuck. I rubbed my temples with my thumb and middle finger. "Not really. What's up?"

"Why didn't you tell me about your engagement yesterday, asshole? I just read about it online."

"I guess I forgot."

He laughed. "What the fuck? Who is she?"

"Felicity MacAllister." I knew I'd mentioned her to Wade before, but I wouldn't be surprised if he didn't remember.

"The girl from back home?"

"Yeah."

"Kinda sudden, isn't it?"

"Not really. I've known her since I was twelve."

"You knock her up or something?"

"Fuck off. No."

"Dude," he said. "Doesn't even matter. Don't do it."

"Huh?"

"Don't fucking get married. It will ruin your life."

"Is this the point of your call, Hasbrouck? If so, I'm hanging up."

"I know it seems like a good idea now, but the shine comes off. As soon as the ink is dry on that marriage certificate, she will not be the woman you think she is. That's what they do—they pretend to be cool so you'll propose, and then they turn into crazy, controlling lunatics once they've got your last name. I've never been so miserable."

"We're different."

He laughed again. "Truth, man. If I was you, I'd still be in L.A. fucking Zlatka in my Porsche."

"I'm sure you would."

"How'd you fuck that up, anyway? She was crazy about

you." He laughed unkindly. "Susie said she read somewhere it was because Zlatka didn't like being submissive in the bedroom. She wanted to be the boss."

"You'd have to ask Zlatka about that."

"Dude, I'd totally let her tie me up and slap me around if she wanted to. You really broke it off because of that?"

"No." My jaw clenched. "We fought all the time. It sucked."

"Tell me about it," he muttered. "I'm stuck on this yacht in the Mediterranean listening to Susie whine about what a shitty husband I am day in, day out. Like, what does she want that she doesn't have? She's got the house, the car, the clothes, the vacations. I pay all her fucking bills. What more does she want from me?"

The answer was obvious, but I kept my mouth shut.

"Anyway, that's all I'm saying. Everyone pretends to be someone they're not to get what they want, and you can't make anyone happy in the long run. Don't even try."

I was on the couch watching a baseball game and brooding over my conversation with Wade when I saw Felicity's headlights in the window. A moment later I heard her come in the back door, and I turned off the TV. She'd be a better distraction than the game, and fuck Wade anyway, for telling me shit I already knew.

I wasn't trying to make anyone happy in the long run. I knew better.

"Hey, you." Felicity came through the kitchen into the great room and sank down next to me, kicking off her sneakers. "How was your day?"

"It was okay. How did everything go with the proposal?"

"It was so great!" She turned to face me, sitting

cross-legged. Her hair was in two low pigtails like Zosia sometimes wore, and her smile, as always, lifted my spirits. "Ellie was completely surprised, and the whole thing went off without a hitch—which is pretty impressive, considering what an elaborate scheme it was."

I listened to her tell me how Gianni had recreated a scene from the Cherry Festival when they were teenagers involving a dunk tank and a pie in the face. "She had a bucket of fifty balls, and she kept throwing one after another, and she could *not* dunk him," Felicity said, laughing. "Lucky for her, my cousin Chip Carswell was in the crowd!"

"The White Sox pitcher?" I asked in surprise. "That's your cousin? How did I not know that?"

"Yes—he's Frannie's nephew. His mom is her older sister, April. And his dad is Tyler Shaw, who was also a Major League pitcher. Tyler and April are married now, but they had him when they were like eighteen and gave him up for adoption. They only reconnected later, when he was a teenager, but he was already off at college by the time you moved here."

My head was spinning. "I guess I have a lot to learn about your family history. I never knew any of that. Carswell is a great pitcher. So was Shaw. Two of the best lefties in the game."

She laughed. "Which Ellie was glad about, because she dragged Chip out there and made him throw for her. Gianni got dunked with every ball Chip threw."

"I bet."

"But it was only fair, because back when they were seventeen, Gianni dunked Ellie that many times. Then she threw a bunch of pies in his face in retaliation."

"So where in all that dunking did he propose tonight?"

"Oh! The last ball in the bucket was a fake—it opened up like a ring box."

"I'm impressed."

She sighed. "It was so romantic."

"I assume she said yes?"

"She said yes. Then he threw a pie in her face."

I laughed, envious of Gianni Lupo's bravado, his willingness to stage that huge production and carry it out in front of an audience. "Sounds like it was quite a show."

"It was amazing. I also spoke to Winnie. She said your mom confirmed the engagement party for thirty people at five o'clock, the last Saturday in July."

I grimaced. "Great."

"Did you practice your toast yet?"

"No." I tugged one of her pigtails. "But I did chat with the Prancin' Grannies for seven whole minutes."

She clapped her hands. "I'm very proud of you. Was it hard?"

"It was okay. I didn't enjoy it, but I didn't feel like my skin was crawling with fire ants."

"I'd say that's a good thing."

"Several of them know Daphne Sawyer. Is that your grandmother?"

"Yes! That's Frannie's mom. She's wonderful. She and her husband John were the original owners of Cloverleigh Farms, but they gave it to their kids, and now they live in Florida most of the year. They spend summers here, so they're probably in town."

"She's likely getting inundated with calls from the Prancin' Grannies right now. They were all very eager to establish a connection to the family. I think they're all hoping for an invitation to the wedding."

Felicity patted my leg again. "Just tell them it's very small."

"I did. They shamed me."

"Shamed you?"

"Yes, they said this whole town is so happy for us and isn't it just a bit selfish of me to have such a small wedding that no one else can share in the joy? They told me to think about that, and they pranced away."

She laughed with delight. "I can picture it perfectly."

"We're all set for New York, by the way. Our flight leaves at eleven tomorrow."

"What? I need to pack!" She jumped off the couch and went running for the bedroom. "How many nights?"

"Two."

"Will I have to dress up for anything?"

"Only if you want to."

She stopped and turned around, throwing her arms in the air. "Hutton! What are the plans? Are we doing fancy billionaire things?"

I laughed. "What are fancy billionaire things?"

"You know—going to a ball or the opera or some sort of gala. Places fancy people go." She held up her palms, her expression growing worried. "Not that I need those things. I'd be just as happy staying at a Motel 6 and eating pizza slices on the street. I just want to pack right."

"I don't know if there are any balls this week, Cinderella, but I would be glad to take you out. Pack something nice."

She smiled and spun around like Zosia did when she was wearing one of her princess costumes. "I'm so excited!"

"Good." I watched her dance into the back hall and heard her humming as she opened and closed drawers.

It felt good to do things that made Felicity smile and twirl and sing. I knew it wasn't about the money—I had no doubt that she'd meant what she'd said about staying in an inexpensive motel and eating pizza on the street—but she deserved nice things, and I could certainly afford them.

Maybe I couldn't make her happy forever, but I could whisk her away to Manhattan on a private jet and treat her like a princess for a couple of days. She'd always have the memory of it, and it would never tarnish.

Because that was Wade's mistake—saying he was capable of something he wasn't. He might blame his wife for pretending to be someone else, but he'd done it too, swearing he'd be faithful and true to one woman for the rest of his life. Making promises he'd never be able to keep.

I knew myself better than that.

Pulling out my phone, I double-checked the flight time my assistant had booked with the private jet company, and scanned my inbox for a confirmation for the hotel suite as well. Noticing I had a new voicemail message from a Manhattan area code, I listened to a velvet-voiced representative from Tiffany tell me I was all set for a private appointment with him at three p.m.

I almost laughed out loud. Felicity was going to be *so mad* at me, but I didn't care.

Everything about this engagement was fake. It would be nice to have one thing that was real.

Later, when Felicity and I were curled up together, our skin still warm and slightly sweaty, our hearts still beating a little too fast, I said, "It's your turn tonight."

"For what?"

"The secret. I feel like it's always me rambling on about shit. Tonight, you tell me something."

"Hmm. What do you want to know?"

The things I really wanted to know—was I the best she ever had, was my dick the biggest she'd ever seen, had anyone ever made her come as hard as I did—weren't really the types of things we'd been sharing, so I refrained from asking those questions. But I was curious about something she'd told me.

"You mentioned that you break up with anyone who says they love you."

"Yes."

"How many times has that happened?"

"Twice," she said, drawing little spirals on my chest with one fingertip. "Once in college, and once in Chicago."

"How long were those relationships?"

"Not that long. A few months."

"And you didn't feel that way about either of them?"

"Nope. I've never been in love. I'm very careful with my emotions." She sounded proud of it. "I'm good at rationing them."

"What do you mean?"

"Well, let's say feelings are like a super rare or expensive ingredient. Truffles or something. You don't just throw them in whole. You shave them, adding a tiny amount to finish off the dish. A little goes a long way."

"Got it. So you shave your feelings?"

She laughed and slapped my chest. "You know what I mean. I give them out sparingly. And when the person I'm dating dishes them out too generously, too quickly, I go into panic mode and just want out. I told you, it's weird."

"No, I get it," I told her. "That's me at a business meeting. Or a party."

"Yeah, but at least you can sneak out. I have to craft an exit strategy."

"Like what?"

She sighed. "Okay, I'm not proud of this, but I told the first guy I was thinking about becoming a nun and wanted to try out celibacy. That was enough to scare him off. I told the second guy I was moving back to Michigan. But he kept coming around, so then I actually had to move."

"Wait a minute. You moved back here to get out of a relationship?"

She started to squirm. "Not *only* for that reason. I'd been thinking about it for a while. But that was a good push—and it was the right decision. I'm happy I came back. And . . . I didn't love those guys. If I had, I wouldn't have been able to walk away so easily. Right?"

"You're asking the wrong person. I've never been in love either. I'm not wired for it."

"How do you mean?"

"I mean, some people are good at getting out of their heads and letting someone else have, I don't know, unfettered access to them—all their flaws and imperfections. Revealing themselves. That's never going to be me."

She was quiet for a moment, her fingers still moving on my chest. "Do you think something is wrong with us? I sometimes wonder if I'm cursed or something."

"No," I said firmly. "I think we're just fine. In fact, I think we're smarter than everyone, because we know ourselves so well."

She sat up and looked down at me. "Yes, exactly. What good does it do to stay in a relationship you know won't work out?"

"If we're cursed, it's with superior intelligence and keen self-awareness."

She laughed. "Yes! We know our strengths and weaknesses. We know that if we can't swim, we don't jump in the deep end of the pool. We stay in the shallow part."

"Or we skip the swim and stay in bed," I said, tugging her close to me again. "There's a lot of fun to be had in bed."

"There is with you." She swung a leg over my hips so she straddled me. "More than I ever thought possible."

Twelve

Felicity

I F THE PRIVATE JET WE FLEW IN TO GET TO MANHATTAN MADE me feel like a rock star, our suite at The Pierre made me feel like royalty.

"Hutton! Look at this view!" I stood in front of the windows overlooking Central Park from twenty-eight stories up.

"I've seen it." He came over and stood next to me, chuckling at my excitement. "But it is impressive."

"It's more than impressive—it's unreal! This whole day is unreal!" I spun around and took in the surroundings. Our suite had a living room with a fireplace, a master bedroom with a sumptuous king-sized bed and views of the Manhattan skyline, and a dining table with six chairs that looked like they belonged at Versailles. I took out my phone and started snapping photos of everything for my sisters. I'd already sent them selfies of me sipping a glass of champagne in the luxurious cabin of the jet and riding in the back of the shiny black SUV with tinted windows on the way to the hotel.

"We should get going," he said.

"Are you going to tell me where?"

"No. That's the whole point of a surprise."

"You hate surprises."

"I hate being surprised," he corrected. "There's a difference."

"Let me just get a few pics of the bathroom."

He laughed as I darted through the bedroom to the master bath, where I captured the long marble vanity, soaking tub with city views, and plush white robes. *Will try to pilfer one for you, Win,* I texted.

"It will still be here when we get back," Hutton said from the doorway. Leaning against the frame, he stuck his hands in his pockets and met my eyes in the mirror.

"I know. Sorry, you're probably used to all this luxury," I said sheepishly. "But I'm more of a budget traveler, so this is pretty cool to me. And chances are I'm only going to be the fake fiancée of a billionaire once in my life, so I want to make the most of it."

He laughed. "Go ahead. We can leave when you're ready."

My stomach muscles tightened—he was so handsome in his blue dress pants and white button-down. He was pretty casual every day, but I loved that he'd dressed up a little to travel. "Am I dressed okay? You look so nice, and I'm in jeans."

"You can wear anything you want."

"And I'll have time to come home and change before dinner, right?"

"Yes."

"Then I just need a minute."

"No problem. I'm going to check in with my assistant on our tickets for tonight."

He left me alone in the bedroom, where I traded my sneakers for flat sandals and my cotton blouse for a nicer top. In the bathroom, I tightened my ponytail, cleaned my glasses, and refreshed my lipstick. I had no idea where he was taking me, but honestly, I didn't even care. Peanuts and beer at a ball game? Great. Views from the top of the Empire State Building? Fantastic. Cruise by the Statue of Liberty? Rice noodles in

Chinatown? Cannolis on Mulberry Street? If it was the two of us, I was in.

In fact, as we rode the elevator down to the lobby, slipped out a side door into the leather back seat of the chauffeured SUV, and traveled along 5th Avenue, I tried to think of another time in my life when I'd been so carefree and happy and alive.

"Hey." I looked over at him. "Thanks for all this. It wasn't necessary, but it's the best vacation I've ever been on."

He smiled. "We just got here. We haven't even done anything yet."

"Doesn't matter what we do, and maybe it wouldn't even matter where we are. I just love being with you."

"Okay, I need you to remember that nice feeling in about three minutes."

"What? Why?"

He looked over my shoulder. "Or one minute."

I whipped around and peered out the window—the SUV was pulling up to the Tiffany & Co flagship store. "Hutton! What's going on?"

"Just relax and have fun."

I faced him again, giving him my meanest stare. "You said no Tiffany. We agreed on a replica ring."

"But we need to know what we're replicating, right? This is just a little exercise in reconnaissance."

"It is?"

"Yes. Trust me."

The driver opened the door on Hutton's side. He got out and reached for me, but I hesitated, peeking at the building behind him with its massive windows and iconic gold lettering.

He smiled at me. "Felicity, come on. It's just for fun."

"Really?"

"Yes. I thought you'd enjoy it, but if you want, we don't even have to go in. I'll cancel the appointment."

"No, no. It's fine." I took his hand and let him help me down from the car. "I trust you."

And I *did* trust Hutton, but as we entered the store and a security guard escorted us to a VIP room on a private floor, my legs felt wobbly and my stomach was tying itself into knots. I remained on edge as we were introduced to James, our diamond expert, and tried on rings with price tags I could not even imagine and didn't ask to see. The secret smile on Hutton's face did nothing to ease my mind.

"Are you okay?" he asked softly when James left us alone for a moment. "You seem nervous."

"Of course I'm nervous!" I whispered frantically. "These rings probably cost more than my college education."

"Stop worrying about that. This is supposed to be fun."

"It is, but I—"

James was back with another ring. "Here we go. Try this one."

I'd already made up my mind that the next ring was going to be the last so I could get out of here and breathe again, but when I slipped the classic solitaire on my finger, I involuntarily sucked in my breath. It was exactly the one I'd described—a round brilliant diamond on a simple platinum band. Elegant. Modern. Stunning.

"Oh," I breathed. "It's so beautiful."

"I think that's the one," said James confidently.

"Is it?" Hutton asked me.

I bit my lip and nodded, admiring it on my hand. "Yes. This is it."

James sized my finger, and then asked if I might like to enjoy a glass of champagne or sparkling water while he and Hutton finished up. "Champagne sounds great, thank you."

While James's back was turned, I tugged Hutton over to the side. "You're not going to buy it, right? That isn't the plan."

"I know the plan," he said easily.

"Then why are you smiling like that?"

"Like what?"

"Like you know something I don't know."

He laughed. "I thought you trusted me."

"I changed my mind."

"Felicity." He took my hand. "You can relax. We'll leave here without a ring."

"Promise?"

"Yes." He met my eyes, and my knees went weak again. "I promise."

"Ms. MacAllister?" James was at my elbow, offering me a slender flute of pale champagne, bubbles rising like the butterflies in my stomach.

Out on the 5th Avenue sidewalk, I inhaled the downtown Manhattan air—bus fumes, car exhaust, a hot pretzel stand on the corner—thankful to be brought down to earth. The smell was real. The traffic was real. The car horns and conversations in different languages and Latin music coming from a passing cab were real.

Hutton and I were just friends.

"What do you think?" I asked him. "Should we look around for a replica ring?"

"Not in this neighborhood. I thought maybe tomorrow we could go down to Chinatown. There are lots of jewelry stores there."

I smiled. We were still on the same page. "That sounds like fun."

"The car should be here any minute. While we were inside, my assistant texted that we have a dinner reservation at 5:30, and our tickets will be waiting for us at the Met box office for a 7:30 ballet."

"Ooooh! What are we seeing?"

"*Romeo and Juliet* performed by the American Ballet Theater."

"Really? That's perfect!" I checked my phone. "But that doesn't leave much time for us to get ready."

"We're having dinner downstairs at The Pierre, so we'll be fine. And if you need more time, I'll have dinner sent up." He glanced over my shoulder. "Here's the car."

The sleek black SUV pulled up to the curb, and Hutton opened the door for me. I slid across the back seat and he joined me, instructing the driver to take us back to the hotel. "Of course, Mr. French," replied the driver.

"Is that the same guy?" I whispered as we pulled into traffic.

"Yes. I hired him for three days."

"So he just waits around for us?"

Hutton shrugged. "That's his job. I pay for his time."

"Sheesh." I laughed a little, rubbing my hand along the leather seat. "How do you get used to this? To being able to afford luxuries like not ever having to hail a cab, and fireplaces in your hotel rooms, and—oh yeah—chartering private jets to take you where you want to go?"

"At first, it *was* really strange," he admitted. "For a long time, I was still riding my bike everywhere, staying at inexpensive places, flying coach. Wade always thought I was crazy. But he'd grown up with a ton of money, so he was used to luxury. My mother doesn't even throw away those plastic containers cream cheese comes in."

I laughed. "How'd you finally get more comfortable with being rich?"

"Little by little, I guess. I'm still not completely used to it, and I do feel guilty about it sometimes."

"But you give a lot of money to charity, don't you?"

He nodded. "Yes, and that helps. I also paid off all my sister's college loans and her grad school tuition. I offered to buy both her and Neil and my parents new houses, but they all told me to fuck off—not in those words, of course." He cocked his head. "Actually, I think my sister did use those words."

"I believe it," I said. "She seems very independent and proud."

"She is all that and more."

Laughing, I rubbed his leg. "I have an older sister too. I know how they can be. It's funny, I haven't been to a ballet in forever, but Millie used to perform in them—not professionally, but she was a pretty serious dance student back in the day."

"Oh yeah?"

I nodded. "She danced until she was maybe fifteen or so and then quit. She even went to a performing arts school for a year."

"Why did she quit?"

"She said she just outgrew her passion for it, but I think a lot of it was related to pressure to look a certain way. Ballet dancers are traditionally very thin and small-boned, and Millie is built differently—it was a constant struggle for her to maintain a certain size and she was just tired of fighting it."

"Was it hard for her to quit?"

"Oh yeah. There were a lot of tears and serious talks behind closed doors. But I think my dad and Frannie were really glad she decided to quit because she was so unhappy. I was only like eleven or twelve, but I remember the tension in the house." I thought back to that time, how Millie had struggled—I'd hear her crying in her room and felt helpless to cheer her up. "But she seemed relieved once the decision was made. Plus, the twins had just been born, so there was a lot of chaos in the house. Frannie was glad to have Millie around more often to help. She was so good with them."

"You weren't?"

I laughed. "Not like Millie was. I thought they were noisy and boring. I liked them better when they got bigger and I could read stories to them—they liked the silly voices I'd do. But anyway, I'm really excited about tonight." Tipping my head onto his shoulder, I took his hand, lacing my fingers through his as New York sped by outside the window. "Thanks again for everything. Sorry I got a little weird back there. I do trust you."

"Good. And you're welcome."

We pulled up at The Pierre, and Hutton told the driver when to come back for us and where we'd be going. Then he got out, offered his hand, and helped me down. I held onto it as we entered the hotel, took the elevator up to our floor, and walked down the hall toward our suite.

He opened the door and let me in first, and as I crossed the threshold, I remembered what I said to Millie about wanting to enjoy this make-believe love affair with Hutton in case I never had the real thing. At that point, my biggest worry was being caught in the lie. Now I realized I was starting to worry about something else.

This love affair might not be make-believe at all.

But that was ridiculous, right?

Of course it was. I was just having a good time living like a Kardashian, and I was confusing that feeling with something else. It was totally understandable. All I had to do was keep reminding myself what this was, and what this wasn't.

Millie called while I was drying my hair.

"Hello?"

"Are you dripping in diamonds?"

I laughed. "No. I tried on a few today at Tiffany though."

She gasped. "Stop it! You really went to Tiffany?"

"Yes, but only to look. We're going to Chinatown tomorrow to buy a fake."

"The best cubic zirconia money can buy?"

"Exactly. Believe me, he's spending enough on this trip."

"How's everything going with you two?"

"Great."

"Are the rumors true? Did he tie you up?"

"Maybe, and not yet."

"Wait, what?"

I glanced at the door and lowered my voice, barely speaking above a whisper. "I think there is some truth to those rumors, but he hasn't really shown me that side of himself yet."

She gasped. "So would you let him?"

I paused, then deflected. "I have to go because we're leaving in like twenty minutes and I still don't know what I'm going to wear."

"Do you have a safe word?"

"Millie!"

"I suggest something else."

"I don't need a safe word."

"Oklahoma. Bumblebee. Roy Kent."

"*Goodbye*, Millie." I could still hear her laughing as I ended the call.

Wrapped in one of those fancy robes, I went into the bedroom and opened my bag to sort through the clothing I'd brought—much of it Winnie's. This morning, after an emergency call from me, she had swung by on her way to work with an armful of dresses and a bag of shoes. I spread three dresses out on the bed and considered them, finally deciding on the little black dress with cap sleeves.

Hutton entered the room as I was hanging up the other two. "Hey, I have to run down to the business center for a fax from Wade. I'll be back in a few minutes."

I glanced at him over my shoulder. "Okay."

I ditched the robe and wriggled into the dress, which zipped up the side. Checking my reflection in the mirror, I smiled. It wasn't too short or cut too low, but fit very snug from shoulder to knee and gave the impression of more curves. Winnie had said to wear it with the strappy red satin heels for a sexy pop of color.

In the bathroom I quickly gathered my hair into a low bun and stuck a few pins in it. Thanks to my self-inflicted haircut, shorter pieces still hung haphazardly around my face, and for a moment I thought about digging out my nail scissors and evening them out a little more, but then I remembered how Hutton had said asymmetry was beautiful too. So I let them be.

I traded my glasses for contact lenses for the night, even though they drove me nuts, and tried to remember how Winnie had done my makeup on Saturday. After about ten minutes, I thought I had a reasonable imitation. I gave myself a quick spritz of perfume and strapped myself into the heels—thanks to a little platform, they weren't too treacherous to walk in, but the dress was so fitted, I did have to take small steps.

I walked out of the bedroom into the living room, where Hutton was standing at the windows overlooking Central Park. "Hi," I said.

He turned around, and his jaw dropped. "Jesus."

"Is that good or bad?"

"You took my breath away. I'd say that's good."

I smiled. "Thank you. You look very handsome." He wore a suit in a shade of blue slightly lighter than navy. His shirt was white, and his tie was a soft amber color.

He ran a hand over his hair, which was neatly combed and sort of slicked back like an old Hollywood movie star's, and then rubbed his jaw. "I feel like I should have shaved."

"Nah, I like the scruff. Gives you some edge."

Smiling, he came toward me, hands in his pockets. "Thanks."

"Should we go?" I glanced at the door. "Our reservation is—"

"Just a minute." He removed his hands from his pockets along with a small blue box.

A Tiffany blue box.

"Hutton."

He opened it, and there was the ring.

Now I was the one who couldn't breathe. I splayed a hand over my chest. *"Hutton."*

"Yes."

"Tell me that is not the ring I tried on today."

"That is not the ring you tried on today."

I met his eyes, catching a twinkle in their midnight blue. "Liar! You said we were leaving without the ring!"

"We did. This one came from another store. It has a stone with better clarity. That one had a blemish."

"A blemish?" I squeaked.

"Yes."

"Hutton." I took a breath. "Tell me this is only on loan, like the necklace was in the movie. Remember? Richard Gere does not actually purchase the necklace for her. He only borrows it for the night."

"Richard Gere's not a real billionaire. I am." He took the ring from its cushion and set the box on the dining table. "Will you wear it?"

I was so torn. I wanted to, but I could *not* accept this ring from him. "Oh, God," I said, feeling like my heart was going to explode. "I want to, I really do—but it's too much."

"It's just a gift, Felicity." He took my left hand and slipped the ring on my finger. "Let me give you a gift."

"For what?" My voice cracked, and tears threatened to ruin my carefully applied makeup. "I don't need a gift for being your friend."

"It's not really *for* anything. It's a symbol of our friendship. It's a gesture of appreciation."

"Huttonnnnn," I whined softly, adoring the way the ring sparkled. "A gesture of appreciation is a latte or a sandwich. This is a diamond ring. It's too *much.*"

He didn't say anything right away, and his eyes stayed focused on my hand, which he still held. "I understand," he said quietly, "that this is unusual. I know most people don't gift diamond rings to their friends—it's traditionally something reserved for the one person you're going to spend your life with. Your soul mate. But you know what?"

"What?"

He offered a hint of a smile. "At the risk of sounding a little crazy, my mom taught me that there are all kinds of soul mates—past-life soul mates, kindred spirits, soul ties . . . She thinks there are certain people you just feel a deep, extraordinary connection with, and it transcends time and place as we know it."

"I believe that," I whispered, remembering how it had felt like I'd known him from the first time I saw him.

"So think of this as a symbol of that connection. Because even though we aren't getting married, you are the person I cherish most, someone I will always want in my life. In fact, I feel one hundred percent certain our friendship will outlast *all* of Wade's marriages."

My throat had closed up, making it impossible to speak, but I managed a smile and a nod.

"This isn't a real proposal, because this isn't a real engagement. But I thought maybe we could have *one* real thing to celebrate our friendship and the way we show up for each other. Something that will outlast this fake engagement." His smile turned a little cocky as he shrugged. "And honestly, I can afford it."

A laugh escaped me, but so did a tear.

Hutton brushed it from my cheekbone with his thumb. "If you never want to wear the ring, you don't have to. But will you accept it?"

I nodded, desperately trying not to cry. "Okay."

"Good." He leaned forward and kissed my forehead. "Let's go."

At dinner, I kept reaching for my wine glass with my left hand so I could admire the ring. I loved the way it glittered in the candlelight. "You know, I've never been the girl who craves fancy, shiny things, but I am head over heels in love with this ring."

"Good."

"But Hutton." I sat up straight in my seat and gave him a death stare. "No more expensive surprises, okay? Promise me."

He reached for his whiskey. "That's no fun. I like treating you."

"But this is all one-sided! How am I going to treat you?"

He took a drink, swirled the liquid in his glass, and sipped again. "We'll talk."

My core muscles clenched.

All I could think was, *Oklahoma. Bumblebee. Roy Kent.*

After dinner, I was dying to try the warm chocolate cake with raspberry creamsicle ice cream, but we were running a little late and still had to pick up our tickets. "Another time," Hutton promised. "I'll make sure you get to taste it before we go home."

Our driver took us over to the Metropolitan Opera House, and we made our way to the box office, where Hutton gave his name. "Do you know where the seats are?" I asked, glancing around the lobby with its massive cascading staircases, deep red carpet, and soaring windows.

"Not exactly." Hutton loosened his tie, and I realized he was probably uncomfortable in such a crowded public place.

"Here. Let me see." I glanced at the tickets and saw that we were in a section called Parterre Box 24. It was easy enough to find someone to ask, and a few minutes later we were shown our very own private box, which had three seats in a front row, and five more in a second and third.

"Wait a minute." I looked around. "Are all these seats ours?"

"Yes. I bought the whole box," Hutton said. "I like privacy."

I laughed. "One of those billionaire perks?"

He smiled. "Exactly."

Needless to say, the view of the stage was incredible. And I had zero chill as I looked around at the sea of red velvet, the sparkling chandeliers, the gold leaf, the marble, the towering ceiling. I don't think I closed my mouth for five full minutes. "This is amazing! It's so beautiful!"

"It is." Hutton sat down beside me.

"Do you come here a lot?"

"Not really. I brought my parents here once—my dad likes opera—and I attended the fundraising gala once."

"Oooh, I bet that was fancy. Ball gowns and tuxes? Cocktails and small talk?"

He nodded. "I lasted about twenty minutes."

I laughed and took his hand. "Well, don't worry. I won't make you talk to me."

"I like talking to you. Among other things."

My heart skipped a beat as the lights dimmed. *I could get used to this*, I thought. But then I corrected myself.

I could *not* get used to this—not this box at the Met, this man beside me, or this feeling inside my chest. In fact, getting used to this would be the worst possible thing that could happen.

I glanced down at our hands.

My ring shone brilliantly, even in the dark.

Thirteen

Felicity

AFTER THE BALLET WAS OVER, WE MET OUR DRIVER OUTSIDE, and Hutton listened to me gush about the music and the dancing and the costumes and the sets and how magical the whole evening had been the entire ride back to the hotel.

And on the elevator. And walking down the hall. And inside our suite, as I awkwardly waltzed across the living room. "The dancers were so graceful," I said. "So elegant and artistic but also strong and powerful. It's amazing how much emotion they can convey just by moving their arms a certain way. Or changing the angle of their head. They have such incredible command of every muscle in their bodies, you know?"

"Yes," he said, and I realized I hadn't heard his voice in like twenty minutes.

I turned around and saw him pouring a drink at the bar cart near the dining table. "Sorry! I'm talking nonstop, aren't I?"

"I don't mind."

"I just loved it all so much."

"I'm glad. Want something to drink? Whiskey or scotch?"

"No, thanks. Mostly I just want to take these heels off."

"Leave them on."

I was already bending down to unbuckle one ankle strap. I looked up and saw him standing there with his glass in his hand. "What?"

"Leave them on. And come over here."

I straightened up and took one tiny step.

"On your hands and knees."

My breath caught. I could feel his eyes on me. Instantly I understood what this was, and even though I was a little nervous, I wanted to play along. I wanted to please him this way.

The only problem was, I wasn't *entirely* sure I could get to my knees in this tight dress. But I said a quick prayer and dropped to my knees on the carpet in one smooth motion. Thankfully, the dress material had some stretch, and the seams didn't pop.

"Good girl," he said quietly, igniting a firestorm in my blood that surprised me. "Now come here."

My heart thrummed fast and loud as I lowered my palms to the floor and slowly closed the distance between us. I'd never done anything like this in my life—*who am I right now?*—but I liked the way it made me feel.

Tempting. Seductive. Alluring. I'd never thought of myself that way before, but here and now, in this tight little black dress with the red satin heels, crawling toward a gorgeous, powerful man in a suit in our Manhattan hotel suite? My billionaire fiancé? It was easy to imagine I wasn't myself at all.

When I reached his feet, I sat back on my heels and looked up. Our eyes met. His lean, muscular silhouette looked imposing above me. Even that rebel lock of hair had been tamed into submission tonight.

He took another sip of his drink and set the glass on the table. Pulled the chair at the head of the table aside. Loosened the knot in his tie. "Are you okay?"

"Yes."

"If there's a point tonight where you are not, you should tell me." He slipped the tie from his collar.

I swallowed hard. "Like a safe word?"

His mouth hooked up on one side. His hand freed the top button of his shirt. "You already have a safe word?"

"No," I said quickly. "I've never needed one before."

"You do now." He undid a second button. "So what will it be?"

Of course, I couldn't fucking think of anything, and I panicked.

"Roy Kent," I blurted.

He cocked his head, his hand still on his shirt. "Who's Roy Kent?"

"Never mind." *Damn you, Millie!* "I'll think of another one."

Do not say Oklahoma.

Do not say bumblebee.

I racked my brain for something else. "Romeo," I said breathlessly. "That's what I'll say. Romeo."

He set his tie on the table and offered me a hand.

Placing my palm in his, I rose to my feet. "Is anything going to hurt?" I asked, picturing whips, chains, ball gags, metal cuffs and clamps, shiny rubber gloves.

"I don't need to inflict pain to feel in control, if that's what you're asking."

"Okay. Should I—"

But that was all I got out because he spun me around and clamped a hand over my mouth, pressing his body tight against my back. "Shhh. From now on, you don't speak until I ask a question. You don't move unless I tell you how. You don't come until I give you permission. Nod if you understand."

I nodded, my heart banging so hard against my ribs I was sure he could feel it on his chest. I was facing the table now—and the window. The drapes were open, and I could see our reflection in the glass. Darkness pressed close on the other side.

I watched as he loosened his hold on me and slowly unzipped my dress. It was so tight he had to pull it down my arms and over my hips until it fell to the floor in a puddle at my heels.

When I went to step out of it, he grabbed my hips. "You don't move unless I tell you to." His tone was low and stern. A reprimand.

I opened my mouth to apologize and caught myself.

He met my eyes in the window reflection. "Good girl. You learn quickly."

Desire hummed beneath my skin.

He noticed what I was wearing—a black lace thong and bra—and murmured his appreciation. "You surprise me," he said, running one finger along the lace that crested each cheek. "All night I've been hard thinking about what you might be wearing under that dress. But I never imagined this. I like it, especially with those shoes." He moved closer to me again, nuzzling the back of my neck with his nose, his breath a warm whisper on my skin. "Those heels have been driving me crazy all night. I want to do *such bad things* to you in those heels."

My breath was coming in short, hot bursts and I felt damp heat between my thighs. My entire body was aching for his hands, but even though he said he'd been thinking about this all night, he was being so agonizingly patient, like he might be content to torture me all night with stories about what he *wanted* to do to me without actually following through.

He reached for his tie and met my eyes in the glass again. "Do you want to watch me do bad things to you?"

I opened my mouth, unsure if I could speak.

"You can answer the question."

"Yes," I whispered.

"Yes, what?"

"Yes, I want to watch you do bad things to me." I saw him smile in the glass—a slow, satisfied smirk.

He took my arms and crossed my wrists at the small of my back. Then he wound the silk tie around them. "You're so beautiful," he said, binding my hands and pulling the knot tight. "So sweet. So polite. Like a princess. And you smell so good." He buried his face in the curve of my neck and inhaled, then pressed his lips to my throat.

It was a struggle not to moan as his mouth moved over my skin, his tongue warm, his lips firm. He kissed his way down one shoulder, and across my upper back, sending chills rippling over my whole body. His hands roamed over my hips, up my ribs. He slid them across my stomach and sternum, and I arched my back slightly, wanting his hands on my breasts, trying to tempt him. But he continued to torment me, putting his hands everywhere but where I wanted them most. He pressed closer to me, his erection grazing my ass.

A little whimper escaped me, and I stepped out of the dress, spreading my legs.

"No." His tone was sharp, and he backed away from me. "That's breaking a rule, princess." He began to unbuckle his belt. "You don't move unless I tell you to. But I can help you remember to obey."

He crouched down, grabbed the ankle with the dress around it, and lifted it up. After tossing the dress aside, he placed my feet side by side and wound his leather belt around my ankles, securing it tightly. When he was satisfied I couldn't move either my arms or my legs, he straightened up.

Locked eyes with me again in the glass.

Removed his jacket.

Unbuttoned his cuffs. Rolled up his sleeves.

Picked up his glass and took a sip of his whiskey.

Every movement was masculine and deliberate, laced

with unspoken power. Nothing rushed or frantic. It was as if he was letting me know by his sheer lack of haste how he relished the tease, that the kick wasn't just in the bad things he wanted to do to me, but in the anticipation of them. In my helplessness to stop him.

And I was as feminist as anybody, but *hot damn*. My legs were trembling. My panties were wet. My nipples poked at the lace of my bra, hard and tingling. It wasn't just being at his mercy that had me turned on, it was the way his eyes traveled over my body, like his desire was almost unbearable.

He set his glass down and pressed up behind me again, locking one forearm across my chest and sliding the other hand into my underwear. He rubbed my clit with slow, firm pressure so it swelled beneath his touch, then dipped his fingers inside me. "You're wet already."

"Yes," I whimpered.

He pinched my nipple, hard. "That wasn't a question. But since you're having such a hard time staying quiet, I'll give you permission to speak. Do you want to watch me make you come?"

I nodded, afraid that if I said something wrong, he'd stop touching me. I couldn't take my eyes off our reflection.

"Say it," he demanded.

"I want to watch you make me come," I panted.

He pulled his fingers from me and brought them to his mouth. "The taste of you. That's another thing that drives me crazy. I can't stop thinking about it." His hand edged beneath the lace again. "I want it all the time."

He held me tightly against his body. At the small of my back, I felt his cock against my palm as he worked his fingers over my clit. I squirmed and writhed over his hand, frustrated at not being able to move freely. I tried to rub his hard length through his pants, hoping to get him worked up, but his arm around me kept my upper body completely immobile. Pretty soon it didn't even matter that I couldn't move—his fingers moved over my clit with the perfect rhythm, the ideal pace, the most sublime pressure. I was hot and sweaty and desperate, frantic little noises escaping my throat, so close, so agonizingly close—

And he slowed down, easing me back from the brink.

My eyes opened—I hadn't even realized they'd closed—and I caught his knowing smile in the glass. "Not yet," he said.

He did that two more times, taking me all the way to the edge, then cruelly yanking me away from it, seeming to enjoy it more every time. I understood then that he didn't have to inflict pain to enjoy control—all he had to do was deny pleasure. I'd never even thought about it before. And at that point, I'd have begged him to hurt me if it meant relief from the tension.

Somehow he seemed to know I was at the breaking point, and the next time I got close, he let me finish. "Don't close your eyes," he warned. "Watch."

I did as he asked, keeping my eyes on our reflection, watching his hand move between my thighs, my cries bouncing off the walls, my leg muscles growing hot and tight, my bones threatening to buckle as the climax shook me.

Finally, I went limp in his arms. "You're perfect," he said, his voice low in my ear. "You're fucking perfect." He kissed my throat, my shoulder, and the back of my neck, before easing my upper body forward so my chest and cheek rested on the cool wooden tabletop. "Yes," he said, running his hand down my spine. "I want you just like this."

He picked up his glass.

The next thing I felt was cool liquid being dripped onto my back, all along my spine from the base of my neck to my tailbone. The smoky sweet scent filled my head as he leaned over and licked the whiskey off my skin. I shivered, and he laughed. Then he popped open the clasp on my bra and poured more whiskey across my shoulder blades. This time, instead of licking it up, he put his hand in it and rubbed the liquid all over my skin.

"Such bad things," he said, his voice somewhere between a growl and a whisper.

He pulled the black lace thong down my legs and picked up his glass. A moment later, what I assumed was some *very expensive whiskey* was drizzled over my ass, running down my thighs, and seeping into places that I'd never imagined pricey booze might seep.

"Fuck yes." Hutton dropped to his knees behind me, his palms on my ass as he licked his way up the backs of my legs, sliding his tongue between my thighs, stroking me from behind. He slipped one hand into the tight, wet space between my legs, rubbing my sensitive clit with the side of his forefinger.

I moaned as he teased and sucked and licked and fucked me with his fingers. No sooner had the throes of the previous orgasm faded than he had me spiraling upward again. My body demanded more. Finally I gave up and begged.

"Hutton," I pleaded. "I want to feel you inside me."

"I want that too, princess." He pushed his fingers deeper inside me. "I want my cock right here. I want to make you come again. But this is a game about patience. About control. We can't just give in to every urge we feel."

"Romeo," I panted. "Now can we give in?"

He laughed. "It doesn't work like that. It's a safe word, not a password."

"But I want you so badly." My body was burning up for him. I felt like heat and desire were emanating from my skin. "I've never wanted anyone this way. I *have* no control."

"You don't have to *have* control." He took his fingers from me, kissed the back of each leg, and rose to his feet. "You have to surrender it. That's what I like."

I moaned, squirming on the dining room table as he

took another sip of his whiskey. "Surrender is harder than I thought."

"I know it is." He set the glass down. "But you're doing so well, princess. You're such a good girl, and I'm going to give you what you want."

"You are?" I grew excited as I heard the zipper of his dress pants being lowered. I couldn't see, but I imagined him pulling out his cock, stroking it with his fist like he had in the bathtub.

"Yes," he said. "But you have to tell me what that is."

"I want you to fuck me," I said without hesitation.

He laughed again. "What happened to my sweet princess? Where are her manners?"

"I want you to fuck me, please?" I tried.

"That's better." He rubbed the tip of his cock between my thighs, damp with whiskey and desire. Both of us moaned as he pushed inside me, every hot, thick inch stretching and filling me until his hips met my ass. Placing his hands on my hips, he pulled back and did it again, and again, and again. "Fuck," he growled. "It's so tight. So hot. And you look so fucking good."

It was tight—having my ankles bound together with his belt kept my legs pressed firmly together. And the way I was bent forward over the table meant he could go in deep. As he moved faster, he moved rougher, and I began to exhale sharply every time he hit the furthest spot.

Suddenly he yanked me back from the table, but only enough to reach one hand around and rub my clit with his fingertips, keeping his cock buried deep just like I wanted. "Come for me," he demanded. "Come right now, on my cock. On my fingers. Let me feel it. Then I'll come for you."

"Yes!" I cried out as the waves crashed through me, relentless and powerful, loud and unceasing, my body completely at the mercy of his touch and his rhythm and his words and his massive, throbbing cock that I wanted to feel pulsing inside me.

But instead, he pulled out. I was so shocked I picked up my head from the table and looked at our reflection in the window. That's how I was able to watch as he grabbed his cock and got himself off as he stood over me, coming all over my back in hot, silken streams, grunting with every savage thrust through his fist.

My mouth fell open and stayed that way, even after I placed my cheek back on the table. "Oh my God," I whispered. "That was—oh my God."

Breathing hard, Hutton propped his hands on the table beside my waist. "I didn't have a condom. That's why I did it that way. Although truth be told, that's what I wanted to do to you."

"I liked it."

He leaned down and kissed my temple. "I'll clean you up. Give me a second to grab a towel."

"Okay, but Hutton?"

"Yes?"

"Can you take my shoes off? My feet are killing me."

Without a word, he dropped down, unstrapped his belt from my ankles, and removed each shoe.

"Thank you." I breathed a sigh of relief to be standing in bare feet on the carpet.

He pulled my underwear up, then undid the knot in his tie and pulled it free from my wrists. "There. But don't move too much. You're a little messy."

I braced myself on my elbows and smiled at him over one shoulder. "It's okay."

He went into the master bedroom and returned a minute later with a warm washcloth, which he used to gently wipe off my back. "You might still be a little sticky. And I also got some, uh, stuff in your hair. Want to take a shower or something?"

"Maybe." I straightened up, my muscles already sore and stiff. I rubbed one shoulder. "Actually yes, that might feel good."

"Let me run it for you."

I smiled. "You don't have to do that. You didn't break me."

"It's not an apology." He kissed my forehead. "I just like doing things for you."

Not only did he run the shower for me, he undressed and got in with me, then insisted on washing my hair, applying the conditioner and waiting exactly two minutes before rinsing it off, and soaping me up with the hotel body wash.

He rubbed his hands together to make suds and sniffed them. "It's nice, but it's not as good as yours."

"I brought some lotion in the scent you like," I told him. "I'll put it on before bed."

After we got out, he dried me off with a giant fluffy towel and brought me one of the plush white robes. I combed out my hair while he put on some pajama pants, then he came into the bathroom and wrapped his arms around me from behind. His hair was wet and wavy, messy in the front like it usually was. As gorgeous and sexy as he was all put together in a suit and tie, there was something so familiar and cozy about *this* Hutton. He made my heart pound just as hard.

"Come here," he said, tugging me out to the living room. "I have a surprise for you."

"You do?" I let him lead me over to the couch. A room service tray sat on the coffee table, a silver cloche over the plate.

Hutton pulled it off. "Tada! Warm chocolate cake with raspberry creamsicle ice cream."

I squealed with delight and jumped up and down. "You made a phone call!"

"I made a phone call."

"How did you get it up here so fast?"

He shrugged. "I paid a little extra."

"It looks so good, I bet it's worth it."

"Your reaction is worth it."

I smiled at him. "You're spoiling me way too much on this trip. I'm going to be terrible to live with. You'll be glad you're going back to California."

He laughed. "Sit down."

I sat on one end of the couch and Hutton handed me the plate and fork. Then he swung my feet onto the other end and sat down, placing them in his lap. "What's this?" I asked as he took one foot in his hand and began to rub it.

"It's a combination of dessert and foot massage."

Was he serious? Simultaneous dessert and foot rub?

How was I supposed to ration my feelings whilst eating warm cake and enjoying his strong, sexy hands on me? He was making it impossible to hold back the tide.

I stuck a bite in my mouth and groaned as Hutton's thumbs pressed into my sore arches. "God, this is insane. I might have another orgasm."

He chuckled. "That would be okay too."

Fourteen

Hutton

"**Y**OUR TURN," SHE SAID SLEEPILY. "TELL ME SOMETHING."

"What do you want to know this time?" I asked, curled up behind her between the soft, cool sheets of our hotel bed.

"If you could do anything else with your life, like if it had gone in another direction, where would you be?"

Here, I thought. Right here with you.

In this place where I felt sure of myself. Comfortable in my skin. Were there still doubts buzzing around in my head? Yes. But they were softer. Quieter. I could endure them when it was only the two of us like this. I could accept them as part of me, because she could—just like she'd accepted the part of me that craved power and control in private because I felt so overwhelmed in public.

So often my mind was ahead of itself, on to the next worry, the next room I'd have to enter, the next time I'd have to be *on*. But when we were alone, it was blissfully quiet in my head. She made it easy to stay in the present—she made it impossible to want to be anywhere else.

She rolled onto her back and looked at me. "You can't think of anything? I guess that's what it's like being a hot billionaire. You've reached the zenith. There's nowhere else to go. Nothing else to achieve."

I laughed. "Hardly."

"Okay, so then what? Like, let's say you never created that algorithm. What would you be?"

I thought for a moment. "Okay. Don't laugh."

"I would never!"

"I'd have liked to teach math. Like be a professor or something."

"I could see that. You'd be great at it."

"Uh, standing at the front of a room with everyone watching me? I don't think so."

"Yes, you would. You were a great tutor back in the day—those middle school kids loved you."

"That was one on one. Teaching a class is very different. You have to be *on* every single minute. You have to explain things exactly right, you can't get a single word wrong. If you say something in error, you look like you don't know what you're doing."

"I'm not saying being a teacher is easy or doesn't take preparation."

"It doesn't matter how prepared I am. I could plan a lecture, rehearse it a thousand times, bring notes into the classroom with me, and still second guess myself to the point where I'm standing up there sweating and shaking, unable to even read my own writing because a hundred pairs of eyes are on me waiting for me to fuck up."

She studied me for a moment. "Did this actually happen?"

"Yeah."

"When?"

"A couple years ago, I was invited to give a guest lecture at M.I.T. to one of my mentor teachers' classes, and I bombed."

"Your mentor said that?"

"No. But I knew she thought that. And I knew every kid

in that room was like, 'who is this fucking hack and why does he make billions of dollars when he can't even form a coherent sentence or write on the board without staring at every problem wondering if he wrote it right?'"

"Wow. That's so cool that you can read minds."

I frowned at her. "That's what it felt like."

"Sorry." She snuggled closer. "But if I don't call you out on this stuff, who will? It's like Winnie with the Wicked Witch of the West."

"Huh?"

"Everyone in my family always wanted to watch the *Wizard of Oz*, but that witch scared the bejesus out of Winnie. She would hide under a blanket every time the witch came onscreen. But then Frannie bought us a nonfiction book about witches. We learned the truth about where the idea behind evil witches came from, and how female healers and priestesses were accused of getting their magic powers from the devil when *really*, it was just terrible men trying to suppress women's influence." She stuck her tongue out at me.

"Sorry for all terrible men," I told her.

"Apology accepted. Anyway, I think your fears are based on something you're guessing at rather than something you know for sure. Just like a witch." She brought two fingers together above her head, forming a pointy hat. "Not real. *Feels* real, but isn't."

"Okay, but that doesn't make my nerves any better. The thoughts are still there. And they cause physical reactions I can't hide."

She sighed and cuddled closer. "Would you consider trying therapy again? This is going to make me sad that you have a dream to teach but won't do it because of the witch."

I paused. "My sister wants me to try acceptance and commitment therapy. There's a woman in her practice who does it."

"Can you get in to see her before you leave?"

"It won't work."

"How do you know?" She sat up. "This is something new, right? An approach you've never tried?"

"Doesn't matter," I said stubbornly. "It won't work."

She looked at me for a moment. "You can read minds *and* predict the future. Maybe *you're* the witch!"

I yanked the pillow from behind my head and swung it at her, and she toppled over dramatically. Rolling on top of her, I pinned her arms to the mattress. "Enough. I'm set in my ways and not going to change. Take me or leave me."

"I never want you to change, Hutton. I'll always take you. I just wish you could see yourself like I do."

I kissed her, glad that she saw me in a positive light, that she thought I was capable of doing things I knew I wasn't. It meant that I was doing a good job playing this role—this version of me that deserved her—and she couldn't see the man behind the curtain.

I had her convinced.

The following day, we slept late and ordered room service for breakfast, which we ate in bed while we looked at photos of us from last night online. I wasn't at all surprised that pictures of us had been snapped without our even realizing it, but Felicity seemed shocked that she was now a figure of public fascination.

Many of the photos were blurry, zoomed-in shots of the ring on her finger. The internet speculated wildly about where it was from, how many carats the diamond was, and what it might have cost.

"Hutton." Felicity looked at me with alarm. "Tell me some of these guesses are way too high."

I shook my head. "I'm not even looking at that bullshit."

The comments, as always, were a mix of effusive praise and shitty garbage.

OMG so cute together!

Seriously? Her??!

Couple GOALS!

He could do so much better.

Omg so pretty DM to collab pls

WTF Zlatka was way hotter

"Wow. People just say what they think, don't they?" Felicity scrolled down through hundreds of comments on one pic. "How do you deal with this all the time?"

I took her phone from her hand and tossed it aside. "Fuck the internet. What would you like to do today?"

"I'd love to sightsee a little bit, but will people be following us everywhere trying to get pictures?" She touched her hair. "I feel weird about that. I'm not Zlatka, and people expect a supermodel, or at least someone with symmetrical hair and—"

"Hey." I pulled her close to me and leaned back against the headboard. "I cannot tell you how happy I am that you are not Zlatka. You are superior to her in every way. You are beautiful inside and out, and you are real."

"Thanks." But her voice was hesitant. "I guess I'm stupid. I didn't foresee this problem. But why *would* a billionaire choose a girl like me?"

Rage burned in my chest—at the idea she thought she wasn't good enough for anyone, at the assholes out there who couldn't just mind their own business, at myself for dragging her into this. "Listen to me. You are way too good for every billionaire I've ever met, and that includes me. Fuck those people."

"I've never worried about, like, leaving my house before. It's kind of a shitty feeling."

I kissed the top of her head and held her tighter. "Being

in the public eye is really fucking hard. Especially when you didn't ask for it."

"How do you handle it?"

"I don't leave the house much. But I'm sorry I dragged you into this fucked-up orbit. I should have known better." I paused. "Want to head home?"

She didn't answer right away, and for a moment I was scared she'd say yes. But then she sat up and looked at me. "No. You're right—fuck those people. They can't steal our joy. Our fake engagement joy."

I laughed. "Damn right."

"We're only here one more day," she said, her voice getting more fierce. "I want to *do* things. If we hide out, the jerks win."

"You tell me what you want to do, and I'll do it. Even if there's a crowd."

"Nothing too fancy. How about the zoo?"

"Done."

"But cancel the driver, okay? Let's just walk. I don't want to call any attention to us."

"Good idea."

We dressed like regular tourists in jeans and sneakers and T-shirts, and wore matching navy baseball caps (which I sent a concierge out to purchase) pulled low over our faces.

"Ready?" I asked her as she finished tying her shoelaces.

She stood up and grinned. "Ready."

We left the room and walked toward the elevator. I was glad to see the excited smile back on her face, and honest to God, if I saw one person with a phone or camera pointed at us, I was going to kick their ass. Reaching for her hand, I pulled it to my lips and kissed it.

That's when I noticed she wasn't wearing the ring.

She saw me studying her hand. "Don't worry, I left it in the safe."

"That's fine."

"It's not because I don't love it or I feel strange wearing it. I just didn't want anyone recognizing us. The ring seemed like a giveaway." Her expression was concerned, like she was afraid I might be upset with her. "I'm sorry."

"Don't be. I understand." And I did—I'd taken my expensive watch off too. "You can wear it or not wear it whenever you want. That ring is yours, Felicity."

She smiled. "Thanks."

I meant what I said, but as the elevator descended, I still felt an ache take root in my chest. It was true—the ring was hers.

But it didn't make her mine.

After touring the zoo, we ate lunch at the little café and strolled through Central Park. "Now what?" I asked her as we ambled down 5th Avenue.

"Shopping?" She peeked at me from beneath the bill of her cap. "I'd like to find a dress for our engagement party."

"That's what the internet is for."

"You don't have to come," she said, laughing. "You can go back to the hotel if you want and I'll meet you back there later. I get it—I'm not a huge shopper either, I just want to find something unique and stylish. Winnie told me to try NoLita or Soho."

"It's fine." I sighed heavily. "I'll go shopping."

"Okay." She jumped in front of me and stopped me with a hand to my chest. "But to be clear, you are not *buying* me anything. Your job is just to stand there and tell me how things look when I try them on."

I groaned. "I have to go *in* to the stores?"

"Yes."

"Is it too late to go back to the hotel?"

"Yes." She moved to the curb and put up her arm to hail a cab. "But I promise it won't be that bad."

I spent the next couple hours trailing Felicity in and out of stores, watching her hold things up and check her reflection in the mirror, and hearing her comment about how great something would look on one of her sisters, but not on her. Occasionally, I waited while she tried something on, feeling like a creeper lurking about, keeping my eyes glued to my phone, positive all the other customers were staring at me and thinking they should call the police.

One time, Felicity came out from the dressing rooms in something and asked me what I thought.

"It looks great," I said after giving her a passing glance. "You should get it."

"Hutton, you didn't even look at it."

"Sorry." I studied the short red dress with the ruffles at the bottom. "I like it."

She stuck her hands on her hips. "What about it do you like?"

"The . . ." I gestured vaguely at the bottom. "Frilly things."

She burst out laughing. "Thanks."

"Can I wait outside?" I asked, wiping sweat from my forehead.

"Why?"

"Because I feel weird. People are staring. They think I'm a pervert here to spy on women changing clothes."

Felicity pressed her lips together, then slowly brought her index fingers together above her head.

"Yeah. I know," I muttered.

She sighed. "You can wait outside."

Grateful to be released, I headed out and waited on the sidewalk. She came out a moment later without a bag. "You didn't want to buy it?"

"Nah."

"Why not?"

"It was expensive, and I—"

I headed toward the shop door. "I've got it."

"Hutton, no." She grabbed my arm. "It wasn't right anyway. I didn't love it."

"Are you sure? Or are you just saying that?"

"I'm sure." She tugged my hand. "Come on, let's keep going."

We strolled down the block in comfortable silence, and then she stopped short. "Oh, look."

I followed her line of sight toward a small boutique named for a designer I'd never heard of: Cosette Lavigne. In the front window were three white dresses. "Are those wedding gowns?"

"I think so," she said wistfully. "Aren't they pretty?"

I couldn't take my eyes off her dreamy expression. "Go try one on."

She shook her head. "I couldn't."

"Why not? Just for fun."

"No, because what if I fall in love for real?"

"Would that be so bad?"

"Yes! I don't want to try something on for fun, get my heart set on it, and then have to walk away."

"You won't," I told her, taking her arm. "Come on."

"Hutton, wait." She braced herself and pulled against me like we were in a tug-of-war. "Why are we doing this?"

"What do you mean?"

"The ring was one thing. Like you said, a symbol of our friendship. And it's something I can wear every day." She looked at the dresses in the window. "I'll never wear one of those dresses."

"How do you know?"

"I guess I don't know for sure, but it seems like a good way to jinx myself—buy a wedding dress when I have no idea if I'll ever get married."

The thought of her walking down the aisle toward some asshole who didn't deserve her jumped into my head. I fucking hated it. "What about wearing it at our engagement party?"

"A *wedding* gown?"

"You don't have to get a big fluffy one. Get something more simple."

She smiled, but still hesitated. "I don't know."

"Cosette Lavigne sounds like a French name," I said. "Wasn't that what you told Mimi? Your dress was French?"

Felicity laughed. "I did say that."

"Then it's meant to be. Come on."

She groaned but let me drag her into the shop. Inside, the air was chilly and smelled like perfume. A saleswoman with jet-black hair and chiseled cheekbones approached with a quick glance at our jeans and hats. "Hello. Can I help you?"

Suddenly, I had no idea what to say, and I looked helplessly at Felicity.

"I'm—I'm looking for a dress," she said.

The woman tilted her head. "A wedding dress?"

"No. I mean, yes, but no." She took a breath and closed her eyes a moment. "Sorry. The dress would be for an engagement party."

The woman seemed to relax a little. "Wonderful. Congratulations. Did you have a style in mind?"

"Something a little more casual than what's in the window. White is fine, but no ball gown or long train or anything. The party is outdoors, on a patio."

"And will you need to leave with the dress today?"

"Yes," she said. "We're going home tomorrow. But if you don't have anything, I—"

The woman held up a hand as she looked Felicity over head to toe. "I have something. We'll need to go off the rack, of course, but I'm seeing something short, perhaps tulle with pearl beading, something to emphasize your waistline, maybe a full skirt, a statement sleeve. Give me a moment."

"Thank you."

The woman disappeared into the back and Felicity and I looked at each other.

"What the hell is a statement sleeve?" I asked. "Is this dress going to talk?"

"I think it means the sleeves will be big and dramatic."

"Interesting."

Twenty minutes later, Felicity stood on a raised platform in front of a half-hexagon of mirrors, up on her toes as if she was wearing high heels. She couldn't stop smiling. The dress was pretty, but I couldn't have told you one thing about it other than it hit her above the knee, had short (big and dramatic) puffy sleeves, no back, and made her glow with happiness.

"Like it was *made* for you." The saleswoman—Olga was her name—shook her head. "It doesn't even need alteration, I can't believe it."

"It's so pretty," Felicity gushed, turning to check out the back over her shoulder. She'd removed her hat and put her hair up in a ponytail on the top of her head, sort of like Pebbles Flintstone.

"Let me see if I have a shoe for you to try on. What size are you?"

"Seven," said Felicity. "But that's okay, I don't know if—"

"I'll be back." Olga disappeared into the back again.

I'd been standing back, out of the way, but now I moved closer. Met her eyes in the mirror. "What do you think?"

"I think we should get out of here while we can. This is nuts."

I grabbed her arm to keep her right where she was. "Or it makes perfect sense," I said with a smile. "Both things can be true."

She shook her head. "Not this time. It's too much."

"Too much money?"

"Just—too much."

"What do you mean?"

She closed her eyes. "I guess I'm getting nervous that the line between real and make-believe is growing a little blurry. Know what I mean?"

Of course I did. I was the one blurring it. But it just felt so fucking good to give her everything she wanted, to be able to spoil her for this short time. "Felicity, it's just a dress."

She turned to face me. Seconds ticked by. "Is it?"

I have to admit, I hesitated too. "Yes."

Her mouth opened, and I thought she was going to call me out on the lie. But suddenly, blood streamed from her nostrils, and she clapped her hands over her nose, her eyes wild with fear. "Shoot!"

Without another word, I whipped off my T-shirt and held it up to her face.

"Get the dress off me!" she cried, her voice muffled by the cotton.

Shirtless, I was fumbling around looking for a zipper when Olga returned holding a pair of high heels. She stopped dead in her tracks at the sight of us, her expression horrified. She probably thought we were trying to have a romantic tryst right there in her shop.

"She has a bloody nose," I explained. "Can you help?"

Olga shrieked and dropped the shoes as she raced for us.

Twenty seconds later, she was cradling the dress and looking with alarm at the red stains on my white shirt. "Should I call an ambulance?"

Felicity shook her head. "It's not that bad," came her muffled reply. "I can wait it out."

"No," I told Olga. "She'll be fine. Is the dress okay?"

"I think so." She held it up and gasped. "No! There is a spot of blood right here on the neckline! It's faint, but I can see it. The dress is ruined."

I smiled at Felicity. "Then I guess we have to buy it."

"I'm sorry." Next to me on a bench in Washington Square Park, Felicity stared down at the garment bag across her lap. She'd tried to pay for it while I ran over to the men's shop next door to Cosette Lavigne to buy a new shirt, but her credit card had been declined.

"Don't be." I put my arm around her.

"This dress was too expensive."

"It's worth it."

"I bled all over your white shirt."

"That's why I bought a black one."

"I'm *so* embarrassed."

"You never have to be embarrassed in front of me."

"No?" She looked up at me.

"No. I guarantee I've made a way bigger fool of myself. Did I ever tell you about my road test when I was getting my driver's license?"

She shook her head.

"I had such a bad panic attack, I had to stop the car, get out, and walk home. It took me another month to try again."

She smiled. Her feet started swinging. "I never knew that."

"I was too ashamed to tell you. Then there was the time

I took an F on a presentation in a college class because I got up to give it but instead of going to the front of the room, I walked out the door."

"The teacher didn't offer to let you redo it?"

"Sure he did. I said no way. And then there was this girl I was kind of crazy about—I totally blew it with her."

Her feet stopped moving. "What girl?"

"This crazy smart, smokin' hot babe in the Chemistry Club."

She laughed, swinging her feet again. "Yeah? What did you do?"

"I worked up my nerve to ask her to the prom, but at the end of the night, I fucking shook her hand instead of kissing her."

"Why'd you do that?"

"I was scared. I never thought she'd want to be with a guy like me."

"Smart? Handsome? Section leader of the marching band?"

"I was a nerd with a filthy mind."

"That's the best kind of nerd." She gave me a little sideways smile. "You should reach out. See if she'll give you a second chance."

"You think so?"

"Definitely."

We sat there for a little while longer, just watching people go by with their friends or dogs or significant others, hands clasped. A little old couple toddled by, arm in arm, and the woman's steps were so tiny and slow, the man took one for every four of hers. They both had glasses and thinning white hair. Hers was sort of short and fluffy and his was combed over from a deep side part.

"He's carrying her purse," Felicity whispered. "How cute is that?"

When the woman spotted the bench, she pointed at it, and the husband led her over. Immediately, Felicity and I scooted down to make room.

"Thank you," said the man, helping his wife sit down next to me, then seating himself on the other side.

"Of course." Felicity leaned forward and beamed at them. "It's a beautiful day for a walk."

"Yes. We've walked in this park just about every Saturday for seventy years," said the woman. Then she laughed. "I just can't get as far as I used to."

I smiled. "That's what benches are for."

"But it's our anniversary," she went on, "and I said, 'Edward, we have to walk today.'"

"Happy anniversary!" said Felicity. "How many years?"

"Seventy-two. We moved here when I was expecting our first baby. We had eight of them," the woman said proudly.

Felicity grinned. "That's a lot of years and a lot of babies."

"Tell me about it," muttered Edward. But he patted his wife's knee. "How's the hip, Clara?"

"A little rusty. I'll just rest a minute." She looked back and forth from Felicity to me. "Are you two married?"

Felicity and I exchanged a look and tacitly agreed we would not lie to this little old couple.

"No," I said.

"We're just very close friends," added Felicity.

"It's so much harder these days," Clara said with a sigh. "Especially for women. The list of things my daughters and granddaughters wanted to accomplish before they got married was a mile long. But finding love is an accomplishment too. That's my two cents."

Edward looked at us. "She's got two cents for everything."

"I'm ninety-three. I've saved up a lot of pennies," said his wife indignantly.

"Well, I think you're right." Felicity smiled at the old lady. "Finding love *is* an accomplishment."

"Holding onto it isn't easy either," Clara went on. "People make such a fuss about weddings these days, I think they forget that after the white dress and the I do's, there's a whole lot of hard work ahead. But that's just my two cents."

"See what I mean?" said Edward under his breath.

"Anyway, I think the best marriages are the ones between two close friends," said Clara. "That's what I was trying to say. Those are the ones that last, because you already know each other so well. You get along with each other. You appreciate things about the other person that you might not if it was just S-E-X all the time."

Felicity tried not to laugh. "Yes, I know what you mean."

"Of course, if you can have both," Clara went on enthusiastically, "that's really the best of both worlds. If you can find that close friend that you love and trust, and the S-E-X is good too, that's when you know. Right, Eddie?"

"Right." He patted Clara's knee again.

"Because one might fade, but the other? Never. That's my two cents."

Edward sighed.

"Thank you," Felicity said. "And happy anniversary."

That evening, we wandered the streets of Little Italy, ate pizza, drank wine, and bought souvenirs for my nieces and nephew. We had fun, but I noticed that Felicity was quieter than usual.

"Everything okay?" I asked her as we turned back the covers and slipped between the sheets.

"Yes. I'm just tired."

"Are you too tired for S-E-X?" I pulled her closer to me. She laughed. "No."

But she didn't kiss me, or sling a leg across my thighs, or slide a hand down my stomach.

"Hey." Rolling to my side, I propped my head on my hand and looked down at her. "What's going on?"

She played with my chest hair, her eyes focused on her fingers. I noticed she'd put the ring on before coming to bed. "I keep thinking about that couple. Seventy-two years."

"That's a long time."

"I think about your parents. My dad and Frannie. Your sister and Neil. Even Winnie and Dex—you can just tell they're going to be together forever." She looked up at me. "How do some people get so lucky, and others just . . . don't?"

"Born under different stars, I guess."

"I guess," she said sadly.

"Hey, listen. Our stars might not come with seven-plus decades and eight kids, but they're not so bad."

She tried to smile. "No."

I wanted a real smile back on her face. "What do you say we do this every year?"

"Do what?"

"Meet up for a weekend in New York—or anywhere else in the world. I'll pick you up in a jet, we'll rent a hotel suite, eat at fancy places, see shows, go shopping, or even better, avoid people and do nothing at all. Just . . . be together. Like this. You and me."

"That sounds nice." But there was no smile.

"You sure you're okay?"

"I'm fine."

I didn't believe her, so I did my best to distract her with my mouth and my hands and my cock—I knew exactly how to kiss her, touch her, make her body arch beneath me. I knew what would make her gasp, what would make her sigh, what would make her cry out again and again. I knew how to bring her right to the edge and pull her back, and I knew when she'd had enough of the game and needed the release. I knew the taste of her, the scent of her, the sounds she made when I was so deep inside it hurt. I knew how it felt to have her fingernails rake across my back and her fists tighten in my hair and her body clench mine as I lost myself inside her.

We fell asleep immediately afterward, but I woke her up the next morning with my head between her thighs.

Because I also knew it was all going to end soon.

Fifteen

Felicity

THE DAY AFTER HUTTON AND I RETURNED FROM OUR TRIP, I met Millie and Winnie for breakfast at Frannie's bakery.

Saturday mornings were always crowded at Plum & Honey, but Winnie had managed to snag a table in the back, and she waved frantically to me as I walked in. Millie was already at the counter, and a moment later she sat down with a plate Frannie had heaped with our favorite treats—monkey bread muffins for Win, blueberry lemon scones for Mills, *pain au chocolat* for me.

After sneaking into the kitchen to hug her hello, I ordered a cup of black coffee and sat across from my sisters, who swooned over the ring, the box at the Met, the story about the dress.

"Nooooo! You and those bloody noses!" moaned Winnie. "Is the dress ruined?"

"Not really," I said. "You can hardly see the spot."

"I love that you had one fancy day and one day just dressed down for yourselves," said Millie.

I smiled. "Me too. We had so much fun both nights."

"I bet you did." Millie's eyebrows peaked above her coffee cup.

Winnie's sister radar perked up, and she glanced back and forth between us. "What's that look? What don't I know?"

"I was just wondering if Felicity had to use a safe word in New York."

Winnie's jaw fell open. "Oh my God. What?"

"Didn't you know?" Millie grinned wickedly and whispered, "Hutton has a kink."

Winnie's eyes bulged as she stared at me across the table. "I cannot believe you have been withholding this information from me, and I demand that you tell me everything immediately."

I rolled my eyes and pushed my glasses up my nose. "Listen. Do I ask you everything about Dex in the bedroom?"

"No, but I tell you everything anyway."

I laughed. "Well, I'm not like that. Some things are private."

My sisters exchanged a look. Winnie blew a raspberry. Millie booed and gave me a thumbs down.

"At least one little detail, please?" Winnie clasped her hands.

I sipped my coffee for dramatic pause. "I did have a safe word. Although I don't think I used it correctly."

Millie burst out laughing.

"Whatever you did, was it fun?" Winnie asked eagerly. "Did you like it?"

"Yeah," I said. "It was hot. I mean, I can see why some people would not like it, and it definitely takes a certain level of trust, but we had a good time."

"And he's okay with the party?" Winnie asked, her eyes worried.

"Winnie!" Millie whacked her on the shoulder. "That is supposed to be a surprise."

"Ow!" Winnie rubbed her arm. "She already knows, okay? She dragged it out of me."

"It was like shooting fish in a barrel." I smiled. "But I was glad she told me. I can't say he's thrilled, but we'll be there."

"And what about a wedding date?" Winnie looked at Millie. "Any progress there?"

"There's one Sunday afternoon available at the end of August," Millie said, shooting me a glance. "I have it reserved for now."

"Thanks, Millie," I said. "I promise to get you an answer in the next day or so."

"I hope so! Invitations need to go out—that's only a month away." Winnie checked her phone. "Shoot. I have to go, I promised Hallie and Luna I'd go swimming with them at eleven. Let me see the ring one more time!"

I held out my hand, and she gazed longingly at my finger before sighing. "It's so beautiful. I'm so happy for you. When do we talk bridesmaid dresses?"

"Uh. Soon."

"Yay!" Winnie stood up and shoved the rest of her muffin in her mouth. "Okay, I'm going."

Alone with Millie, I felt her eyes on me. "What?"

"A real wedding dress? A real ring?" She shook her head. "What's going on? I'm starting to wonder if the joke's on me. Maybe I *should* save the date."

"We had to buy the dress because my nose bled on it," I insisted. "It doesn't really look like a wedding gown. Just a party dress. And I even tried to pay for it."

"What about the ring?"

"The ring was just a gift," I said, trying to ignore the uneasy feeling in my stomach.

"A gift." Millie blinked at me. "From Tiffany."

"Yes. Look, I know it's a bit extravagant, and I told him that, but he wouldn't listen. He said he knows diamond rings are normally reserved for people you're asking to spend the rest of your life with, but since he knows he always wants me in his life, it's fine." I picked up my coffee for a sip. "We're not really getting married, and it's fine."

"It's fine?"

"It's fine. I'm fine." But my fingers trembled as I set down my cup.

Millie glanced at my shaky fingers a moment, then met my eyes. "I don't think you are. What's wrong?"

"Nothing." I sipped my coffee, cradling the cup in both hands. "I'm tired is all. I didn't get much sleep in New York, and I had to work last night."

My sister broke off a piece of her scone and put it in her mouth. As she chewed, she kept looking at me.

"What?" I said, uncomfortable with her scrutiny.

"I know you. Something has you nervous. Jumpy."

"That's ridiculous." I tried to sound dismissive.

She took another bite, never taking her eyes off me. "Did Hutton tell you he loves you or something?"

"No!" I laughed as if she'd said something hilarious. "Things aren't like that with us. This isn't a real relationship or a real engagement. It's something I made up, remember?"

Millie rolled her eyes. "I remember."

I took a bite of *pain au chocolat* without tasting it. Glanced out the window. On the corner, a woman took a small child by the hand and looked both ways before crossing the street. "I know it might look real on the outside, but that's just because we're having a good time. It's one hundred percent fake. We are not together."

"If you say so," she said.

"I do." My head was spinning, my breath was short. "It's not real."

I'm fine.

Nothing's the matter.

Everything's good.

As days went by, I said it out loud to anyone who asked if I was okay, and I said it to myself, trying to convince myself that this pit in my stomach wasn't anything to worry about.

So I had the ring and the dress—so what? They were just gifts.

So there was a wedding date on hold at Cloverleigh Farms—it was part of the act.

So I was lying to people who loved me—it wasn't hurting anyone.

So the internet continued to obsess over photos of Hutton and me—some sleuth had even managed to get their hands on a prom photo (I suspected Mimi, who kept texting me asking to meet, like we were old friends), and even reputable news sites ran it along with captions about "the hometown honey that bagged herself a billionaire." It was fine—I only let myself read a couple hundred shitty comments before putting my phone down and walking away. And I deleted Mimi's messages without a second thought. The *last* thing I needed was her voice in my ear.

So I spent every night in Hutton's arms, woke up next to him every morning, and desperately tried not to think about the day it would all be over—all good things must come to an end, right?

I threw myself into work.

I responded to lots of inquiries about catering and booked half a dozen new jobs for the fall. I created new recipes and took stunning photos in Hutton's kitchen. I took phone calls regarding some of the offers for collaboration that had come in.

Hutton spent a lot of time alone in his office getting ready for the hearing, but he'd warned me on the flight home from New York that would happen. "I'm sorry," he said. "It will seem like I don't care or like I'm self-obsessed, but that's not it. When something like this is hanging over my head, I just get really focused. I can't think about anything else."

"I get it," I told him. "And you don't have to apologize or worry about me. Concentrate on you."

He wasn't exaggerating—I hardly saw him the week after we got home. And when I did, he was quiet and introspective. But we still had mind-blowing S-E-X before falling asleep in each other's arms every night, and in many ways, it was the happiest I'd ever been.

It was also the most terrified.

Which made me crazy mad at myself. Because it's not like I didn't know what was going to happen. It wasn't like walking into my bedroom imagining there might be a witch about to jump out—the fucking witch was in there and I knew precisely when she'd show her face. This thing with Hutton had an expiration date.

Every time I booked a catering gig for the fall, I'd think, *He'll be gone by then*, and my stomach would pitch and roll. My breath would catch.

But it was fine. I was fine.

Until the voicemails.

The first one came on Monday. I waited three days to listen to it, which I did sitting in my car in the grocery store parking lot.

"Felicity, darling, it's Mom. I heard the big news! At first I just couldn't believe it—it seemed so unlikely for you—but I've seen the photos and don't you two look cute together? And wow, a billionaire. That's really something. I'm sure your father is happy about that. He'll never have to worry about money again, right?" (Unkind laughter.) "Anyway, I'm dying to talk to you. Give me a call, it's been too long."

I was fuming by the time I got to the end. *Unlikely* for me? My father happy about the *money*? It's been *too long*?

"Not long enough," I snapped, deleting the message.

Later that night, as we were getting ready for bed, Hutton asked me what was wrong.

"Nothing," I said, unable to meet his eyes. I opened a dresser drawer and messed around in it, not looking for anything.

"You've been so quiet tonight. Actually, all week."

"Have I? Sorry." I shut the drawer and took off my glasses so I could rub my eyes. "Just tired, I guess."

"Hey." He came over and turned me into his arms, the place where I felt safest in the world. "Talk to me. I know I'm distracted with work, but I'm still here for you."

I wrapped my arms around his middle and pressed my cheek to his bare chest. It was on the tip of my tongue to tell him about the voicemail from Carla, but I didn't want to do it. Hutton had enough to worry about—the hearing was only a week away. I refused to add more stress to his life. "It's nothing. I promise."

She left two more messages over the weekend, whining that I hadn't called her back, reminding me she was still my mother, and faking enthusiasm for my wedding. "I just can't wait to meet a real billionaire," she said. "And I'm dying to see that rock up close. It looks huge. Is he paying for out-of-town guests to stay somewhere nice?"

I deleted them both immediately, mad at myself for even listening.

Monday night, Winnie asked me to come over and help her create a vegetarian menu for a wine dinner she and Ellie were planning at Abelard. Glad for the distraction, I spent the evening at her condo helping her plan, eating takeout, and sipping wine. Hutton had said he needed to work late, so I lingered at Winnie's, envying the easy affection between her and Dex. What would it be like to know you could have forever together?

I left around nine, and my phone rang just as I got behind the wheel. I should have checked the number before answering.

"Hello?"

"Finally," Carla said, slurring the word a little. "I was wondering when I'd actually get you."

Fuck, I mouthed, closing my eyes. "What do you want?"

"I want to talk."

"About what?"

"About life." She laughed drunkenly. "About this wedding thing. Why would you want to get married anyway? You're too young."

"Do you even know how old I am?"

"Don't be rude," she snapped. "I'm still your mother."

"When did you decide that?"

"Hey. I'm trynna do you a favor. I get wanting the money, but make sure he signs a prenup. You need to protect yourself for when he leaves you."

My blood boiled. "I don't need a prenup."

"Yes, you do," she slurred. "You think everything will be wine and roses, but it won't. The good times don't last. He'll make promises he won't keep, just like your father did."

"You leave Dad out of this," I said furiously. "He's never broken a promise to me my entire life. And I bet he never broke one to you either!"

"He promised to *love me*. Instead he drove me away. He took my children from me," she accused.

"Leaving was *your* choice," I shot back. "You betrayed Dad. You betrayed Millie and Winnie and me."

She laughed again. "You don't know what you're talking about. You don't know *anything*."

"I know enough," I said. I ended the call, blocked her number, and tossed my phone on the passenger seat.

I will not cry. I will not fall apart. I will not give her that power over me.

But it wasn't just her call that had me bawling into my hands—it was everything. The lying to my family, the dread of losing Hutton, the fear that my feelings were hopeless, the envy of anyone who'd found love, the doubt that my heart would remain in one piece . . .

What had I done?

Hutton was still working at the kitchen table when I walked in. "Hi," he said, giving me a tired smile.

My gut instinct was to run for him, bury my face in his chest, and let him hold me while I sobbed. But I refrained—I couldn't be dependent on him to comfort me. He wouldn't always be here to put me back together when I felt myself coming apart.

"Be right back." I dropped my keys and purse on the floor and made a beeline for the bedroom. Slipping into the bathroom, I shut the door behind me and braced myself on the vanity. Stared at my reflection in the mirror. Inhale. Exhale. Inhale. Exhale.

I opened the top drawer and messed around, looking for scissors. Then the second drawer. The third.

Found them.

I pulled them out of the drawer and was about to start cutting when the ring on my finger caught my eye. I hesitated.

Then I heard a knock on the door behind me.

"Felicity?"

Ashamed, I shoved the scissors back in the drawer and slammed it shut.

The door opened. "Felicity."

I spun around, hands behind my back, leaning on the vanity. "What?"

"What are you doing?"

"Nothing." I bit my lip.

He glanced at the sink behind me. "Were you going to cut your hair?"

I shook my head. Stopped. Nodded.

And burst into tears.

Wordlessly, he came forward and pulled me into his arms, holding me, rubbing my back, letting me cry my eyes out into his chest. After a few minutes, he reached over and grabbed a tissue. "Want to tell me what's up?"

"No." I took the tissue from him and blew my nose.

"Why not?"

"Because you're busy and need to concentrate on work, not my bullshit. The entire point of this arrangement was for you to have time and space to work, and I don't want to be a burden."

"You are not a burden. Do I need to remind you how we promised to be there for each other when one of us needed a friend? I know you didn't use the code, but I'm sensing the bat signal here." He peeked behind me. "Those scissors are a cry for help. Now talk."

I grabbed another tissue. "My mother called."

"Oh."

Mopping up my face, I told him about the messages she left, how she managed to push all my buttons, how mad I was at myself that I let her get to me. "After all this time," I said angrily, yanking another tissue from the box. "Why should she still have that power?"

"Because she's your mother and what she did left a scar," he said.

"But I don't need her. I don't even like her." I struggled to keep the sobs from erupting. "Why should it matter what she says?"

"Maybe it doesn't matter whether you need her or like her. Maybe just the fact that deep down, you know she was your mother and was supposed to love and protect you, and instead she hurt you, is enough to fuck with your head."

"Yeah." I took some shuddery breaths. "I guess."

"Maybe you should talk to my sister," he said. "Or she could give you the name of someone else. While I *am* an expert at head fuckery, I'm not a therapist."

That actually made me crack a smile. "Look at you promoting therapy."

He shrugged. "Just because it didn't solve my issues doesn't mean it can't help you with yours. My shit is my own fault. Your shit was done *to* you—I bet a good therapist could help you work through it."

"Maybe. But how do you ever work through the fact that your own mother didn't want you? Or love you enough? It's like this stupid voice in the back of my head that I can't turn off."

He pulled me close again. "I wish I had a good answer. I can't turn off the voices in my head either."

Everything about his embrace soothed me—the hard body beneath the clothes, the clean masculine scent, the warmth of his skin. "Thanks for chasing me in here. I guess I did need you."

"I like when you need me." He didn't speak for a moment, and then I heard him swallow. "I wish things were different."

"Different how?"

"All kinds of ways." He paused. "I wish I had my magic powers back."

I laughed. "You're enough without them."

"What would you wish for?"

I'd wish for the guts to tell you I love you. Because I don't need you to be perfect or magical. I just need you to stay with me.

But a wound had been opened up tonight, and it was too big a risk. In New York, when we'd talked about the forever kind of happiness, he hadn't offered me hope. He'd offered to meet me in New York once a year. He'd offered me a piece of his life, of his time, maybe even of his heart, but not the whole thing.

I'd never wanted anyone's whole heart before, and I didn't know how to ask for it. I'd spent too many years being afraid, running away, convincing myself love was a losing game.

"I'd wish for some ice cream, a bubble bath, and an orgasm—probably in that order," I said instead.

He laughed, probably relieved. "Now that I can deliver."

Sixteen

Hutton

I HADN'T SLEPT WELL SINCE WE'D GOTTEN BACK FROM NEW YORK. It was easy to blame my restlessness on the upcoming hearing, my nerves about public speaking, my irritation with Wade, my fears that things would not go well and not only would HFX go under, but my credibility would be shot too. Then my net worth would crumble, and I'd go down in history as the guy who single-handedly tanked the digital currency industry in a day.

It was a lot.

But there was more to it.

Beneath the surface of my anxiety was this creeping unease that somewhere I'd made a wrong turn with Felicity. I couldn't pinpoint the moment where things had gone off-track, I just sensed that things were not okay. When I did manage to fall asleep, I had nightmares about being caught in a storm, flood waters rising all around me. I could hear Felicity's voice but couldn't see her.

I'd wake up sweating and shaking, unsure what it meant. Did the flood symbolize my fear of things out of my control? But things *weren't* out of control. We'd mapped this out so carefully. We had a plan, and the plan made sense. We had a timeline and an exit strategy. We wouldn't be caught by surprise.

No one was going to be rejected. Nobody would be hurt. That was the beauty of it. We'd stay friends.

Except . . . I didn't *want* to make an exit.

I hadn't gotten enough of her. I hadn't gotten enough of the way I felt when we were together. I'd showed her more of me than I'd ever showed anyone, and she accepted me.

But I wasn't an idiot. I knew that would change with the pressure of a real relationship, especially long-distance. The whole reason we were so good together is because it was all for fun. We were in on a secret in a way that pitted us against the world, not one against the other. If we were dating for real, she'd grow tired of my bullshit. She'd stop teasing me and making her little witch hat and start rolling her eyes, sighing heavily, and thinking I wasn't worth the hassle. I'd been through it before.

You're being ridiculous.

Stop being selfish.

You need to get over yourself.

She wouldn't look at me the same way. And that was unthinkable.

But what was the alternative? Never having her in my arms again? Never kissing her? Tasting her? Never knowing the unbelievable ecstasy of moving inside her, feeling her body wrapped around mine?

Fuck that. I couldn't give her up. Not yet.

But time was running out. It was Monday. I was leaving for D.C. on Wednesday, back on Friday. Our party was Saturday, and then we'd have two weeks at most to break up, move away from each other, and go on leading separate lives. Unless I thought of another way.

I tossed and turned as the hours passed.

Toward dawn, a solution came to me.

When I got back from my run, Felicity was still asleep. I showered and dressed, then stood at the foot of the bed, watching her for a moment. She was so damn adorable—she hugged a pillow when she slept like a kid holds a teddy bear. I envied that pillow and wished I had the time to crawl back in bed with her.

Instead, I went and kissed her cheek.

Her eyes opened, her lips curving into a smile. "Hey."

"Hey. I'm heading to my sister's to hang out with the kids for a while. You want to come with me? I can wait for you to get dressed."

"I can't." She sat up, holding the pillow to her chest. "I'm behind on a bunch of things, and I have to work at Etoile tonight."

"Okay." I lingered at the side of the bed, eager to share my idea with her. "So I was thinking."

"About what?"

"I have to be out of here by August fifteenth."

She took a breath and nodded. "I know. It's okay. I'll move back home."

"Why don't I rent you another place?"

"Rent me another place?" She reached for her glasses and slipped them on, as if her vision might have affected her hearing.

"Well . . . yeah. That way you don't have to move back in with your parents when I go back to San Francisco."

"So you wouldn't live in the new place? It would just be for me?"

"Right. But I'd have a place to stay when I came to visit." I smiled. Problem solved. "You can stock the kitchen with everything you like. You can take all the things I bought for here and keep them in the new place."

But she shook her head. "That won't make sense, Hutton. We're supposed to break things off after the party, remember?"

"I've been thinking about that too." I took a breath. "Maybe we don't have to break things off *entirely*. Maybe we just say we've decided not to get married, but we're still together."

"We're still together, but you live in San Francisco and I live here?"

I felt a slight ache behind my right eye. "I know it's not ideal, but it's better than nothing, right?"

She dropped her eyes to the pillow she held. "Better than nothing. Right."

"Maybe we should talk about this later," I said. "You're not fully awake yet, and I kind of ambushed you with this."

"I'm awake enough to say no."

"Huh?"

She lifted her chin. "No. I don't want you to rent me another place. I don't want to be together but never together."

"So you'd rather just break it off completely?"

"No, but—"

"Because those are the options," I went on, angrier than intended. Why couldn't she see that my plan made perfect sense? What more did she want from me?

"Those are the options? Something or nothing?"

"Yes."

She nodded slowly. "Then I guess it's nothing."

"Felicity, come on. We've talked about this." I shifted my weight from foot to foot. "I've never been dishonest with you about what I can offer."

"I know." Her voice broke. "And I'll be honest with *you* now, and say that what you have to offer isn't enough for me. I'm sorry."

"We agreed," I said testily. "We agreed that it's foolish to jump into the deep end of the pool when you can't swim."

"I didn't jump, Hutton." Her shoulders rose. "I fell."

Her words stabbed me in the heart, but I was a pro at masking what I felt inside. "You're asking for something I can't give."

"I'm not asking for anything." She wiped her eyes beneath her glasses. "You know, I've spent years being terrified of this very situation. Years of being careful with my heart so I wouldn't ever be rejected."

"Felicity. Stop." I couldn't take her tears—or the fact that I'd caused them.

"I thought I was so smart," she said. "But here I am anyway. And even though I won't ask for what I want, I won't settle for less than I deserve."

What the hell was I supposed to say to that? I didn't want her to settle for less than she deserved either, but I couldn't deliver it. She was insisting on all or nothing, and my all would never be enough.

Rather than admit my fears, I stormed out of the bedroom. A moment later, I slammed the front door behind me.

My idea had been a good one, dammit! It allowed us to keep seeing each other without the pressure of having to make an every-day relationship work. I'd been up front about the fact that I didn't want that. I didn't need that. I couldn't handle that.

I hadn't thought she wanted that either, but clearly I'd misjudged her. It wouldn't be the first time I'd read the signs all wrong.

I started my car and threw it in gear, tearing down the driveway too fast.

Jesus, I was as bad as Wade, trying to be someone I wasn't.

I should have just stuck to the fucking plan.

Seventeen

Felicity

BETTER THAN NOTHING?

When I heard the front door shut, I burst into tears. Which was so stupid—even if we weren't faking everything, I'd known all along what we were doing was temporary. I wasn't a kid anymore, blindsided by an ugly truth in the middle of the night. No one had lied to me. No one had made me any promises.

But *better than nothing?* Being his girlfriend when he came to town? Living alone in a house he was paying for? What the fuck?

I rolled over and sobbed into my pillow. This was my fault.

He'd told me from the start he was shitty at relationships and didn't want one. He told me he was never lonely. He told me he didn't have the temperament to be a husband or father, and since those were things I was hoping to have one day, did it really matter if I was in love with him or not?

He was who he was, and I'd always said I would never want him to be anybody else. In New York, he'd flat out said, *I'm set in my ways and not going to change. Take me or leave me.*

I said I'd always take him. It wasn't fair of me to change my mind.

I'd get through this week and the party, and then we'd have to call it quits.

My heart was already broken anyway.

Eventually, I dragged myself out of bed and checked my phone—the first thing I saw was yet another text from Mimi. **Hey, not sure if you've been getting my messages, but really need a chat. Trust me when I say you can't afford to ignore me.**

Disgusted, I deleted the message and went to make myself some coffee. She probably wanted to give me tips for growing my social media following—although, at this point, my follower count far exceeded hers. Or maybe she wanted to offer hair and makeup advice. Get a close-up look at my ring. Hound me for more details about my wedding.

I distracted myself with work, editing some photos, drafting posts, responding to emails, replying to comments on social media. My one-star review on Dearly Beloved had finally been removed—thank heavens—but I was anxious to have some good ones in its place. I flipped through my calendar, looking at the coming months' catering gigs and shifts at Etoile.

The engagement party date was circled in red.

When the calendar blurred, I got up from the table, changed into workout clothes, and took a walk through the woods surrounding Hutton's house. When I got back, I put a towel out on the deck and did some yoga and stretches in the sun. Breathing deeply, I reminded myself that I still had a plan. I still had goals. I still had dreams. And just because Hutton was leaving didn't mean I'd never see him again. With some time and distance between us, maybe we could repair our friendship.

But would I ever feel this way about anyone else?

When tears threatened once more, I got up and took a shower. Afterward, wrapped in a towel, I walked into the closet to get dressed for work.

And saw the Cosette Lavigne garment bag.

Unable to resist, I unzipped the bag and took out the gorgeous white confection of a dress, took in its full skirt and deep V neckline and statement sleeves. I recalled Hutton asking what the hell that meant, and a laugh turned into a sob.

Hanging the dress up, I spun around and raced into the bathroom. Dug out the scissors.

And this time I cut.

Less than an hour later, I knocked on Millie's front door.

She pulled it open and gasped. "Oh no. More bangs."

Nodding, I began to cry, and she quickly ushered me into the house and wrapped her arms around me. "Shhhh, it's okay. They're a little extreme, but at least they're even . . . ish. Did you cut any off the back?"

"No," I blubbered. "I stopped myself for once."

"Good girl." She released me and stood back, hands on my shoulders, taking in my black pants and white chef's coat. "Got time for some tea or lemonade?"

"Yes. Thank you." I followed her back to the kitchen and sat at the table while she poured us some lemonade and hulled some fresh strawberries. Muffin and Molasses twined around my feet, and Muffin jumped into my lap.

"Here." Millie set a glass and the fruit in front of me. "I'd open some wine or something, but it looks like you have to work, and something tells me we'd kill that bottle pretty fast."

"Yeah. I better stick to lemonade."

She picked up her glass from the counter and lowered herself into the chair next to me. "So what's going on?"

"It's this thing with Hutton," I said, struggling for composure. "I think it might have turned real."

She pressed her lips together, like she didn't want to say *I told you so*.

"It didn't start real," I said defensively. "It *was* all an act. A way for me to save face in front of Mimi Pepper-Peabody and for Hutton to get his mother off his back. Plus, I got to move out of Dad and Frannie's house."

"You know, both Winnie and I said you could move in with us, just saying," Millie pointed out.

"That isn't the point," I said irritably.

"Of course not. Sorry. Go on."

I took a breath. "Everything was fine until we got to New York. That's where I started to get . . . confused."

"Can't imagine why," she muttered, taking a sip of her lemonade.

"I was overwhelmed by the . . ." I rolled my hands like wheels on a bus. "Whirlwind of fantasy. It's not easy to keep your feet on the ground when your head is in the clouds, you know? I was never the girl who dreamed about being the princess, but Hutton just has this way of making me feel so beautiful and special and deserving."

"You are, Felicity." Millie's voice was firm. "Don't doubt that."

My throat hurt, it was so tight. "I don't know what to do, Millie. Hutton is the only guy I've ever felt this close to. The one guy on the planet who gets me, who's seen me at my best and worst, who knows the crazy inner workings of my mind and doesn't judge me."

Millie sat back and draped her arm over her head, half-eaten strawberry still in her hand. "Are you listening to yourself? The *one* guy, the *only* guy? You're in love with Hutton."

"Shhhhhhhh!" I made frantic erasing motions with my hands in front of her face. "Don't *say* it!"

"Why not? I feel like that's the one thing that's been said in this kitchen in the last couple weeks that makes any sense at all. This whole fake fiancé routine is insane. You guys love each other. You're good together. The whole reason people swallowed your whole cockamamie story to begin with is because it's so obvious to those around you that you two are meant to be." She shook her head. "I know you've got some weird allergy to love, which I have never fully understood, but it's time to get over it, Felicity."

I stared at her for a few seconds. "You want to know why I have an allergy to love? I'll tell you."

She swallowed and picked up her lemonade. "Yes. Please."

Muffin purred on my lap, and I was grateful to have something soft and warm to hold as I finally spilled the secret I'd kept from her for over twenty years. "When I was six, I overheard the fight Dad and Mom had the night she told him she was leaving. She said she never wanted us."

Millie's jaw fell open. "Oh my God."

"But that's not all I heard her say." In a calm, monotone voice, I laid out the details of what I'd heard, or at least what I remembered hearing. "And within days, she was gone."

My sister's face was stricken, her eyes full. "Why didn't you say something about what you'd heard? To me or to Dad?"

"I didn't want anyone else to be hurt," I explained. "What she said meant she didn't want you or Winnie either. And I knew I wasn't supposed to be listening. I was worried I might get in trouble."

Millie got up and disappeared into the bathroom off the front hallway. When she came out, she had a roll of toilet paper in her hand. "Sorry, I'm out of tissues."

"I'm not going to cry over this," I said evenly.

"I am." She set the roll on the table, sat down again, and wept into her hands.

"Millie, don't." At seeing my sister upset, my heart broke.

"She doesn't deserve your tears. I'm sorry, I shouldn't have told you."

"I'm not crying about her. I'm crying about you," she said, her shoulders heaving. "Carrying that around all these years and never saying anything about it."

The lump in my throat grew bigger. "It was a long time ago. I'm fine."

"No, you're not!" she blubbered, looking up at me with a tear-streaked face. "You're totally messed up over it. Now I understand why you left your relationships when someone told you they loved you. You never believed them."

"Even if I did," I said, shaking my head, "it wouldn't matter in the end. People can love you one day and not the next. You won't even know what you did until they're gone."

"Oh, Felicity." Millie tore off some toilet paper and blew her nose. "Mom didn't leave because of something you did. She left because she met someone else. She ran off with some other guy. She did it to get back at Dad for not paying enough attention to her."

"But if she really loved us, she'd have stayed," I insisted.

"Maybe, maybe not." Millie dabbed beneath her eyes, but her eyeliner and mascara was a mess. "Some people are just bad at love, you know? They're too selfish or narcissistic, or deep down they don't love themselves, so they don't know how to accept it from others."

Something about that struck a chord in me. "Do you think some people just aren't wired for love?"

Millie sighed and blew her nose again. "Me, personally? No. I think some people choose to behave in ways that keep them closed off from it, but I think everyone is capable."

I looked down at the ring on my finger. "Hutton says he's not wired for love, because of his anxiety. He thinks he's better off alone."

"People say a lot of things they don't mean when they're scared."

My eyes filled and I grabbed some toilet paper. "That's what I mean! You can't trust people to tell the truth!"

"Does Hutton know how you feel? Did you tell him?"

"No, but I *implied* it."

"Felicity." She put a hand on my arm. "Tell him the truth about your feelings. I'm not saying you have to get engaged or married or even keep living together. But why not at least be honest? What if hearing the words is the push he needs?"

I shook my head. "He doesn't want to hear those words from me."

"But you just told me—"

"I'm not done. He has to be out of the house two weeks after the party. Our plan was to end things by then."

"I remember the plan," she said drily.

"But then this morning he comes into the bedroom with a *new* plan. He said maybe he'll rent another place here and I can live in it. This way he'll have a place to stay when he comes to town."

Millie shrank back and wrinkled her nose. "What?"

"He wants to keep me like a pet," I said, gesturing to Muffin.

"This makes no sense." Millie seemed genuinely perplexed. "Why would he say that? He loves you."

"Not enough," I said quietly.

For once, Millie had no rebuttal.

My phone buzzed on the table, and I looked at it. "Jesus Christ, this woman is so annoying!"

"Carla again?"

"No, fucking Mimi Pepper-Peabody. She keeps wanting to meet up with me." I read the text. "Now she's making threats. This one says 'If I don't hear from you within twenty-four hours, you won't have a chance to tell me your side of the story.'"

"What the hell does that mean?"

"I have no idea. I'm fucking exhausted." Setting my phone down, I rubbed my face with both hands. "But I have to go to work."

"Me too. I'm sorry—I feel like I wasn't much help." She walked me to the door. "Want to hang out tomorrow?"

"Maybe. I'll text you." I gave her a hug, and she didn't let go right away.

"I wish you would have told me about that night," she said, her voice cracking. "I feel awful you went through that alone."

"It's okay."

"Are you going to tell Dad?"

"No." I let her go and stood back. "Dad does not need to hear it at this point. He was hard enough on himself, and I don't want him feeling guilty about this. He's happy."

"He is happy. Thank goodness for Frannie." She laughed a little. "It's funny to me—Frannie was younger than we are now when she married Dad. Didn't she seem so old?"

I had to smile. "Yes. I'd never seen two old people act so stupid. Especially Dad."

"Think they would have gotten together if we hadn't told him what was what?"

I shrugged. "Probably. It would have taken longer, since Dad was so stubborn, but they were obviously in love."

She poked my shoulder. "So you're saying love finds a way?"

"It's different for us." I frowned. "We're not Dad and Frannie."

"What's so different?"

"We're just—" I struggled for an answer, then I heard Hutton's voice in my head. "We were born under different stars."

Twenty minutes later, I arrived at Etoile. After pulling myself together in the parking lot, I went in the kitchen door.

Gianni glanced at me as I passed by his office. "Oh, hey. Someone's waiting to see you."

"What? Where?"

"I think she's in the tasting room now, but she walked right into the kitchen a little bit ago."

I rolled my eyes. "Tall blonde?"

"Yeah. I told her she couldn't wait back here." He grinned. "Sent her Ellie's way."

"Sorry about that. I'll deal with her." I checked the clock. "Should only take a few minutes."

"Go ahead."

Annoyed, I hurried through the empty restaurant, across the lobby, and down the steps to the winery. Inside the tasting room, I spotted Mimi at the near end of the bar checking her phone. Her back was to me, but I'd recognize that sleek golden blowout anywhere. Frowning, I touched my new bangs.

"Hey," I said, approaching her from behind. "You're looking for me?"

She turned on her stool and gave me a fake smile. "There you are."

I held out my arms. "Here I am."

She studied me critically. "Did you get your bangs cut again? You really should fire that stylist."

"What do you want, Mimi? I have to get to work."

"You know," she said, folding her arms. "I was *wondering* why you'd still work as a cook since getting engaged to a billionaire."

"I like my job," I said stiffly.

She laughed. "That's good, because now that I know the whole thing was a scam and you're not really engaged to a billionaire at all, you'll probably be working it for a while."

Eighteen

Hutton

"SO HOW'S IT GOING?" MY SISTER ASKED AS SHE CLEANED up the post-breakfast kitchen mess. "I haven't even seen you since you got back from New York. You ignore me now that you have a fiancée."

"Sorry." I was sitting at her kitchen table watching the kids play in the yard through the window.

"Looks like you guys had fun. I saw some pictures."

I folded my arms over my chest. "We had fun. Despite the people who felt it necessary to intrude on our privacy and take photos."

"The ones I saw were good." She collected some more dirty plates from the table. "I mean, you knew people were going to be interested. The love lives of celebrities sell."

"But it's fucking annoying. I don't want to be a celebrity. And Felicity didn't ask for that kind of attention."

Allie shrugged. "No, but it sort of comes with the territory. She knows who you are."

She did. She knew me better than anyone. Why was I mad at her for it?

"Quite a ring you gave her."

"Yeah."

"Have you guys settled on a date yet?"

"No."

She wiped off the table with a sponge. Then she stood there with her hands on her hips. "What's wrong?"

"Nothing." I clenched my jaw a little tighter.

"Is it the hearing?"

"That's a lot of it."

"So what's the rest of it?"

I averted my gaze out the window again. The kids were drawing with sidewalk chalk on the cement in front of the garage.

"You know I'll get it out of you."

"Maybe I'm dreading that stupid engagement party."

"Hutton! You're not supposed to know about that."

"Too late."

"Who told you?"

"Felicity. She heard it from her sister that works at Abelard, because unlike my family, her family knows how much I hate parties and gave us a warning."

Allie tossed the sponge in the sink and sat down at the table, flashing her palms at me like she was innocent. "It was not my idea, okay? But Mom consulted some crazy celestial calendar that said to throw a party on that date. When she found out it was available, she took it as a sign from the stars."

"Of course she did."

"Is that really what's bothering you?"

I exhaled, wishing I was outside drawing with chalk instead of in here under the microscope. "There's just a constant loop of negative shit running through my brain, okay?"

"They're just thoughts. You don't have to give them power."

"Don't go therapist on me. I don't fucking need it right now."

"Okay, okay." Her tone softened and she sat back. "I just want to help."

I dug in deeper. "You can't help."

"All right. Then I'll just say I'm really proud of you for having the guts to finally admit your feelings for Felicity and asking her to marry you. I know how hard that must have been. And I think you made the perfect choice. She's really amazing."

She was amazing. Goddammit.

"She's so good for you," Allie went on. "She's always understood you so well. You really need someone who's a safe place, someone to ground you. But also someone who can stand up to you when it's necessary."

"I know," I snapped. I didn't need to be told Felicity was one in a million. This wasn't helping.

"I'm just so glad you got out of your head and told her how you feel before it was too late. I mean, it took you long enough—but also, it came out of nowhere. One minute you won't even go to a reunion, and the next—poof, you're getting married."

I looked at her. "Allie."

"Yes?"

It was so obvious. "You know."

"Know what?" She blinked innocently at me. "That your sudden engagement is totally ridiculous? That it was a ploy to get Mom off your back? That you two *are actually in love* but somehow feel more comfortable faking it? Which thing that I know should we talk about first?"

"Fuck. Why didn't you say something?"

"What good would that have done? You two clearly had your reasons, you're consenting adults, and people work out their shit in different ways. I just figured this was your way of finally crossing the line without fear. If you could call it all for show, it was less pressure." She grinned. "Plus, it was a riot to watch you two react that morning at your house."

I groaned. "I can't believe you knew. You made us take all those pictures! You made us *kiss*."

"I know." She chuckled. "So did you guys plant the story yourselves?"

"Not exactly." Taking a deep breath, I launched into the story—how Felicity had blurted it out at the reunion, how she'd asked me to come rescue her, how the story had leaked, and how I'd convinced her to keep up the act.

"To get Mom off your back? Was I right about that?" she asked, since she was still my big sister, and being right mattered.

"Yes. Also . . ." I rubbed the back of my neck.

"Also, you wanted to be with her. And this handed you the opportunity without the vulnerability."

I frowned. "You don't have to make me sound like an asshole. We both agreed to the plan."

"I'm not here to judge you, Hutton." She sat back. "But I have a feeling something went wrong with your plan."

"Nothing was wrong with the plan," I argued. "The plan was perfect. What went wrong was that I tried to make it better, and she got mad."

She put her chin in her hand. "Go on."

"We were going to get through the party, then break it off and tell everyone we'd decided we were better off as friends when I went back to San Francisco."

"But then you realized you're in love with her and that plan sucks?"

I jumped out of my chair and started pacing. "Look, it doesn't really matter how I feel. We can't stay together."

"Why not?"

"We just can't, okay? I'm going back to San Francisco and her life is here."

She cocked her head. "So it's the distance?"

"Yes," I lied.

"But you're a billionaire. Can't you work from anywhere?"

Honestly, I probably could. But that wasn't the point. "No, I can't. I have to live where my company is based."

"Felicity won't move?"

"I didn't ask her." I avoided Allie's eyes.

"Why not?"

"Because her family is here, and her business is here, and she won't want to upend her life that way for me. Why should she? My relationships always end badly, and so do hers. We wanted something different. Something safer."

"Interesting choice of words," she mused. "So you thought you were protecting yourself by giving the relationship a deadline? That way neither of you would have to do the hurting or get hurt? You could stay friends?"

"Exactly!" I snapped my fingers, glad she finally understood. "Foolproof."

"So how did you attempt to improve upon this totally safe and foolproof plan?"

"We have to be out of the house we're in by August fifteenth," I explained. "But I suggested that I could rent or buy another place and she could live there when I go back to San Francisco. I was trying to do her a *favor*."

My sister's jaw dropped. "By suggesting she become a kept woman?"

"It wouldn't be like that. I care about her."

"But that's not what you said to her, is it?"

"She knows I care," I insisted.

"She doesn't know you love her."

I shook my head. "I can't tell her that."

"Because . . ."

"Because then I'm just like her mother, okay?" I yelled. "I'd have to say it and walk away, and I can't do that to her."

My sister rose to her feet. "You're missing the point—I'm suggesting that maybe you *don't* walk away, Hutton. You tell her you love her and you find a way to stay." She held up a hand to prevent me from arguing. "You accept that you're not perfect, you accept that you'll probably always have that shitty voice in your head, but you accept that you're still deserving and fucking *capable* of love. Or you let her go. That's your choice."

Infuriated, I stood there glaring at her for a full ten seconds, my jaw clenched, my chest tight, my head pounding. "I said no therapist shit."

"That wasn't therapy shit. That was big sister shit." She pointed to the yard. "Now you go out there and think about what you did."

While Allie ran errands, I hung out with the kids, took them to the park, made them lunch, and bought them ice cream from the truck Zosia and Jonas chased up the street. All afternoon, my sister's words ran through my head, but I refused to admit she was right.

I knew myself better than she did. What she was telling me to do was impossible.

"Why are you in such a bad mood?" asked Zosia as we walked home. Her ice cream was dripping all down her hand.

"I'm not." I glanced behind me to make sure Keely was okay in the wagon I was pulling.

"Yes, you are. You've been grumpy all day."

"I just bought you an ice cream cone, didn't I?"

"Yes," she allowed. Then she held it up toward me. "Want a lick?"

"No, thanks."

"When you get married, will Felicity be my aunt?"

It felt like she'd kicked me in the gut. "I guess so."

"And when you have kids, will they be my cousins?"

I swallowed hard. "They would."

"Cool. I want some cousins." Then out of nowhere, she said, "You'll be a good dad."

I stared down at her. "What makes you say that?"

"You like the park, you never care about getting sandy or messy or wet, and you buy us ice cream."

"That's all it takes to be a good dad?"

She shrugged. "Pretty much, yeah."

After Allie got back, she walked out to my car with me. "Good luck in D.C. Call me if you need a pep talk, okay?"

"Okay."

"What time is your flight?"

"Early. Six."

She stuck her hands in the back pockets of her shorts. "What will you do about Felicity?"

"I don't know." I exhaled. "First I have to get through that fucking hearing. And maybe after a few days apart, I'll be able to think more clearly."

She shrugged. "Sometimes distance does add perspective."

"I wish I could see the future," I blurted. "To know how it would play out."

"Me too." Allie spoke quietly. "But unfortunately, no matter what Mom thinks, there's no way to know what the future holds. No dream, no crystal ball, no palm reading, or tea leaves or tarot card is going to give you the answer."

"Yeah."

She gave me a hug, patting me on the back. "Even though we want the path to be clear and easy, the truth is, sometimes there's a lot of shit in the way. And the only way out is through."

Nineteen

Felicity

THE HAIRS ON THE BACK OF MY NECK STOOD ON END. "EXCUSE me?"

"Your engagement. It's all a lie." She snapped her fingers twice. "Keep up."

I forced myself to laugh. "What are you talking about?"

"I will admit you two put on a pretty good show at the reunion, but it never sat right with me—maybe you'd have made a cute couple back in high school, but a guy like Hutton is out of your league now."

"Well, I'm wearing a ring that says otherwise." I held my hand out, hoping she wouldn't see how my fingers trembled.

"Yes, I know all about the ring and the dress and the . . ." She brought her hand up like a blade and spoke on one side of her fingers, like a stage whisper. "Kink."

I sucked in my breath. "What?"

"I was there, at the coffee shop last Saturday morning. I came in after you were already there and sat in the booth right behind you, but you were *so* preoccupied with your story that you didn't even notice me. I do find it odd that you'd have sex with someone you're not even really dating."

"You were at Plum & Honey? Sitting behind me?"

She nodded, her eyes dancing. "I heard you say all kinds of interesting things."

I closed my eyes as the breath left my body, realizing too late it was a dead giveaway that everything she'd heard was true. "You're crazy."

"I have notes, in case your memory is faulty. I didn't want to forget a single word, so I wrote down what I was hearing." She picked up her phone from the bar and read, "'Things aren't like that with us. This isn't a real relationship or a real engagement. It's something I made up, remember?'" She looked up at me. "Does that ring a bell?"

I couldn't find words to answer.

"Oh, there's also this. 'I know it might look real on the outside, but that's just because we're having a good time. It's one hundred percent fake. We are not together.'" She set her phone down and picked up her wine glass. "I also heard the part about the safe word and the bloody nose—so good! I mean, really, this story has everything, humor, sex, deception . . ." She sipped her wine. "I was thoroughly entertained."

My pulse was racing. "Mimi, I have to go to work. I don't know what your problem is, but—"

She laughed. "I don't have a problem, Felicity. You do."

"And what's that?"

"I'm going to make sure this story gets out, and then what will your perfect family think? It's obvious to me only one sister knows you're scamming everyone."

"We're not scamming anyone," I snapped. "This is none of your business."

"Oh really? Because I was chatting with your mom at her coffee shop before I left on Saturday, and it was obvious she doesn't know you're a liar. She was just so happy."

"Leave my family out of this," I said through my teeth.

"And Hutton's family too. I happened to run into his

mother at her shop last week, and she was simply beside herself about your upcoming nuptials. She couldn't say enough sweet things about you." She picked up her wine for a sip.

I was seething. Nostrils flaring. I wanted to strangle her with her perfect blowout.

"I was also thinking," she said, swirling what was left of her wine, "how terrible it would be for Hutton if this got out. I know he's testifying this week down in D.C. The last thing he'd want people saying about him is that he's crooked and shady."

It was like a punch in the stomach. I could handle people talking shit about me, but I would not tolerate anyone implying Hutton was dishonest. If this story broke, it would cause his anxiety to skyrocket. He would imagine people calling him a con artist. Whispering behind their hands. Looking at him strangely. He'd probably suffer panic attacks, maybe even be unable to answer questions.

And it would be my fault. Not only for telling people we were engaged in the first place, but for talking about it being fake in a public place.

"Why are you doing this, Mimi?" I shook my head. "I don't get it."

She sat up taller on her stool, her expression imperious. "I'm doing this because I don't think it's right that people can just lie and get away with it."

"So you're doing this in the name of truth?"

"Exactly."

"Bullshit!" I was so loud that several people at the counter looked over at me. I lowered my voice only slightly. "You're doing this because you're jealous."

Mimi shrank back, her jaw dropping. She touched her chest. "Jealous? *Moi?*"

"Yes." Fired up, I gave her my meanest stare. "You. Are. Jealous."

She laughed, but it was one hundred percent fake. "What would *I* have to be jealous about?"

"I don't know. My ring? Hutton's money? The attention we're getting? Or maybe," I went on, remembering the way Thornton kept looking around and checking his watch at the reunion, "maybe it's my relationship with Hutton. The way we look at each other. Respect each other. How close we are."

"That won't last, you know," she said frostily. "Thornton used to look at me that way, the way Hutton looks at you. It goes away. The business trips get longer. The rumors about other girls will start. His clothes will smell like cheap perfume. His lies will get more clumsy, until he won't even bother to lie anymore."

I shook my head. "We're different."

"Anyway." She blinked back tears, the first crack in her armor I'd ever seen. "People deserve to know the truth. But I'm not totally heartless. I'm giving you a chance to offer your side of the story. Explain why you faked an engagement." She tilted her head. "Was it about money? Was he paying you to make him seem more normal? There are all those rumors about him being weird and anti-social. Then there are the things Zlatka said about him wanting to be cruel to her in the bedroom. Tie her up and boss her around."

Unwilling to give her the satisfaction of getting a rise out of me, I shook my head. "I have no comment."

"You don't want to defend yourself?"

"I haven't done anything wrong."

"You lied to me!"

"Okay, fine!" I tossed a hand up. "You want an explanation? Here it is. I was sick and tired of you making me feel small. You did it all through high school and I vowed that I was not going to let you do it again. So when you stood there at the reunion cutting me down to size, instead of telling you to fuck off like I should have, I made up the lie about being engaged to Hutton to save face."

"You did it for me?" She actually looked pleased.

"I did it to take you down a notch," I clarified.

"Oh." She looked less thrilled.

"I did it for girls like me who never had the guts to stand up for themselves in high school," I went on. "I did it because it's not okay to treat people like you're better than they are just because you have really great hair. And then I snuck off to a coat closet and called Hutton, begging him to come rescue me, even though he hated high school, hates parties, and dreads being in public."

"And he showed up?" She looked incredulous.

"Yes. He showed up. That's what friends like us do for each other."

"God. Thornton would *never* have done that for me. I had to drag him to that reunion, and he complained the whole time, even though I'd done so much work to put on a nice event. He doesn't appreciate me." Mimi pouted. "It's almost not even worth the money."

I rolled my eyes. "So find someone else."

"Easy for you to say." She scowled. "Everyone likes you. Everyone thinks you're so clever and talented and sweet. Even in high school, no one ever said a bad word about you."

"Mimi, give me a break. You were the most popular girl in school."

She shook her head. "They were scared of me. It's not the same as being liked."

"They were scared because you were mean. Why don't you try being kind?"

"Then I wouldn't be respected." She shrugged. "But I'll give it some thought. I've been working on self-love."

I held up my hands. "Look, I don't have time to argue

about this. What can I do to persuade you not to leak this story?"

"Nothing. I promised Thornton's sister a big story. She runs dirty-little-scoop-dot-com and she hates me, so I need this to butter her up. She's always in Thornton's ear saying shit about me."

"Can't you give her another scoop?"

"Do you have one?" she asked hopefully.

I chewed my lip. "No."

"Then I have to use you. Sorry." She started to get off the stool.

"Wait a minute." I put my hand on her arm. "Can you at least wait until after the weekend to tell her?"

Mimi thought for a minute. "I guess. What's in it for me?"

I exhaled through my nostrils. "I'll give you my side. Complete insider scoop."

One of her brows peaked. "Including the part about the kink?"

"No. But I'll spill everything else." At least this way, I could control the narrative. I'd make sure Hutton was spared any embarrassment, and I'd take full responsibility. I'd make him out to be a friend who'd come to my aide.

"When can it run?"

"Monday." That way the party would be over too. I felt horrible about it, but I didn't see a way to come clean in time for Mrs. French to call it off—there was only one day in between the hearing and the party. Maybe I could offer to cover the cost once all was said and done. That would make me feel better.

"Fine," said Mimi. "But you have to give me your side of the story this week."

"You'll get it no sooner than Sunday. I don't trust you."

Mimi looked offended. "I'm not a monster, Felicity. I'm just a woman looking out for herself."

I shook my head in disbelief. "You know, Mimi, there's something other than self-love I think you need to work on," I told her. "It's called empathy."

As horrifying as the conversation with Mimi had been, I couldn't help being sort of proud of myself for finally standing up to her. It felt good to call her out on her mean-girl behavior, even if I had to admit that I'd lied to out-Mimi her.

My first instinct was to tell Hutton about it, but then I remembered this morning—our first fight? The beginning of the end? The end of the beginning? Where were we now?

During my shift, I made up my mind that I would not tell him about the bullshit with Mimi before the hearing. He needed to be at his best over the next couple days, and the tension between us was stressful enough.

What would happen tonight when I got home? We hadn't spoken all day, and he was leaving first thing in the morning. Would he be asleep? Would he be awake and want to talk? Would he apologize for being insensitive earlier, or would he stubbornly refuse to see why I didn't like his idea?

When I arrived, I discovered that he'd already gone to bed, leaving just one light on for me in the living room. His roller bag was already by the front door, and his laptop case was beside it.

I locked the front door and went into the dark, silent bedroom. Quietly as possible, I undressed, pulled on a T-shirt, and went into the bathroom, pulling the door shut behind me. I switched on the light and saw Hutton's leather toiletry bag on the vanity, and beside it were the last few things he'd use tomorrow and then pack up.

I brushed my teeth, washed my face, and rubbed

moisturizer into my skin—that's when I thought of something I could do for Hutton that might make him a little less anxious.

It was a small thing, but hopefully it would help.

When I was ready for bed, I turned off the bathroom light, entered the bedroom, and slid beneath the sheets. Hutton's breathing was deep and even, and I made sure not to disturb him.

But it struck me that this was the first night I'd been here that we hadn't reached for each other in the dark.

Rolling away from him, I squeezed my eyes shut against the tears and curled into a ball.

When I woke up, he was gone.

Twenty

Hutton

I LISTENED TO HER COME IN, GET READY FOR BED, AND SLIDE IN beside me. But rather than pull her close like I wanted to, I feigned sleep.

My heart ached when she rolled away from me, and I heard her sniffle.

But I kept my eyes shut and my body still.

Avoidance was my specialty.

I arrived in D.C. exhausted and miserable, and spent the day being dragged around by Wade, who wanted me to schmooze a bunch of politicians ahead of tomorrow's hearing.

But schmoozing was not in my skill set on a good day. I was terrible at remembering names, I had no idea where anyone was from, my head was pounding, and Wade constantly telling me to chill the fuck out was not helping.

By five o'clock, I was beyond done.

I pulled Wade aside at the cocktail reception I was suffering through. "I'm going back to the hotel," I told him in a voice that said *don't fuck with me*. "I'll see you tomorrow."

"Dude, don't leave now. Orbach isn't even here yet."

I had no idea who Orbach was or why I needed to care that he hadn't arrived. "I'm out," I said. "Sorry."

Wade rolled his eyes. "Fine. I'll stay and gather the intel. We'll have breakfast tomorrow before the hearing. Answer your fucking phone in the morning."

Ducking out of the reception without another word, I caught a car back to the hotel, went up to my room, kicked off my shoes, took off my jacket and tie, and crashed. I hadn't slept at all last night, and I'd felt like a complete asshole leaving this morning without saying goodbye or even kissing her cheek. Instead, I'd left her a note on the counter.

Didn't want to wake you. I'll text you later.

Lame as fuck, and after I left, I thought of a hundred other things I could have and should have said.

Sorry about yesterday.

I was a dick.

Let's talk when I get home.

I'll miss you.

I buried my head under the pillow and fell asleep.

I woke up groggy and confused. It took me a minute to remember where I was. Checking my phone, I saw that I'd been asleep for three hours and had missed texts from my assistant in San Francisco, my mother, my sister, and Wade, but not Felicity.

My assistant wanted to make sure I had the most updated schedule for tomorrow. My mother wanted to make sure Felicity and I were still planning to meet her and my dad for dinner at Etoile Saturday night—the ruse for getting us to the party. My sister wanted to wish me luck and also offer advice about dealing with negative thoughts.

You can separate yourself from the thoughts. Create some space between yourself and those negative feelings. Acknowledge them, but don't struggle against them. The fight makes it worse. They're not as powerful as they seem.

Frowning, I set my phone down and rubbed my face. My stomach growled loudly, and I realized I hadn't eaten much of anything today. I scanned the QR code for the room service menu and ordered dinner. Then I took off my shirt and dress pants, tugged on some sweats, and opened my laptop to go over my notes.

But I couldn't think. I felt horrible about the silence between Felicity and me. Should I call her? She was at work, but she'd see it eventually. At least she'd know I was thinking about her, and that I cared enough to actually make a phone call.

Before I dialed, I rehearsed what I'd say. I even wrote it down on the hotel stationery.

Hey, I want to apologize about yesterday. I can see now that it wasn't a good idea. This thing with us has sort of taken me by surprise, and I'm not sure how to handle it. Anyway, I miss you and I'm sorry. Give me a call when you can.

I read it aloud ten times. Then I dialed her number.

My pulse kicked up a little as it rang, and I took a few deep breaths, scanning the words I'd scribbled out.

"Hello?"

Oh, shit. She answered. "Uh . . . hi."

"Hi."

"I didn't think you'd answer. I thought you were at work."

"I wasn't feeling well tonight. I took the night off."

"Are you okay?" I asked, immediately concerned.

"I'm fine. Just . . . needed a night off."

"Oh." I was scrambling for words when I heard another voice in the background. "Is someone there?"

"Millie. She's, um, helping me with something."

"Oh."

"She says good luck tomorrow."

"Tell her thanks." I looked at the handwritten message I'd planned to leave and wondered if I should still read it. I felt a little weird about it now that I knew she wasn't alone.

"How's your trip so far?"

"It's fine."

"How are you feeling about tomorrow?"

"Nervous."

"You're gonna be amazing. I know it."

"Thanks." I felt like a goose egg was stuck in my throat. "Felicity, I . . . I want to say something, but I don't know how."

"Hang on." Her voice grew muffled, but it sounded like she was telling Millie she was going outside for a minute. A moment later, she said, "What do you want to say?"

I love you. I need you. I want you in my life, by my side. Let's find a way to make it work.

But what I said was, "I'm sorry."

Silence. "For what?"

"For what I said yesterday morning. I shouldn't have made the offer about the house."

"Oh. It's okay," she said. "You did it to be nice. I understand."

It sounded like she might be crying, which made my chest feel like it was splitting in two. I was desperate to hold onto her, but I felt like my hands were tied. "You know I would do anything for you, if you asked."

"I know." Her voice trembled. "But some things you can't ask for."

"Felicity—"

"It was a good idea we had. To end things how we planned."

That caught me off guard. "What?"

"It's the right way. The only way. We'll get through the party, and then figure things out. But it's nothing you need to worry about now. Focus on the hearing, and we'll talk when you get back."

I tried to swallow and couldn't. "Is that what you want?"

"It's what we agreed to, Hutton." Her voice broke on my name. "It's how this was always going to end."

That night, when I got ready for bed, I found the small plastic bottle of lotion she'd tucked into my toiletry bag. At first, I thought she'd done it by mistake, but then I noticed she'd written on it—in one of those eyeliner pencils?—using our code.

Breathe, it said. *You got this.*

I unscrewed the top and held the lotion to my nose, inhaling. The lavender and vanilla scent hit me like a tidal wave.

Allie was right. Felicity was so good for me.

Was it possible I could be good enough for her?

Twenty-One

Felicity

I STOOD OUT ON HUTTON'S DECK FOR A FEW MINUTES, ALLOWING myself a good cry. Eventually, Millie came out with two glasses of wine.

She handed one to me. "Hey. Thought maybe you could use this. Hope Hutton doesn't mind I opened a bottle of wine."

"He won't. I probably bought it anyway. But what I really need is a tissue."

"Be right back."

She went into the house and returned a minute later with a box of Kleenex, setting it on the wooden rail. "Here you go."

"Thanks." I set my glass next to the box, plucked a tissue, and blew my nose.

"God, it's beautiful here." Millie breathed in the fresh, woodsy air. "I wouldn't want to leave either."

"It's not the view I'm going to miss most."

She glanced at me. "I know. I loaded the last bag in the car."

"Thanks. I promise I won't stay with you too long—just until after the party, when it will make more sense that I had to move out of here."

"You can stay with me as long as you need to." She sipped her wine. "So what did he say?"

"He said he was sorry for offering me a place to live when he leaves."

"That's it?"

"He also said he would do anything for me, if I asked."

Millie sighed. "But you can't ask him to love you."

"Nope," I said, my voice breaking again. "I can't."

All day Thursday, I kept checking the news online, hoping to hear how the hearing was going. It was live-streamed, but I couldn't bring myself to watch it, scared that I would either jinx him or fall apart.

Finally, my search results turned up a nine-minute video of hearing highlights with key takeaways by a few talking heads. I watched the entire thing, gasping when they showed a clip of Hutton speaking. I could tell he was nervous, and he kept his eyes on his notes, but his voice was strong, he sounded smart and confident, and the talking heads commented that of all the crypto CEO's who spoke today, "Hutton French was the most articulate, and gave measured, thoughtful answers to all questions, admitting when something was uncertain and offering solutions that addressed major concerns."

I nearly wept with relief.

I was watching it a second time, sitting at Millie's table having an early dinner before going into work, when Winnie walked in.

"Oh, hey," she said, clearly surprised to see me. "I need to borrow Millie's hand mixer, and she said I should just come get it. Mine broke. What are you doing here?"

"Um . . ." My mind searched frantically for an excuse before I gave up. "Actually, I'm staying here right now."

Winnie's eyes widened. "What? Why? Did you and Hutton have a fight?"

"Not exactly." Tears filled my eyes, and I tried to blink them away. "We're just taking a little time-out."

"A time-out? But you just got engaged! Your party is in two days!" Her eyes narrowed. "Is that why you cut those bangs?"

I pushed my salad around on the plate. "Yeah."

Winnie sat down at the table. "Need to talk?"

"There's really not much to talk about. We're just—thinking things over. Taking a step back." I tried to smile, but it was pretty pathetic. "We did move kind of fast."

Winnie was distressed. "I guess, but . . . but you've been so close for so many years! You had these feelings buried deep inside you! He was pining for you from afar, and you were locked in a tower of longing, knowing you were meant to be, and suddenly there he was!"

I raised my eyebrows. "Wow. A tower of longing?"

She waved a hand in the air. "I'm a romantic, okay? Sue me."

"Look, it's just not that simple." I picked up my plate and went over to the sink. "Hutton and I both have some baggage that makes it difficult to trust."

"Everyone has baggage! Dex's baggage could sink a ship! His parents' marriage was awful, his dad was absent and emotionally abusive, his divorce was difficult, he's a single dad . . . believe me, it was not easy to work through. But if you love each other, you do the work."

"I get it." I stared out the window over the sink. "And maybe we'll figure it out."

"You have to. You love each other . . . right?" Winnie sounded scared.

"There is love between us," I said carefully.

She was silent for a minute. "What should I do about the party?"

"Nothing." I turned around and faced her. "Just let it go on as planned. We don't want to cause anyone any stress."

"But if you guys aren't even together, what's the point?"

"We're not *not* together," I said, attempting to inject a little hope into my voice.

"So why are you living with Millie?"

"For some space. But Winnie, you can't tell anyone I'm here." I spoke seriously. "I mean it—not Mom, not Dad, not Hutton's family, not anyone. I know it's hard for you to keep secrets, but I need you to keep this to yourself."

"I promise," she said solemnly. "I'm locking my lips and throwing away the key." She mimed turning a key in front of her mouth and tossing it away.

"Thank you."

"But I'm really sad about this." Her shoulders slumped. "I love you guys together. I want you to have a happily ever after."

My breath hitched, and I tamped down the sob threatening to erupt. "We'll always be friends, no matter what. That might be what our happily ever after looks like, okay?"

She folded her arms and pouted. "No. That is not how a romance ends. I don't accept it."

I had to laugh, even though the sadness was heavy in my heart. "Try. I will too."

Before leaving for work, I sent Hutton a text. Congratulations on the hearing. I'm very happy for you. Have a safe trip back.

Fighting tears, I stuck my phone in my bag and went out the front door.

He'd find the letter when he got home tomorrow.

Twenty-Two

Hutton

I READ THE TEXT MESSAGE FROM FELICITY AND FROWNED. NOT because it wasn't kind, but because it didn't sound like her—there was no levity, no joy, no smile behind the words. She said she was happy, but it was obvious she wasn't.

She was hurt, and she was pulling away from me.

My initial thought about the distance between us being helpful seemed ludicrous now. I missed her too much. I wanted to hear her voice. I wanted to call her and tell her how much it meant that she'd stuck that lotion in my bag, how I'd put it on my hands and occasionally brought my knuckles to my nose during the hearing to inhale the scent, how it helped keep me grounded in the moment and prevented my mind from spiraling.

Had my performance been perfect? No. I sweated profusely for five straight hours, struggled to breathe normally, and battled the urge to bolt for the exit sign when it was my turn to be questioned.

But I'd gotten through it. I'd faced the lions and won, or at least hadn't let *them* win.

It was enough. And it was her victory too—why wasn't she here with me to celebrate it?

"Dude, come on. Let's go get drunk." Wade came up behind me in the hallway and shouldered me forward. "This smokin' hot intern told me where she and her friends hang out after work. She said they'll be there by five-thirty."

"I'm not interested."

Wade groaned. "You're never interested. But you killed it in there, don't you want to celebrate? One drink. Come on."

A drink did sound good. My nerves were totally shot. "Fine, one drink. But I'm not going to some bar crowded with interns. Let's just grab a drink somewhere close, then I'll go back to the hotel."

"You're such a fucking old lady. But fine." He slung an arm around my neck. "Let's go."

"So what's the deal with this engagement?" Wade asked after we'd rehashed the hearing. "You really gonna marry this chick?"

I took a swallow of whiskey. "I don't want to discuss it."

He laughed. "Trouble in paradise already?"

I remained silent. Took another sip.

"Listen, I get it. Women are a fucking pain in the ass. They're never satisfied. You give them one thing, and then they want more. They say they don't want you to change, but they do. They claim they're happy if you're happy, but that's the biggest fucking lie of all." Wade finished off his drink and put his hand up to order another. "They don't want you to be happy. They want you to be miserable, and they go at it like it's their *job*."

"Felicity isn't like that."

"Well, she's not like that *now*. But it changes once that ring is on your finger. Mark my words."

"I've known her for fifteen years. She'd never want anyone to be miserable, least of all me."

Wade shrugged. "If you say so. But think about it—marriage is fucking permanent. You can't just get out of it. One woman until the end. One body. One piece of ass for the rest of your life."

I frowned at him. "You're a dick."

He laughed and picked up his second drink. "I'm just trying to be a good friend, dude. Warn you about what's ahead—but if you like eating the same meal every night until the end of time, be my guest and get married. Because that's what it's like. Even if the steak is good, you get bored. And I can't help it if I sometimes want to taste something else."

"If you don't stop talking, I might actually punch you in the face."

Wade looked at me in surprise. "What's your problem?"

"My problem is that I love this woman you're talking about like she's a fucking piece of meat. And I can't think of anything better than having her to myself for the rest of my life. The thought of being with someone else is absurd. The thought of *her* being with someone else makes me want to put my fist through the wall. The thought of losing her because I'm a fucking idiot is unacceptable."

Wade shrugged. "Okay. Then get married. But don't blame me when it all goes to hell and you wish you were banging hot interns instead of getting your ass chewed out."

"I have to go." I pulled out my wallet and threw some cash on the bar.

"When are you back in the office?"

"I don't know." I stood up, stood taller. "Maybe never."

"Huh? What the fuck does that mean?"

"It means I did what I came here to do, but it doesn't matter as much as I thought it would—or rather, the reason it matters has nothing to do with HFX, and everything to do with me realizing I might fail but taking the risk anyway, because not taking it would have been the greater failure."

"Dude. You lost me."

"Never mind." I was already heading for the door.

Losing Wade, I could handle.

Losing Felicity, no fucking way.

In the car on the way back to the hotel, I changed my flight so I could get out of D.C. tonight. Then I packed in a hurry and raced to the airport.

It was late when I got home, after midnight, so I wasn't surprised that all the lights were off. I let myself in, dumped my bags at the door, and rushed into the dark, silent bedroom.

"Hey." I sat down on her side of the bed and put a hand out. "I'm home."

But she wasn't there. I felt around for a few seconds, then panicked and switched on the lamp. The bed was empty.

I jumped to my feet. "Felicity?"

No answer.

Frantic, I checked the bathroom and noticed all her things were gone. I looked in the guest bedroom across the hall, even out on the deck. I went downstairs and looked in every room. I went into the garage—her car was gone.

"Fuck!" I pulled the door shut and went into the kitchen, my heart racing.

That's when I saw the envelope on the island. It was white, and my name was written on it in her loopy, girlish handwriting.

My chest grew tighter as I ripped it open, smoothed out the page, and began to read.

Dear Hutton,

By now you've realized that I moved out while you were in D.C. I'm so sorry for doing it without telling you, but I didn't want you to be worried or distracted during the hearing. You needed to be able to focus one hundred percent on your testimony. I didn't want to add any additional stress.

I think this time apart is a good thing. As much as I have loved living with you and pretending to be a couple, it feels like the right time to step back from the fantasy and remember what's real.

If you could please respect my need for a little space, I'd really appreciate it. I'll get in touch on Saturday and we can make a plan for attending the party. Maybe on Sunday we can discuss the best way to handle the breakup where our families are concerned.

I hope you don't think I'm upset with you—I'm not. I am upset, but only with myself for getting carried away. I forgot that it was all for show, and my feelings for you have grown beyond make-believe.

This isn't your fault.

I'll never forget this time we had together.

Love,

Felicity

P.S. I have been and always shall be your friend.

The postscript was written in code, and that, almost more than anything else, made my throat constrict and my heart threaten to splinter.

I had to fix this. I had to win her back.

Friday morning, I skipped my run and showed up at my sister's house before eight a.m.

She looked surprised when she answered my knock. "You're back already?"

"Yeah. Can I come in?"

"Of course!" She grabbed me in a hug. "Congratulations. You did so great!"

"Thanks."

"How'd you get through it? Was it my stellar advice?"

"Your suggestions did help," I admitted. "Thanks for the text."

"You're welcome." She let me go and gave me a smug grin. "The things I said were based on the principles of acceptance and commitment therapy, by the way. I asked Natalia for a few ideas. She's still open to talking with you."

"I might take her up on that." I exhaled and adjusted the cap on my head. "But first, I need your advice."

Her jaw dropped. She put a hand by her ear. "Did I hear that right?"

"Please don't joke. This is serious."

She studied my face. "Okay. Want something to eat? Coffee?"

"Coffee sounds good. I didn't sleep much."

"I can tell. You've got some major circles under those eyes."

I sat at the table. "Where are the kids?"

"They slept at Mom and Dad's. I have early appointments this morning, so I have to be at the office in about forty-five minutes." She brought me a mug of black coffee and sat down. "Speak."

"Felicity moved out while I was gone. She did it without telling me."

She nodded. "How do you feel about that?"

"At first I was angry that she just up and left without saying anything—we've been friends a long time, and it felt shitty."

"That's understandable."

"But she left me this letter that explained why she moved out, and it fucking tore me apart inside."

"What did she say?"

"She said she didn't want to tell me because she didn't want me to have additional stress while I was in D.C."

"That was thoughtful of her."

"She said she left because she needed to step back from the fantasy of being a couple and remember what was real.

She said she got carried away and her feelings grew beyond make-believe."

Allie nodded. "She's scared. She ran away."

"She said it's not my fault and she doesn't blame me."

"Do you blame yourself?"

"Yes. No. I don't know." I leaned forward, elbows on the table, head in my hands. "She's everything to me, Allie."

"She needs to hear that."

"She told me not to contact her. She asked me to respect her need for space."

"What about the party?"

"She said she'll call me tomorrow and we'll make a plan to attend it, and then afterward figure out how to end things." I jumped up. "But I can't let that happen. I can't go a day without trying to get her back."

Allie looked surprised. "Okay."

"That's why I need your advice." I started to pace. "What can I say to convince her to give me another chance? How can I prove to her that she can trust me?"

"You could start with telling her how you feel," she suggested. "If you love her, she needs to hear it."

"I do love her. I do. But . . ." I stopped in my tracks. "I can't get over this fucking thing in my head telling me I'm not good enough for her."

My sister shrugged. "Maybe you're not."

I stared at her. "Huh?"

"I mean, maybe the thing in your head is right. Maybe you're not good enough for her. Maybe you're going to fuck it up. Maybe she'll decide you're not worth the trouble."

I frowned at her. "You're not helping."

"But *maybe*," she went on, "*maybe* you risk it. Maybe you get to spend the rest of your life doing things to make every day better for her. You've already got her heart, Hutton. So

maybe you find ways—big and small—to deserve it forever."
She tilted her head. "Doesn't that sound like a nice way to live?"

I could picture it—life unfolding in a series of days, some good, some bad, but all of them worth living, because she was mine and I was hers and we would always have each other.

But first, I had to find her.

"Thanks," I said as I ran for the door.

"You're welcome!" she called after me. "I'll bill you for the session!"

I drove by her parents' house, but her car wasn't there. I wasn't sure where else she might be staying—with one of her sisters?—so I drove home and called her before going in the house.

As I suspected, her voicemail picked up. I left a message. "Hey, it's me. I found your letter. I want to respect your need for space, but I also really want to talk to you. Can you call me back please?"

Inside the house, I began to overthink every single word I'd said in the message and wondered if she'd even think twice before deleting it. But when I caught my mind getting stuck in that negative loop, I decided to go work out instead of sit there and speculate about how she might react. I pictured her making her little witch hat over her head, and she'd be right. I was letting fear have too much power. I needed to give her a chance to think and breathe.

But when she hadn't called me back by two o'clock, I was losing my mind. I drove by her folks' house again, but her car still wasn't there. I had no idea where either of her sisters lived, but I knew one of them worked at Cloverleigh Farms and one worked at Abelard Vineyards.

Abelard was closer, so I headed up Old Mission Peninsula.
After parking in the guest lot, I rushed into the lobby of

the French chateau-inspired inn, and frantically looked around. A few people stared at me, and I started to sweat. "Can I help you?"

I looked at the reception desk, where a young woman stood smiling at me. I had no idea what to say. I may have grunted.

"Hutton?"

When I heard my name, I spun around and saw Felicity's sister Winnie standing there.

"What are you doing here?" she asked.

"Can I talk to you?" I strode toward her. "Please?"

She looked nervous. "Um, okay. Let's go to my office."

I followed her into an office off the lobby. "Thanks," I said as she sat down behind her desk. "I appreciate this."

"Of course." She gestured to the chairs across from her. "Please have a seat."

But I was too worked up to sit. "I need your help," I blurted.

"Okay." Her fingers kneaded together. Two lines appeared between her brows.

"I'm looking for Felicity. Do you know where she might be?"

"Do I know where she might be?" she repeated.

"Yes."

"Um." She looked off to one side. "I can't say."

"Winnie, please. I need to talk to her. It's important."

A high-pitched whimper escaped her, and she began to rock back and forth. "But I promised."

"Okay. Okay." I sat down in one of the chairs. "I know she probably told you not to say anything to anyone. But did she specifically mention me?"

"No," she admitted, still not meeting my eyes. "But she said not to tell anyone. And I can't let her down."

"I understand." I took a breath. "But this is sort of an emergency."

She looked at me. "Are you okay?"

"Yes and no. I will be if I can talk to Felicity. There's something I have to tell her."

Winnie continued to rock back and forth, murmuring to herself. "I can keep a secret. I can keep a secret."

"I'll give you a billion dollars." I was only half-kidding.

She reached over to her tape dispenser, ripped off a piece and put it over her mouth.

I blinked at her. "Is that necessary?"

She nodded, ripped off two more pieces and taped her mouth shut.

"Okay." I held up my hands. "I get it. You don't want to betray her, and I appreciate that. But . . ." I closed my eyes and exhaled. "I've never been in love before, and I'm not handling it very well."

She made a little squeak of surprise, or maybe sympathy. Her blue eyes were bright.

"I don't know what I'm doing. I'm scared every word out of my mouth will be wrong. I'm scared she won't believe me when I tell her how much she means to me. I'm scared that I blew my chance to be with the only girl who has ever made me feel like I'm okay."

Winnie squeezed her eyes shut and sighed. Then she peeled off the tape. "You didn't. You can win her back. But maybe it should be something more than words."

"Like what? Tell me," I begged. "I'll do whatever it takes."

She thought for a moment. "You know, Felicity has always been a little different from Millie and me," Winnie said. "Smarter and quieter and not into the same kinds of things we were. She was never overly obsessed with clothes or makeup or boys. When we played Cinderella as kids, I was the princess, Millie was the fairy godmother or the evil stepmother, depending on her mood, and you know what Felicity always wanted to be?"

"What?"

"Merlin the wizard."

It made me smile, despite everything.

"We'd be like, 'There's no wizard in this story! Can't you be the prince?' And she'd be all, 'No! The prince sucks! What does he do to deserve her, ask her to dance? Kiss her? He never knows a thing about her, not even her name!'"

"I mean, she's not wrong," I said.

"So she put Merlin the wizard into Cinderella. And somehow, in the end, it was always Merlin's magic that really saved the day." Winnie laughed. "I guess what I'm trying to say is, Felicity doesn't *need* a prince. She doesn't *need* to be rescued. But . . ." She shrugged. "Every girl wants to feel like a princess sometimes."

"I understand." I paused. "No, I don't."

Winnie laughed gently. "You know her, Hutton. I think you can figure this out."

Something came to me. "Can you get a message to her?"

Winnie nodded.

"Do you have a piece of paper I could use? And a pen?"

She took a sheet of paper from her printer and slid it across the desk for me along with a pen.

Using our code, I wrote the only words I knew she couldn't ignore. *I need you. Please be there for me.* Then I folded the paper and handed it to Winnie. "You're a good sister."

She smiled. "Thank you. My family is everything to me."

Outside, I took a few deep breaths and turned my face to the sky, praying for inspiration to strike me. Why hadn't I watched more romantic movies in my life? There were never any big romantic gestures in science fiction. A jet went by overhead, leaving a white trail against the bright blue.

That's when it hit me.

Twenty-Three

Felicity

WHEN I GOT TO WORK FRIDAY, GIANNI TOLD ME WINNIE wanted to see me. "She's been in here a couple times looking for you," he said. "She tried calling and texting but said you didn't respond."

"Yeah, I'm taking a break from my social media, and it seemed easier to just take a break from my phone altogether," I said. "I'll go see what she wants."

I found Winnie in the lobby, directing guests to the patio, where a rehearsal dinner was taking place. "Hey," I said. "You were looking for me?"

"Yes. Hutton was here." She beamed. "But I kept the secret. I had to tape my mouth shut, but I kept it."

"Today?" My voice rose. "He was here today?"

"Yes. Earlier this afternoon."

"What did he want?" My heart had started to race.

"To know where to find you. I didn't tell him," she added quickly. "But I promised to give you this." She reached into her pants pocket and pulled out a small, folded square.

[A handwritten coded message made of dots and lines]

I took it from her and unfolded it.

It took me less than ten seconds to decode the dots and lines on the page. My eyes filled.

"What is it?" Winnie asked. "Some kind of secret language?"

"Yes." I sniffed. "It says 'I love you.' But it's written in the code we promised each other we'd always honor."

"Aww, that's so cute. He looked really miserable—he does love you, Lissy. So much."

"You think so?"

"Of course I do! He told me he's never been in love before, and he doesn't know what he's doing, and he's scared he blew his only chance to be with the one person who means everything to him."

Goosebumps blanketed my arms. "He said all that?" *He loves me. He loves me.*

"Yes! And I'm sure I was not supposed to tell you any of it, but in my defense, I did make it obvious I'm terrible at keeping secrets. He also offered me a billion dollars for your whereabouts." She lifted her chin. "I want you to know I didn't take the money."

I laughed. "Thank you."

She bent down in a little curtsy. "You're welcome. I think maybe you should hear him out, Felicity. Guys aren't perfect, you know? Sometimes they need a second chance to get something right."

Later that night, when I got back to Millie's, I called him.

"Hello?"

I couldn't help smiling. "That's new. I was expecting your usual greeting."

"I'm working on some things about myself."

"Good for you." I paused. "I got the bat signal. Are you okay?"

"No. There's something I have to tell you, or it's going to eat me alive."

"Okay."

"Can I see you?"

"I guess so. I'm at Millie's."

"Text me the address," he said. "I'll be there as fast as I can."

We hung up, and I sent him Millie's address. I had just enough time to change out of my work uniform into shorts and a T-shirt, and although I debated fussing with my hair and makeup, I decided against it. Hutton knew what I looked like morning, noon, and night. I didn't need to paint my face for him.

But I did take the ring from the blue box and slip it on my finger.

When he pulled up, I was sitting on the porch with my arms wrapped around my knees. My pulse skittered as he came up the front walk. "Hey," I said, getting to my feet.

"Hey." His smile was boyish and charming. "Will you go for a drive with me?"

"Sure."

He took my hand and led me to the passenger side of his car, where he opened the door for me and closed it after I got in. A few minutes later, we were heading toward town.

"Are we going anywhere in particular?" I asked.

"You'll see."

I tried to guess where he might be taking me, but we stayed in so much that there weren't a lot of places that had a ton of memories for us besides his house. Since we weren't going in that direction, I was completely baffled.

For a moment, I wondered if he was taking me to some airfield where a private jet was going to whisk us away to some exotic location. I hoped not—I didn't want him to think that I needed those kinds of things to be happy.

I shouldn't have worried. Hutton knew me better than that. Even better, he knew us.

We pulled up behind the public library, where a little old lady was waiting by the door with a set of keys. She was short and plump and had a head full of coppery curls.

"There you are," she whispered excitedly. "I was getting nervous."

"Sorry, Gladys. Thanks a lot for this."

"You're welcome, dear. I'm glad to help." She unlocked the door and put a finger over her mouth. "Don't turn any lights on, okay?"

Hutton nodded. "We won't be long."

"I'll just wait in my car." Gladys looked back and forth between the two of us and sighed before hurrying over to a Buick, the only other car in the lot.

"What on earth?" I whispered as Hutton took my hand and pulled me through the dark, silent library. "Why are we here?"

"I need a second chance at something." He led me into the study room off the main section of the library, and over to the table where we'd once sat studying for our AP calculus exam.

I laughed softly as Hutton pulled out the chair for me. "Thank you."

He sat down next to me. "I don't know what would have happened if I'd had the nerve to kiss you that night. But I do know that I have always regretted not taking that chance when I had it."

"Is this a do-over?" I asked, my heart pounding just as hard as it had been when I was seventeen.

"It's a do-better." He leaned in, his lips nearly touching mine, and paused. "You're not chewing gum, are you?"

I shook my head.

"Good." Taking my head in his hands, he pressed his lips to mine, sending sparks shooting every which way beneath my skin. "Everything is going to be different from now on."

"It is?"

"Yes. That night, you told me something you'd never told anyone before. I'm going to return the favor."

"Okay." I tried to swallow and found it difficult.

"I love you, Felicity. I've always loved you. And if you'll let me, I will love you for the rest of my life."

I gasped. "Oh my God. Hutton, I—"

"Hold on. I want to hear every single word you want to say, but I'm afraid if I don't get everything out all at once, I'll lose my nerve. Or I'll forget something important."

"Okay," I said, laughing softly.

"That day my family showed up at my house and I asked you to keep pretending we were engaged, it wasn't only because I wanted my mother off my back. It was because I wanted the chance to *be* with you without the risk of losing you. I didn't trust myself not to screw things up. I didn't believe that someone like me could hold onto someone like you. I was convinced that if you got close enough, you'd see all my flaws and idiosyncrasies and know you could do better."

"All I want is you," I whispered. "But I understand your fear. I was scared too. I thought I could ration my feelings the way I usually did."

"Like truffles?"

I smiled. "Like truffles. But it didn't work. Every day we were together I just fell deeper and deeper."

"I did too," he said. "I was a wreck when we got home from New York."

"Same! Even *in* New York—that day I tried on the dress." I shook my head. "I knew it wasn't just a dress, no matter what you said."

"You were right."

"And the ring." I looked down at my hand, at the band circling my finger. "You gave me a real ring."

"I wanted to buy you all the real things, because my feelings were real. But it was easier to spend money than to admit them."

"Let's make a promise that we'll be honest with each other from now on."

"Deal."

"Is this where I can tell you I love you too?"

He smiled. "Sure."

"I love you too—everything about you. What you see as flaws and idiosyncrasies are what make you different and special. I'm not perfect either," I said with a laugh. "I'll probably always cut my hair when I'm stressed, never walk right in high heels, and continue to blurt random things when I'm nervous."

"I might think you were the wrong girl if you didn't."

"And I know that you might not always be in touch with your earthy bull feelings, but I promise to be patient and not snatch them back into my little crab shell."

"Good." He leaned forward and kissed me. "Because there's only one crab for me."

"So what happened that made you realize all this?"

He laughed. "My sister. Turns out, she knew the engagement was bullshit, but she didn't say anything, because she thought it was just how we were working up the nerve to admit how we felt for real."

I gasped. "Just like Millie!"

"She saw me wrestling with my feelings and pretty much told me I had to get over myself or let you go." He shook his head. "Letting you go was not an option. So here we are."

"Here we are." I smiled and glanced around. "How *are* we here, anyway?"

"Turns out, one of the Prancin' Grannies is the boss here."

"Gladys?"

"Gladys." He shrugged. "Also I made a very large donation to the Friends of the Public Library Foundation."

I laughed. "Will there be a Hutton French wing sometime next year?"

"Possibly." He took my hand again, playing with my fingers. "What are the chances I can get you to come home with me tonight?"

"Hmm. Are we talking theoretical probability here?"

He shrugged. "If you insist."

"Then I would say the desired outcome is highly likely. In fact, I would say it is a mathematical certainty."

The following morning, Hutton woke up early as usual for his run, but I grabbed his arm and snatched him back into bed. "Five more minutes," I begged.

Laughing, he pulled me close once more, and we lay tangled up in each other as the sunlight streamed through the window. We hadn't even bothered pulling the drapes closed last night, we'd been in such a hurry to tear each other's clothes off. Our reunion had been hot and frantic at first—we'd gone at each other as if we'd been apart for months, not days. But the second round was slower and sweeter, like we were settling into it and knew we didn't have to rush. There was no deadline, no end in sight. No one was going to take this feeling from us.

"So about tonight," he said, brushing his hand up and down my naked back. "I have a surprise for you."

"You do?" I smiled and snuggled closer.

"Yes—that is, if I have permission to surprise you."

"You do." I giggled. "I like your surprises."

"I just have one request. Can I pick you up for the party at your sister Millie's house?"

"Sure. But why?"

"If I tell you, that will spoil the surprise." He kissed the top of my head. "You just have to trust me."

"I do." I closed my eyes, blissfully happy. "I do trust you."

"I haven't mentioned this yet, but I told Wade I'm not coming back to San Francisco."

I picked up my head and stared at him. "What? You're leaving HFX?"

"I haven't decided that yet. But I want to live here—with you. I'll start looking for a new place this week."

My eyes filled. "Really? You'll stay here? Because I'd go with you to California if that's what you wanted. My business can go anywhere with me."

"Nah. I've had enough of that life. I like it here. My family is here, your family is here, it's peaceful and quiet . . . I don't want to leave."

I put my cheek back on his chest, and he held me tight.

"Everything is going to be okay," he promised.

It felt like a dream, but we were finally real.

Twenty-Four

Felicity

MY SISTERS HELPED ME GET READY.

Winnie came over to Millie's house—Hallie and Luna in tow—with an entire suitcase full of shoes, accessories, and cosmetics. While Millie blew out my hair, Winnie painted my nails and the girls came over with one pair of heels after another, slipping them on my feet and standing back to judge them.

"This is like Cinderella's stepsisters after the ball," said Luna excitedly.

"Except she's not mean or ugly and all the shoes fit," Hallie pointed out.

I laughed. "Which one do you think will go best with the dress?"

"The sparkly ones!" Luna said, pointing at my left foot. It was a sandal with rhinestone-studded straps and dangerously high heels. "Those look the most like glass slippers."

"Of course you'd pick those. Isn't there a princess who wore sneakers?"

"No. What should we do with her hair?" Millie asked Winnie.

"Hmmm." Winnie wrapped one arm around her middle and tapped her lips with a finger. "What about a high bun? Sort of an Audrey Hepburn look?"

Millie nodded. "That could work."

I slipped the dress on, Millie put up my hair, and Winnie did my makeup. Hallie and Luna helped me strap on the shoes, and then all four of them stood back and looked at me.

"Well?" I asked, turning in a circle. "How do I look?"

"Perfect." Millie's eyes were shining.

"I love that dress," Luna gushed.

"Yes, even the hair isn't bad." Hallie nodded her approval. "I like it!"

I took one final look in Millie's full-length mirror and had to admit I'd never felt so pretty. Maybe I didn't have Winnie's golden hair or Millie's curves, but I was me, and I looked *good*. "Thanks, you guys."

"I thought the party was a surprise," said Luna. "How come you know about it?"

"Because Winnie can't keep secrets," Hallie reminded her.

"Shhh." I held a finger to my lips. "We're going to pretend I didn't know. You all look wonderful too. I'm so glad you'll all be there tonight."

A moment later, there was a knock at the door.

"I'll get it!" Both younger girls took off running for the stairs. The next thing I heard was loud squealing and clapping.

My sisters raced out of Millie's room. I took one last look in the mirror, picked up my tiny evening bag, and carefully wobbled out to the top of the stairs. I held onto the banister and started down, but I only got halfway before I saw Hutton standing at the bottom, looking up at me.

My breath caught. He wore a black suit, white shirt, and the blue tie he'd worn to the reunion, the one that matched his eyes. His hair was combed in that movie star way that made my insides dance—although that one contrary piece had sprung loose—and his scruff was trimmed close.

Best of all was the way he looked at me.

"You're so beautiful," he said quietly, shaking his head like he couldn't believe his eyes.

"Thank you." I reached the bottom, and he took my hand.

"He rode here in a carriage, Felicity!" Hallie jumped up and down, clapping her hands.

"With two white horses!" Luna added, pushing the door open for us.

I looked at Hutton, my mouth agape. "Is this *true*?"

He shrugged. "I heard that was how billionaires got around back in the day."

Laughing, I stepped onto the porch and sucked in my breath, bringing both hands to my cheeks. "Oh my God!"

At the curb was an open white carriage, the kind tourists rent to be driven around town during the summer, harnessed to two beautiful white horses.

"Our driver's name is Alfred," said Hutton, offering his arm. "And he did warn me that it will take a little longer to get to Abelard by horse than by car, so we should probably get moving."

"Wait, let me take a picture!" Millie raced back into the house and came out with her phone.

We posed for a few photos, then Hutton helped me into the carriage. The driver tipped his hat in my direction. "Miss."

"Hello, Alfred," I said. "Nice to meet you."

"We'll see you there!" Winnie called, while Hallie and Luna looked wistfully at the carriage. "And remember—you never knew about the party!"

I laughed and blew them a kiss. Hutton climbed in next to me and sat down. A moment later, we were on our way.

I took his hand in mine. "I cannot believe you did this. For someone who doesn't like to be the center of attention, this is insane. Are you really Hutton French, the friend I've known for fifteen years?"

He laughed. "Yes and no. I'm really Hutton French, but I don't want to be just your friend anymore."

"Good. Because I'm wildly in love with you."

His eyes traveled over me. "You're stunning, Felicity. I know I have to share you with a lot of people tonight, but I can't wait to take you home."

My face warmed. "I missed you so much while you were gone. I hated sleeping alone."

"You don't ever have to sleep alone again, if you don't want to." He took my hand. "I meant what I said last night. I want to love you forever."

"That's what I want too." Scooting closer to him, I rested my head on his shoulder, and he wrapped an arm around me. The sun was warm on my face, and I closed my eyes. "So what now? Should we just pretend like we've decided to postpone the wedding? We can always say that Millie couldn't—"

"Hey." He gave me a squeeze. "How about we just enjoy the ride for now?"

I smiled. "Sounds good to me."

About thirty minutes later, the carriage turned into the drive-way of Abelard Vineyards. I sat up and smoothed the full skirt of my dress.

That's when Hutton groaned. "Oh, Jesus."

"What?"

He pointed a little way up the drive. "Looks like our public is here to greet us."

I looked up and started to laugh. The Prancin' Grannies, all decked out in their pink bedazzled shirts, lined either side of the gravel road, waving and shouting. "Hello! Congratulations! We're so happy for you!"

I recognized Gladys as I waved back and smiled, calling out, "Thank you!"

"One of them—Mona—is married to Alfred," he explained. "That's how I arranged this so quickly."

"Wow, you and the Grannies are tight these days," I teased.

"They were very eager to help me make this special for you."

"Awww. That's so nice of them."

The carriage pulled up to Abelard's entrance, and Hutton helped me down. "We might have to invite them to our wedding."

My heart thumped hard as my feet hit the ground. "Our what?"

He pointed to the sky, and I followed the line of his finger.

And gasped—there in the sky was a small airplane with a banner behind it that read *Felicity, will you marry me?*

Stunned, I looked at Hutton, who'd gone down on one knee.

"This is the real thing," he said, taking my left hand in both of his. His mouth hooked into a boyish grin. "I already got you the ring, and you're already wearing the dress, so I thought maybe I should ask you the real question."

"Oh my God." I touched my heart with my free hand. "Oh my God, I can't believe this is happening."

"Felicity MacAllister, I've loved you longer than you know, and there will never be another human on this earth that matters more to me. I may not have magic powers, but you understand me, you accept me, you make me happy. I know this is probably a shock to you, and if you don't want to say yes today, that's okay too, but you are the only one for me, today and always."

"Yes," I said, tears slipping down my cheeks. "Of course yes! A thousand times yes!"

He stood up and embraced me, our lips meeting in the sweetest, realest kiss we'd ever shared. Behind him the Prancin' Grannies cheered, and even the horses whinnied their approval.

I smiled up at Hutton. "You *do* have magic powers—you turned this thing into a *real* engagement party!"

He held a finger to his lips.

I laughed, happier than I'd ever been. "I'll never tell."

"What do you say, ladies? Alfred?" Hutton turned to our audience. "Would you like to join us?"

"We thought you'd never ask," said a granny with thick penciled-in eyebrows.

Hutton turned to me. "Felicity, this is Jackie. Her grandson is flying the plane up there."

"It's so nice to meet you, Jackie." I smiled at all the grannies. "And thank you all for being here."

"You're very welcome." Jackie patted Hutton's back. "Lead the way."

They pranced behind us all the way to the patio, where our families greeted us with a loud, exuberant, "Surprise!" As we caught our breath, the Clipper Cuts launched into "Let Me Call You Sweetheart."

"Guess this is our song," I whispered to Hutton.

He pulled me in front of him and wrapped his arms around my waist. "Their repertoire is limited," he whispered back. "But it works for me."

I wasn't sure whether it was the old-fashioned harmonies, or the simple sentiment of the lyrics, or being surrounded by everyone we loved that made me so emotional, but I couldn't help weeping as the song ended.

"Awww," Mrs. French said as she embraced me. "I'm so happy, I could cry too!"

Frannie, also misty-eyed, hugged me next, followed by my dad—who held me so tight, I choked up again—then Millie, Winnie, Audrey and Emmeline, Allie, and Dex's girls.

"We passed you on the road!" Luna told me. "But we weren't allowed to yell out the windows."

"Or honk the horn," added Hallie.

"Thank you so much for coming," I said to them. "I'm so glad you're here."

"We *love* engagement parties," said Hallie. "Last time we went to one was the day we met Winnie!"

"We're hoping our dad will ask Winnie to marry him, but he says to stop bugging him about it," said Luna.

Hallie shook her head. "We'll never stop bugging him about it."

"Never," agreed Luna.

"But there's one thing I don't understand," Hallie said, pointing at the plane, which was still flying overhead. "Why does that sign say 'Felicity, will you marry me?' Weren't you already engaged?"

Hutton and I looked at each other, and he smiled.

"Yes and no," I said, taking his hand. "Both things can be true."

The party was still in full swing when I saw Hutton standing alone beyond the edge of the patio, his back to me, his hands in his pockets as he studied the rolling hills of the vineyard in the light of the setting sun.

I excused myself from the conversation I was listening to and made my way over to him. "Hey," I said, tucking my arm inside his. "How are you? Sorry we got separated."

"I'm fine." He smiled at me. "Just needed a minute or two to catch my breath."

"You've been amazing tonight. Thank you for this." I tipped my head onto his shoulder. "For everything."

"You're welcome."

I inhaled the sweet summer evening and let my gaze wander over the neat rows of grapevines and fruit trees. "It's so beautiful here, isn't it?"

"Would you like to live here?"

"At Abelard?" I laughed. "Who wouldn't?"

"Maybe not this exact spot, but maybe we could find something nearby. Or something on the water. Or something with some acreage and you could have your own small farm." He chuckled. "I might like being a farmer. Seems like a job with a lot of solitude."

I faced him. "You're serious?"

"Yes." He shrugged. "I told Wade I might not come back to HFX."

My jaw dropped. *"What?"*

"It will likely mean a significant drop in my tax bracket, but I was thinking of moving back here and doing something else with my life—starting with marrying you."

My throat closed up and I shook my head. "I feel like someone is going to wake me up any minute. This is a dream. You'd give up being a billionaire for me?"

He laughed. "I'll still be a billionaire. But on a smaller scale. Hopefully small enough that no one will care about me anymore."

I wrapped my arms around his waist and rested my head on his chest. "I'll care. Not about your billions. Just about you."

He embraced me, kissing the top of my head. "Will you move back in with me?"

"Of course I will."

"And stay for seventy-two years?"

I smiled and hugged him tighter. "At least."

"Speaking of home, how much longer do we have to stay

at this party? As much as I love you in that dress, I'm going to love you out of it even more."

"You know what?" I tilted my head back and looked up at him, my blood rushing hotter at the thought of his skin on mine. "I think we've given them enough of us tonight. Should we say our goodbyes and sneak out?"

He pressed his lips to mine. "You never have to ask me that question twice."

Hutton had arranged for Neil to drive his car to the party, so we were able to get home quickly. Actually, quickly was an understatement—I'd never seen Hutton drive so fast.

When we arrived, he threw the SUV into park and hustled around to open the passenger door for me. We entered the house through the kitchen, which was dark and shadowy. I started to walk toward the bedroom, but as soon as the door was closed behind us, Hutton grabbed my wrist. "Come here."

Crushing his mouth to mine, he kissed me hard and deep, his hands sliding into my hair. Pins clattered to the floor. Our lips and tongues met, caressing and consuming. He backed me into the refrigerator, his hard body pressing close, his mouth moving down my throat while I struggled to breathe.

This man will be my husband.

Desire radiated from deep inside me, and I shoved at the lapels of his jacket, trying to push it off his shoulders. He shrugged out of it and let it fall to the floor before putting his hands on my bare back, sliding them inside the dress, his fingers digging into my ribs as his mouth renewed its assault on mine. Frustrated, I tried to yank his shirt from his pants, but he was bigger and stronger and held me too tight.

I moved one hand to his crotch and stroked the thick, hard

bulge, gratified when he moaned. "I want this," I whispered against his lips, rubbing his cock. "I need it."

"You'll have to wait." He grabbed me around the waist, spun around. And set me up on that gorgeous marble island. "I'm hungry."

Before I knew it, he'd pulled my lace panties down my legs and tossed them aside. Then his head disappeared beneath the tulle skirt of my dress. I dropped back onto my elbows, crying out as his mouth descended on me with long, decadent strokes and quick, hard flicks and glorious, swirling motions that turned the dark kitchen ceiling to a sky full of stars. He slipped his fingers inside me, working in tandem with his tongue. I hooked my legs over his shoulders, crossing my ankles behind his head. In minutes, my entire lower body tightened and tensed, every nerve ending alive and humming.

He sucked my clit into his mouth and my head dropped back, my cries bounced off the walls, and my body contracted around his fingers as my orgasm rippled against his tongue.

Before I even caught my breath, he straightened up and swept me off the island, carrying me toward the bedroom. Panting and dizzy, I hung onto his neck for dear life, afraid that if I let go, my body would just slither to the floor because he'd melted my bones. Miraculously, I managed to stand when he set me on my feet at the foot of the bed.

"I'd rip this dress to shreds just to get it off you, but not if you want to wear it again," he said, caging my ribs with his hands. "So tell me now."

"No ripping!" I said frantically. "I want to get married in this dress. Side zipper."

He unzipped the dress and slid the sleeves from my shoulders. It fell to my feet in a cloud of white. Carefully, I stepped out of it, scooped it up, and laid it across the chair in the corner of the bedroom.

"But wait," I said, slipping out of the heels. "You've seen the dress already. Is that bad luck?"

"Nope. We make our own luck," he said, loosening the knot in his tie and pulling it from his collar. "I mean, I could spend a couple minutes trying to convert our odds to implied probabilities, but I'm afraid my cognitive abilities have been hijacked by my dick and I'm likely to misjudge the variance of the payout. Now get over here."

Laughing, I went running straight for him and jumped into his arms, lassoing my legs around his still fully clothed body. Taken by surprise, he was knocked off balance and we tumbled onto the bed. I sat up, straddling his thighs, and unbuckled his belt. "You're such a math nerd."

"Some things never change," he said, palming my breasts, teasing my nipples with his thumbs.

Somehow, I managed to get the rest of his clothes off, although he didn't make it easy since he kept distracting me with his mouth and his hands. But finally, he couldn't wait another minute either, and he flipped me beneath him and reached for a condom.

I held my breath as he eased inside me, one hot, thick inch at a time, and we moaned in sync as he buried himself deep. "I love you," I whispered, pulling him closer.

"I love you too," he said as he began to move. "And I don't care what the odds are. I'd bet on us every time."

He covered my mouth with his, and I surrendered—to the sinuous motion of his hips, to the friction and heat between us, to the driving rhythm of his cock deep inside me, to the final throes of our shared release, where it was impossible to tell where he ended and I began.

I felt no fear in my heart—just love and belonging and hope.

When our energy was finally sapped—it took a while—we finally collapsed and snuggled close.

"If anyone comes to the door in the morning, we're not answering it," Hutton said gruffly. "I'm not sharing you."

"Deal," I said. "We can stay in bed all day, and then go get the rest of my—shoot!"

"What?"

I'd forgotten about fucking Mimi—I'd promised her a story by tomorrow. I sat up and put a hand on his warm, breathing chest. "I have to tell you something, and you're not going to like it."

"Now?" He yawned. "Because I'm really fucking content, and if it's like a big brunch or something you want me to attend in the morning, I'd rather not know."

"It's not brunch. It's Mimi Pepper-Peabody." I told him about her overhearing me at Plum & Honey, and then accosting me at work.

Hutton propped himself up on one elbow. "Wait. She's trying to blackmail you?"

"Not exactly. I don't think she wants money or anything. She just wants a story."

"Well, fuck her. She can't have ours." He lay down again. "I'll fucking buy that stupid tabloid tomorrow and put it out of business."

I laughed. "I know you would, but you know what? I'd rather have the satisfaction of telling Mimi she has no power over me anymore."

"Good. She's the one who's going to look like an asshole anyway, since we actually *are* getting married."

"True."

"When do you want to do that, anyway?"

"Get married?" I thought for a moment. "You know, unless you want to wait, we could just keep the wedding date Millie set aside for us at Cloverleigh Farms."

"I don't need to wait. I know what I want."

I smiled at the conviction in his voice. "Then let's do it. We can let everyone know tomorrow to save the date." I snuggled up to him again.

"Oh yeah. I forgot there would be other people involved. I don't suppose I can convince you to elope, huh?"

"No, but I don't need a three-ring circus either. Just our families."

"And the Prancin' Grannies."

I laughed. "And the Prancin' Grannies."

The next afternoon, Hutton and I met Mimi at Plum & Honey. I told him he didn't have to be there, but he said he wouldn't miss the opportunity to see me tell Mimi to go fuck herself—although I didn't plan on using those words. I wouldn't need them.

When she slid onto a chair across from us, she looked surprised. "You're here *together*?"

"Of course we are," I said. "And we only have a few minutes because we're heading to Cloverleigh Farms to finalize plans for our ceremony."

Mimi's jaw dropped. "Ceremony? As in, you're really getting married?"

"We're really getting married. Last Sunday in August."

"But you said it was fake! I *heard* you!"

"You must have misunderstood," I said calmly, taking a sip of my coffee.

Mimi scowled. "I did not. You admitted it to me in the tasting room at Abelard."

"I'm sure I have no idea what you mean. You were drinking that day. Perhaps you're confused—wine can do that to you."

"I wasn't confused," Mimi insisted. "You told me you'd made the whole thing up to take me down a notch. Now you're saying it's real?"

"Exactly." I snapped my fingers twice. "Keep up."

She sat back and folded her arms over her chest. "I could still leak the story."

"You could," I agreed, "but you're the one who will look like a fool when we tie the knot."

Mimi pouted. "This isn't fair. I'm not the one who lied, but I'm being punished."

"You lied to Felicity at the reunion when you swore you wouldn't reveal our engagement," Hutton pointed out.

"Oh, come on." Mimi rolled her eyes. "Felicity knew I was going to tell everyone—I'm the mean girl. I've always been the mean girl. People are only friends with me because I intimidate them."

"Tell you what, Mimi," I said. "You stop trying to intimidate me, and I'll try being your friend for real."

"Seriously?" She perked up a little. "Can I come to your wedding?"

"We'll see."

"And will you cater my bridal shower? I can't stop thinking about those watermelon crostinis."

I shrugged. "Sure."

"And maybe . . ." She fussed with the ends of her hair. "Maybe you could give me the name of your stylist? I've been thinking about trying some little bangs like yours."

I burst out laughing.

"What's so funny?" Mimi asked.

"Actually, Mimi, I cut them myself."

"You cut your own hair?" She was visibly horrified.

"Sometimes. It's a nervous habit, something I do when I feel like my life is out of my control." I shrugged. "I shouldn't do it, but you know what?"

"What?"

"It's okay if I do. I don't have to be perfect. Or fashionable. Or even symmetrical." I looked at Hutton, and his smile was everything. "I can just be me. And that's enough."

Epilogue

One Month Later

"ARE YOU READY?" MILLIE POPPED INTO THE ROOM AT Cloverleigh Farms that my sisters and I were using to get ready.

"Definitely." I studied my reflection one last time. "Do you think it's lame that I'm wearing the same dress? Everyone here will recognize it."

"Not at all," Winnie said, handing out bouquets to everyone. "It's gorgeous on you, and this time you've got the veil. That totally changes the look."

I reached up to touch it—it was Frannie's veil, and none of us had thought it would look right with the dress, but somehow the long, traditional veil gave the short, modern dress just the right touch. We'd all shed tears when Frannie had brought it out of the box so I could try it on, remembering the day she'd married our dad.

"Also the sneakers." Millie laughed, shaking her head. "It's a look all your own."

I looked down at my feet. "Yeah, I couldn't do those heels again. At least they're clean and white!"

"You look amazing. You can't even see the blood on the dress," Emmeline said generously.

I laughed. "Thanks." The dress had been dry-cleaned after the party, but you could definitely still see the faint stain. That was okay—little imperfections didn't bother me.

Audrey fussed with my bangs a little. "And your hair is so cute. Good job staying away from the scissors today."

"You know what?" I smiled at all four of my sisters. "Believe it or not, I wasn't even tempted. But I think Hutton took all the scissors out of the house yesterday just in case."

Hutton and I were renting a place in town while we looked for land to build on. He'd left his position as CEO of HFX and sold most of his shares to Wade, but he'd agreed to stay on as a consultant as long as he could work from home. He had several offers from other companies, both in the crypto industry and outside it, but so far, he'd turned them all down.

He wanted to devote more time to his charitable foundation, and he'd also been offered an adjunct professor position in the mathematics department at a university nearby. The department head was one of our old high school math teachers, and she and I had persuaded him to try teaching just one small class this semester.

Natalia, his new therapist, was also on board with the plan, and even though he complained about her all the time—she reminded him too much of Allie—he hadn't fired her.

I thought that was a good sign.

"You all look beautiful," I said, my heart swelling with love and gratitude as I looked at the women surrounding me. They'd each chosen their own dresses in different styles but in complementary shades—the twins in peach and watermelon, Winnie in coral, Millie in scarlet. "I could not be more proud to have all four of my sisters beside me today."

Winnie fanned her face. "Don't do this to me. My mascara isn't even dry yet."

"No tears! We're all happy today. Have you seen Hutton?" I asked Millie.

She smiled and nodded. "He looks like a million—sorry—a *billion* bucks in his suit and tie, but also a little nervous."

"Yeah, fifty pairs of eyes on him is not his thing," I said. "He's definitely doing this for me."

"Honestly, Dad's probably a bigger mess," said Millie, laughing. "He keeps tearing up and pacing."

"He puts on such a tough front, but he's really a softie," said Winnie. "Giving away one of his girls for the first time is probably killing him."

"If you're ready, Felicity, we should go down," Millie said. "Frannie's already been seated, and Dad's waiting outside. I don't think we should leave him alone too long."

"Let's go," I said, giving myself one last look in the mirror. "I'm ready."

"Just give it like two minutes, okay?" Millie looked over her shoulder from me to our dad. We were standing on the patio of the restaurant at Cloverleigh Farms, in the shade and out of sight of the ten rows of chairs that had been set up on the edge of the orchard. The sound of the Clipper Cuts floated over the lawn toward us.

The twins had walked down the aisle side by side, and Winnie had followed. Millie was serving as maid of honor, and she'd be the final attendant before my dad and me.

"Okay." My stomach was full of jitters, but I felt steady on my feet. I smiled at my father, so strong and handsome in his gray suit. Suddenly I felt like crying, so I made a joke. "Bet you never thought I'd be first, huh?"

His smile was sweet and sad at the same time. "I never thought about this at all, or I'd have fallen apart."

A lump popped into my throat. "No fair, Dad. Do not make me ruin this moment with ugly tears."

"Sorry." He held out his arm, and I slipped my hand through it. "I couldn't be happier for you, honey. It doesn't surprise me at all that you're first, because it's Hutton. Maybe if it had been a stranger, I'd have questioned it . . . but you two have always been there for each other, and that's what marriage is. The fireworks are cool, but it's the friendship that matters."

I kissed his cheek. "I love you, Dad."

"I love you too, sweetheart." He glanced in the direction Millie had gone. The Clipper Cuts had launched into our song. "I think it's our turn."

"Let's do it."

We stepped out of the shade and into the warmth of the late afternoon sun. I felt surprisingly confident on my dad's arm as we walked through the guests that had gathered for us. Maybe it was the sneakers. Maybe it was the weather. Maybe it was all the familiar faces—not only the MacAllister and French clans, but the entire extended Sawyer family as well. All Frannie's sisters and their husbands, their children, John and Daphne, who'd been like grandparents to me. The Prancin' Grannies were all in attendance, and even Mimi was there, sporting some freshly cut bangs, as short and choppy as if I'd done them myself.

Maybe it was Hutton, who watched me walk toward him as if he'd never imagined this kind of moment would belong to us. When we reached him, I saw some nervousness in his eyes, yes—but also love and pride and gratitude. My dad shook his hand and kissed my cheek, then took his seat next to Frannie, who blew me a kiss and dabbed beneath her eyes with a tissue.

I glanced at my sisters, all grinning widely, Winnie and Millie with eyes full of tears. I touched my heart and faced Hutton—my friend and my forever.

The love of my life.

That disobedient lock of hair had overpowered his styling product and sprung free onto his forehead. Self-conscious, he tried to brush it off, but I reached for his hand and smiled. "Leave it," I whispered. "I love an imperfection."

But standing there, in this place full of warm memories, next to my best friend in the world, in front of the people we loved most, looking forward to our happily ever after, I had to admit that even with imperfections, some moments in life were still perfect.

Both things could be true.

THE END

I hope you enjoyed *Tease*! Want a peek into Hutton and Felicity's future? Subscribe to my mailing list and you'll get instant access to an exclusive TEASE bonus scene! Just use the QR code below.

Already subscribed? Just check your last newsletter for the link to my bonus materials! If you can't find it, you can simply resubscribe and the scene will be yours in minutes.

Also by
Melanie Harlow

Acknowledgments

As always, my appreciation and gratitude go to the following people for their talent, support, wisdom, friendship, and encouragement . . .

Melissa Gaston, Brandi Zelenka, Jenn Watson, Hang Le, CE Johnson, Corinne Michaels, Melissa Rheinlander, the Social Butterfly team, Anthony Colletti, Rebecca Friedman, Flavia Viotti & Meire Dias at Bookcase Literary, Nancy Smay at Evident Ink, Julia Griffis at The Romance Bibliophile, Stacey Blake at Champagne Book Design, One Night Stand Studios, the Shop Talkers, the Sisterhood, the Harlots and the Harlot ARC Team, bloggers and event organizers, my Queens, my betas, my proofers, my readers all over the world . . .

I'd especially like to thank my sensitivity readers who so generously answered my questions about Social Anxiety Disorder, shared their experiences, and read the book early to provide feedback. I am so grateful.

About the Author

Melanie Harlow likes her heels high, her martini dry, and her history with the naughty bits left in. She's the author of the Bellamy Creek Series, the Cloverleigh Farms Series, the One & Only series, the After We Fall Series, the Happy Crazy Love Series, and the Frenched Series.

She writes from her home outside of Detroit, where she lives with her husband and two daughters. When she's not writing, she's probably got a cocktail in hand. And sometimes when she is.

Find her at www.melanieharlow.com.